- A Hope Springs Novel

Valerie M. Bodden

Not Until Us © 2019 by Valerie M. Bodden.

This is a work of fiction. Names, characters, places and incidents either are products of the author's imagination or used in a fictitious manner. Any resemblance to any person, living or dead, is coincidental.

Cover design: Ideal Book Covers

Valerie M. Bodden
Visit me at www.valeriembodden.com

Hope Springs Series

Not Until Christmas
Not Until Forever
Not Until This Moment
Not Until You
Not Until Us
Not Until Christmas Morning
Not Until This Day
Not Until Someday
Not Until Now
Not Until Then

River Falls Series

Pieces of Forever
Songs of Home
Memories of the Heart

Contents

A Gift for You . . .

Members of my Reader's Club get a FREE story, available exclusively to my subscribers. When you sign up, you'll also be the first to know about new releases, book deals, and giveaways.

Visit valeriembodden.com/gift to join!

Remember, LORD, your great mercy and love,
for they are from of old.
Do not remember the sins of my youth
and my rebellious ways;
according to your love remember me,
for you, LORD, are good.

—PSALM 25:6–7

Chapter 1

*H*ow had she messed up again?

Jade swiped at her cheeks as she slid the key into the lock of her apartment door. If the God her roommate Keira kept telling her about had any decency, Keira would still be in bed. She wasn't in the mood to be reprimanded by her squeaky clean friend right now. She already knew last night had been a mistake.

One she'd made far too many times.

She inched the door open slowly but let out a frustrated breath as her eyes fell on her roommate, perky as ever, sitting on the couch with some kind of kale-soy-banana-protein drink in hand.

Apparently God didn't have any decency. Or he had one wicked sense of humor.

"Good morning." Keira eyed Jade's clothes—the same ones she'd been wearing when she'd left for work last night.

Jade held up a hand. "Don't say it."

"Say what?" Keira took a long sip of her drink, still watching Jade.

"Fine. I screwed up. Again." She tried to sound defiant, but even as the words came out, a bone-crushing weariness descended on her. She was trying to be a better person. She really was. But old habits were hard to break. Last night had been just one more name to add to her list of lifelong mistakes. Or it would be if she knew his name.

She buried her face in her hands. She was an awful person. "I don't know why I keep doing this."

When the guy had walked into the bar where she worked, she'd told herself to ignore him. But she'd been bored. And he'd had nice eyes and witty banter. Plus, he was only passing through town on business. There was no chance things would get messy or complicated. He'd go on his way, she'd go on hers, and neither of them would worry about it again.

Besides, he'd practically challenged her to go back to his hotel room with him. What was she supposed to do?

Walk away. The voice in her head sounded an awful lot like her big sister Violet. Not that Violet had any idea what Jade's life was like, aside from the sanitized version Jade fed her on their weekly phone calls.

Keira crossed the small space and pulled Jade's hands away from her face, holding the protein drink out to her. Jade wrinkled her nose and pushed it away. After eight years in Los Angeles, she still had no interest in the stuff that passed for breakfast around here. Give her a donut and a strong cup of coffee any day.

"Change is hard." Keira wrapped an arm over her shoulder and steered her to the couch. "You should pray about it."

Jade shook her head. If there was anything she was less interested in than protein shakes, it was prayer. "I need to pack. My plane leaves in a couple hours."

She still wasn't sure what had compelled her to give in to her sister's pleas that she spend the summer in Hope Springs. But maybe it would do her some good to get away from this town of broken dreams for a while.

Besides, the way Violet talked about Hope Springs made Jade almost homesick for it.

Almost.

Mostly, though, she was going because she owed it to Vi. After six years of completely cutting her sister out of her life, Jade didn't deserve the second chance Vi had given her. The phone calls they'd been exchanging for the past couple years weren't enough. The least she could do was spend the summer helping her sister finalize plans for her wedding.

"Well, look at it this way." Keira sucked down the last of her shake. "Maybe you'll meet a nice, wholesome man in Hope Springs, and you'll get married and live happily ever after."

Jade snickered. "You read too many small town romances. Trust me, there's no one in Hope Springs I'd consider dating, let alone marrying. Besides—" She flopped onto the couch. "I'm not really the happily ever after kind of girl."

Keira tipped her head to the side, studying Jade. "Everyone's a happily ever after kind of girl. It just takes some of us longer to get there than others." She moved to the cramped kitchen to rinse out her glass.

Jade stared after her. Keira could dream about happily ever after all she wanted. But Jade knew the truth. There was no such thing. She'd learned that lesson early, and she wasn't going to forget it anytime soon.

Chapter 2

*D*an hadn't known it was possible to sweat this much.

This had to be the hottest Hope Fest parade on record. Of course, that might have something to do with the heavy lion costume he was wearing. Grace had borrowed the local high school's mascot, insisting that if they were going to have a Noah's ark float, they needed the animals too. Lucky for him, he was exactly the right size for the costume.

Despite the sweltering heat, Dan had to admit that the float had turned out better than he could have imagined. And judging from the crowd's cheers as they walked past, he wasn't the only one who thought so.

Dan swiveled to catch a glimpse of the others marching with him. There had to be nearly one hundred people representing Hope Church in the parade—all of them in some sort of animal costume or another.

His heart filled. He knew many of them were there in tribute to his father, who had been their spiritual leader for nearly forty years. Dan had almost canceled the church's entry in the parade this year. His grief over Dad's death was still too raw for him to dedicate the time needed to plan it. But when he'd brought it up to the church board, they'd reminded him that the congregation was looking to him as their new head pastor for guidance in how to move on. He was glad now that he'd listened to them. The parade seemed to have brought his members together in a way nothing else had lately.

"Hey. This turned out really well." His sister Leah sidled up to him, decked out in a colorful parrot costume. "Dad would have loved it. I could totally see him hamming it up in that costume."

"I was just thinking that. Thank goodness Grace came through with all this stuff." It was almost a miracle, considering he'd asked her to be in charge of the parade only two weeks earlier. And she'd done it all with a smile.

"Speaking of which—" Leah poked him in the side, and Dan knew what was coming. "How was your dinner last night?"

"You mean the one you tricked us into?"

Dan, Leah, and Grace had worked on the float until late the night before, and afterward Leah had suggested they grab a bite at the Hidden Cafe, before conveniently remembering she had to take care of a friend's cat.

"How was the cat, by the way?"

"What cat?" Leah waved to the cheering crowds. "Oh, yeah. The cat was good."

Dan gave her a little shove. "There was no cat."

Leah laughed, completely unashamed. "Nope. But you didn't answer my question. How was dinner with Grace?"

Dan sighed into his costume, then wished he hadn't, as his breath only made the small space steamier. "It was fine."

"And?" Leah poked him, as if waiting for more.

He lifted his hands, the claws of his costume clacking. "And that's it."

There'd been no fireworks. No amazing revelation that this was the woman for him. Just some good food, a bit of conversation, and a wave goodnight.

Which was fine.

Just fine.

"You should ask her to the fireworks tonight."

11

This time Dan managed to contain his sigh—barely. "I just don't see this going anywhere, Leah."

It wasn't like he was looking for a relationship anyway. Sure, he'd been performing marriage ceremonies for his friends more frequently lately, and every once in a while, he longed for what they had. But mostly, he was too busy with his ministry to consider marriage and a family.

"Famous last words." Leah flitted away to pass out candy to the parade goers.

Dan shook his head at her. His sister was a meddler, there were no two ways about it. Her heart was in the right place, but sometimes he sure wished that place was somewhere else.

By the time they reached the final stretch of the parade, Dan was tempted to pull his lion head off. But he forced himself to wait until they'd gone past every last spectator.

When he'd finally taken the costume off, he grabbed an abandoned water bottle from the float and poured it over his head. The few kids whose parents hadn't yet plucked them from the realistic-looking ark giggled, and he grabbed another half-empty water bottle and gently tossed a few drops their way. They shrieked but laughed harder.

"You're good with them." Grace came up next to him, looking cool and comfortable in her shorts and t-shirt. She'd ridden along in the truck to manage the speaker system. She started pulling decorations off the float.

"Ah, kids are fun." Dan lifted a little guy dressed as a turtle down from the ark and passed him a lollipop from the bag of extra candy. Soon, a group of kids had gathered around him. Dan couldn't help but smile. He knew the kids were surrounding him more for the candy than for his company, but that didn't make him feel any less like a rock star.

"Bribing them again?" Dan's friend Nate, who really was a rock star—or at least the lead singer for the church's worship band—clapped him on the back.

Dan grinned. "Whatever it takes. I'd better bring some of these along to camp next month." Dan was excited to resurrect the annual trip to Camp Oswego that the church had taken when he was a kid.

"Oh." Grace popped up from the other side of the float. "I almost forgot to tell you. Cassandra Murphy said she could chaperone, so we should be all set."

"Seriously?" Dan could have hugged her. He'd been trying for weeks to find one more female chaperone. He'd asked Cassandra himself at least twice, but she'd said it'd be impossible to get time off. Apparently Grace really was a miracle worker.

"I don't know how you did it, but thank you." He pulled a stuffed giraffe off the side of the ark. "And thank you for putting this float together. It looked amazing."

Grace ducked her head. "It was nothing."

Leah bounced over to them. "What was nothing?"

"The float." His voice was guarded. The last thing he needed was for his sister to overreact to his compliment to Grace. Next thing he knew, she'd have them walking down the aisle.

But to his relief, Leah turned away from him to Grace. "Oh my goodness, yes. Thank you so much for designing it. My attempts the last few years have been kind of . . ."

"Pathetic," Dan filled in for his sister.

"Ouch." Leah swatted at him. "But yes. Pathetic is a good word to describe it." She slid the parrot wings off. "Are you coming to the fireworks tonight, Grace?"

There it was. Dan shot his sister a look, but she only winked at him.

Grace shifted the handful of stuffed animals she'd picked up from the float. "There are fireworks?"

"Oh yeah, better than the fourth of July." Leah gestured toward the sky, as if she could see them already.

Even though he knew what was coming, Dan couldn't figure out a way to prevent it. He took a step away from the float, but that didn't stop his sister.

"Actually, I know Dan is going. I bet he could pick you up on the way. He has to drive right past your house anyway."

Dan froze but didn't turn around.

After last night, Grace would recognize his sister's blatant matchmaking and say no.

Wouldn't she?

"If that wouldn't be too much trouble, I'd love to go."

"It's no trouble," Leah assured Grace, and Dan almost snorted out loud. Of course it was no trouble for her. She'd just set her little brother up on a date. He'd have to thank her later. Once he'd come up with a suitable revenge.

But for now he turned to Grace. It wasn't her fault he had a meddlesome sister. And he really did owe her after all she'd done to make the parade a success. "It's no problem at all. How about I pick you up around eight?"

Leah beamed at them both, then sashayed off, saying something about making sure everyone handed in their costumes.

"I'm sorry if you don't want—" Grace said. "I don't need to go."

"No, it's fine. I'm looking forward to it." He offered her the most genuine smile he could muster. "It'll be fun." Anyway, it wasn't like a trip to the fireworks was a marriage proposal.

He stood awkwardly, trying to figure out something else to say. Thankfully, Nate's fiancée, Violet, walked up at that moment, winding her arm through Nate's as he leaned down to kiss her forehead. Dan couldn't have been happier for his two friends, whose wedding was coming up at the end of summer.

"We'd better get going. We need to be at the airport by seven." Violet tugged Nate toward the parking lot.

Nate patted her arm. "It's only four now."

"I know, but there could be traffic, or . . ." She gave him a playful swat on the arm. "Stop laughing at me. I'm excited."

"Are you two skipping out of town? Without seeing the fireworks?" Dan's heart fell. He'd been hoping he and Grace could sit with them, so it'd seem less like a date.

"Nope." Violet's face lit up brighter than any firework. "We're going to the airport to pick up Jade."

Dan fought to keep his expression neutral, even as his heart surged at the name.

It had been eight years. He shouldn't still react that way to something as insignificant as her name.

"I didn't know Jade was coming home."

If possible, Violet's smile got even brighter. "I've been begging her for weeks to come home for the summer, and she must have gotten sick of it because she finally said yes. She's staying until after the wedding." Violet pulled on Nate's arm. "Come on. We have to go."

Nate shrugged at Dan, then followed his future wife toward the parking lot.

"Save us a seat for the fireworks," Violet called over her shoulder. "We may be late."

"Who's Jade?" Grace's question made Dan jump.

"Violet's sister." And his— His what?

His almost-girlfriend?

They hadn't dated. Not officially. But they'd spent so much time together in the last few months of high school that they'd forged a connection deeper than dating ever could.

At least that's what he'd thought.

Right up until she disappeared, leaving him only a note. He hadn't seen or heard from her once since then.

But apparently that was about to change. So he'd better get a grip on how he felt about it.

Fast.

Chapter 3

Thirty thousand feet in the air probably wasn't the best place to change her mind. As the captain announced over the intercom that they had started their descent, Jade's eyes went to the window, where the sun was low on the horizon, throwing a blinding light across Lake Michigan. She pressed a hand to her stomach.

She'd left eight years ago with the intention of never returning. So what was she doing here now?

She had let herself get caught up in her sister's excitement, had let herself believe that she'd left behind all the shame and regret that had driven her to flee Hope Springs in the first place. But now that she was almost home, it squeezed against her lungs, as if someone had over-pressurized the cabin.

It may have been eight years since she was in Hope Springs, but one thing she knew about small towns—they had long memories.

And Jade had given the people of Hope Springs plenty to remember—even if no one there knew the worst of it. None of them knew the real reason she'd fled.

Jade straightened in her seat. *And they never will.*

She caught her breath as the plane skimmed over the runway, then bounced lightly as the wheels touched down.

Her heart was suddenly thrumming faster than the jet's engine. She couldn't do this.

Maybe she could sneak off the plane and skip picking up her luggage. Then Vi wouldn't see her, and she could sneak onto another plane to somewhere else—anywhere else—and no one would ever have to know.

Jade let herself indulge in the fantasy for all of ten seconds. But the thought of what that would do to Vi put an end to it.

She was lucky her sister had forgiven her for running the first time. She couldn't do that to her again.

Anyway, she was stronger than this.

She steeled her shoulders and stood. She wouldn't worry about what any of them thought.

She was Jade Falter, and she was proud of it.

A nagging voice at the back of her head said she shouldn't be, but she shoved it away, along with all the other nagging voices she'd ignored over the years.

She clutched her carry-on and followed a white-haired woman off the plane, forcing herself to keep her chin up.

But the moment she stepped off the plane and into the airport, a wave of memories slammed against her. Of course she'd have to be in the same terminal she'd fled from that last day. Everything looked almost identical to how it had then. There was the bank of chairs in the corner she'd huddled in as she'd waited for her flight to be called. The terminal had been crowded, and at least a dozen people had approached the seats next to her. But they'd all walked away the moment they'd spotted her. Not that she blamed them. She'd been unable to stop sobbing, her arms wrapped around her middle, rocking back and forth.

Tears sprang to her eyes for the scared girl she'd been then, but she blinked them away.

She wasn't that girl anymore.

She pointed her head forward and made her way to the baggage claim without another look back.

The moment she neared the luggage carousel, she heard her name shrieked, and then arms were engulfing her.

"I'm so happy to see you. I can't believe you're here. You look so good." Violet squeezed so hard that Jade couldn't lift her arms to return the hug.

"It's not going to do much good to have your sister home if you crush her before she gets out of the airport." A man with a light layer of scruff and slightly shaggy hair gently pulled Violet's shoulder.

Vi laughed, wiping at her cheeks as she took a step back. "I'm sorry. It's just so— I can't believe this is real. That you're really here."

"I'm here." Jade swallowed down her own unexpected tears. When was the last time someone had been so happy to see her? "I just need to grab my bag."

She stepped around Violet toward the luggage carousel, giving herself a minute to collect her composure. It wasn't like her to lose it over a little thing like this. Probably just all the emotions of the day catching up with her.

Nate insisted on taking her bag for her as they made their way to Violet's car. At the vehicle, he opened the door for each of them. Jade climbed into the backseat with a weary sigh. All she wanted was her pajamas and a bed.

She settled back into the seat, training her gaze out the window. The familiar sights were more of a balm than she'd expected, and her eyes drooped with fatigue from the long day.

"I don't think we have time to stop at home. Hope Street will be closed by now anyway." Vi's voice broke into her half sleep, and when she opened her eyes, dusk had already fallen. As she peered into the graying night, she picked out the town's various landmarks. The Old Lighthouse. The giant sunfish. The church.

Her heart jumped as her gaze swept over the beach below the church. The beach where she'd thought maybe her life would change. Where she'd let herself hope that she'd found a man—he was really a boy then, she supposed—who could love her in spite of her reputation, in spite of her past. Who could believe that she'd changed. The man she'd fled the moment she'd had to confront the fact that there was no changing who she was.

She briefly considered asking Vi what had ever become of Dan but then thought better of it. There was no point in rehashing old dreams that could never be. Besides, Vi would probably find the question odd, since Jade had never told her—or anyone else, for that matter—that she and Dan had spent time together at the end of senior year. Had developed feelings for each other. Anyway, that was a long time ago. If Dan had followed his plans, he'd moved far away by now.

"Why don't you park here? It's probably as close as we're going to get." Nate gestured down a side street, which was almost parked full.

Vi nodded and pulled up to the curb. Throngs of people funneled down the sidewalk toward the lake.

"What's going on tonight? Why's everybody out?" Jade leaned forward to watch a mother trying to quiet a crying baby. The familiar pang jabbed her behind the belly button, and she looked away. She kept waiting for the guilt to end, but it was always there, hovering like her own personal cloud of regret.

The young mother moved down the street, and Jade sat back. If things had been different, if *she* had been different, would she be like that young mother?

"It's Hope Fest." Vi put the car in park and opened her door. "We're going to have to hurry or we'll miss the beginning of the fireworks."

Jade's stomach plummeted. Vi didn't really expect her to go to the town's annual celebration, did she?

"Come on." Vi opened her door.

"I'll wait for you guys here. I need a nap." Jade forced a yawn that even she could tell wasn't believable.

"It's going to be too loud to sleep." Vi planted a hand on her hip. "Come on, everyone is dying to see you."

Jade sincerely doubted that. If there was one person besides Vi in this town who wanted her to come back, she'd eat her left shoe.

Nate opened her door. "I didn't think I'd like it either when Violet made me come last year. But it was actually pretty fun. Come on. I'll buy the popcorn."

Jade threw her hands in the air. "If you two are going to gang up on me, I guess I don't have much choice, do I?" She slid to the door, and Nate stepped aside to let her out.

Vi and Nate closed the car doors, and she let them pass in front of her. The two linked hands, and Nate leaned over to drop a light kiss on Vi's cheek.

Jade's stomach clenched as she fell into step behind them.

She was happy for her sister. No one so young should have to experience the loss of a spouse like Vi had.

But Jade hadn't even gotten one happily ever after. So how was it that Violet had been given two?

As they approached the marina, Violet glanced over her shoulder, as if to make sure Jade was still there, and Jade offered her a tight smile. It was the best she could do.

"Dan texted that he's saving us a seat in front of the gazebo," Nate said.

Jade almost stumbled but caught herself at the last second. "Dan?" She forced the name out.

Violet's brow wrinkled. "Dan Zelner. You remember him, don't you? I'm pretty sure he was in your class."

Jade nodded but couldn't answer. Her mouth went completely dry. Dan was here? As in *here* here?

A huge crowd covered the hill of the public park above the marina, and Jade let a momentary relief wash over her. The gazebo was on the far side of the hill. There was no way they'd be able to get through the crowds to it—and even if they did, the chances they'd find Dan in this mess of people were small at best.

"There he is." Nate held up a hand to wave, then started weaving through the people toward the gazebo.

Jade's feet wanted to remain planted, but Violet reached back and grabbed her arm, tugging her forward.

She was about to be reintroduced to her past. Whether she wanted to be or not.

Chapter 4

"*Y*ou were saying?" Grace's voice reached Dan's ears, but he had no idea what he'd been saying. He'd just spotted Violet and Nate—and being dragged behind them as if being taken to detention—Jade.

His stomach rolled uncomfortably, and his pulse rocketed past any heart rate he'd ever achieved on the treadmills at the gym. He had a sudden urge to give himself a quick sniff test, even though he'd gone home and taken a shower after the parade. How was it that one glimpse of Jade had sent him right back to feeling like a self-conscious teen?

He kept his hand raised in the air until he was sure Nate had seen it, then turned toward the lake as if he couldn't care less that the woman he'd once dreamed of spending the rest of his life with was coming his way at this very moment. Anyway, he reminded himself, she was also the woman who'd torn his heart out and left it to rot in the sand.

"About camp." Grace's prompt reminded Dan that she was still sitting next to him on the blanket Leah had called to tell him to pack. If his sister micromanaged this date any more, she might as well be the one on it. Then again, since she was sitting right behind them, she practically was.

"Look who I brought with me." Violet stood to the side and motioned Jade forward, but Jade barely moved. "Sophie, Dan, you remember Jade, right? Everyone else, this is my sister, Jade."

"Welcome home." Sophie stepped forward to hug Jade, her husband Spencer following with a handshake. The rest of the group—Jared and

Peyton, Emma, Grace, and Tyler—stepped forward and introduced themselves.

Finally, Dan was the only one left who hadn't said hi. Jade lifted her eyes to meet his for a second, then let them dart away. A tiny worm of satisfaction crawled through Dan's gut. At least she had the grace to look embarrassed to see him. But a moment later he reprimanded himself. He'd forgiven her long ago, so he had no right to hold the past over her head.

He took a step closer, thinking he'd give her a hug, but then changed his mind at the last second and held out a hand instead. She stared at it, as if not sure what to do with it, then put her hand in his. He tried not to notice the warmth her grip sent up his arm.

She could have stepped right out of the pages of their high school yearbook. Same white-blond hair, same smooth complexion. Same standoffish confidence she'd worn like a shield through most of high school, except in those rare moments when she'd dropped it with him.

"It's nice to see you again, Jade." Lame, but what else was he supposed to say?

Jade's nod was slow and deliberate, but her eyes drifted from him to Grace, and he groaned inwardly. She was going to think he was here with Grace.

You are here with Grace.

Dan shook himself. Of course he was here with Grace. And so what if Jade knew? She wasn't here to see him. And he most definitely wasn't here to see her.

"I think the fireworks are about to start." He laid a hand on Grace's elbow to steer her back to her seat on the blanket, then sat next to her. "Have a seat, you guys. There's plenty of room."

He kept his gaze directed toward the lake as he felt people shuffling next to him.

A second later, someone's leg brushed his as they sat. He risked a glance over.

23

His eyes landed on Jade just as the first firework exploded overhead, lighting her in a wash of blue.

She tilted her face up at the sound, but he noticed the lines of tension around her lips.

As if she felt him watching her, Jade turned toward him. Her eyes were the same shade he'd remembered—like a summer sky on a perfect day. But there was something new in them—something broken. Dan pressed down the urge to ask what it was.

She'd chosen to run. Whatever had happened to her since then was none of his concern.

Still, he had to say something, or this would get awkward. "How have you been?"

"Good." She bobbed her head vigorously. "Fabulous."

"Oh. Good." Dan fumbled for something else to say. What did you say when the girl of your dreams suddenly showed up in real life again?

Girl of your former dreams, he reminded himself.

His new dreams had nothing to do with her.

A sharp prod in his back made Dan jump. He cast a quick look over his shoulder at his sister, who jerked her head toward Grace on his other side.

Dan returned Leah's glare but turned his attention back to Grace. Her legs were stretched out in front of her as she leaned back on her elbows to watch the fireworks, her lips slightly parted like she was mesmerized. Her relaxed demeanor was a perfect contrast to the tension exuding from Jade on the other side of him.

As Dan lifted his eyes to the sky, Grace leaned a fraction closer. "Your sister wasn't exaggerating. These are the best fireworks I've ever seen."

Dan nodded, fighting every impulse to glance at Jade when she shifted next to him, causing her arm to brush his.

"I didn't think you'd still be in Hope Springs." Jade's voice was low but closer to his ear than he'd expected, and he leaned slightly away. It would be dangerous to let her get too close. He'd made that mistake once already.

"I thought you were going to go to seminary and then go off and do big things for God." Her words held a trace of a sneer, but under that he sensed something softer—curiosity, maybe?

He frowned at the white streaks flashing above them. "I guess I was meant to do smaller things for him." He let himself glance at her out of the corner of his eyes, but she was looking toward the sky. "I'm actually head pastor at Hope Church."

In his peripheral vision, he saw her head snap toward him. "You are?"

"Yeah. I am. I was serving with my dad, but he died a few months ago." He swallowed past the sharp jab the words brought.

"I'm sorry." Jade set a hand on his arm for the briefest second.

But the touch was enough to send him back to those few months in high school, when the touch of her hand meant everything to him.

Sometimes, he wondered if it had all been a dream after all—their relationship was just too unlikely. He was the pastor's son. She was the rebel.

All through grade school and middle school, she'd teased him mercilessly. In high school, she'd finally lost interest and ignored him.

Until they were paired as lab partners for chemistry senior year.

He'd nearly groaned out loud when Mr. Burns had read out their names. So much for a peaceful final year of high school.

To his surprise, though, she hadn't said an unkind word to him all year. Hadn't said more than a handful of words to him at all, actually.

She always showed up to class with one guy or another. Dan lost count of how many boyfriends she went through during first semester alone. One constantly called her crude names, another couldn't seem to keep himself from grabbing at her, and another was always giving her compliments on various parts of her anatomy.

Dan had kept his head down and his mouth shut.

But one day right before spring break, she'd walked into the room earlier than usual, with a hand pressed to her ribs.

Dan tried to focus on the homework he'd come in early to finish up. He told himself not to say anything, but when she winced as she sat, he couldn't help it. "Are you okay?"

He could have sworn he saw tears in her eyes. But if there was one thing he knew about Jade Falter, it was that she didn't cry. Ever. Not even in grade school when she'd taken a baseball to the nose.

He leaned closer, keeping his voice low. "What is it?"

She shook her head and blinked hard enough to clear the tears. "Let's just say Brett wasn't a big fan of being dumped." Her laugh was sardonic.

The lead of Dan's pencil snapped, leaving a jagged line across his paper. He threw it down.

"Did he hurt you?" He fought to get the words out past his gritted teeth.

Jade shrugged, but her hand tracked to her side again.

"Let me see." Dan reached toward her, but Jade slapped his hand away.

"I didn't expect you of all people to try to take my shirt off." Her smirk was calculated to irk him.

"Whatever," he muttered under his breath, picking up his pencil and crossing the room to sharpen it.

"What?" Jade watched him as he sat down again. "Now you're not talking to me?"

"You wouldn't listen anyway."

"You never know." She gave him an exaggerated wink. "I just might surprise you."

He almost let it go at that. But something about her tone told him she needed to hear what he'd been wanting to say to her for months.

"I don't understand why you keep dating all these jerks." He clamped his mouth shut. He shouldn't have said it. He knew it the moment the words were out.

But Jade fixed him with a look he'd never forget. One that told him whatever she was about to say was from her most vulnerable place.

"The good guys don't tend to ask me out." She shuffled through her bookbag and pulled out her textbook. It was the first time he'd seen her with the book all year. A curtain of hair shielded her face, but he could have sworn her cheeks were tinged with pink.

"I'm sure—" Dan stuttered, not knowing where he was going with the sentence. "I'm sure there are plenty of good guys who want to go out with you. They're probably just scared of you." Now he could feel his own neck warming. That wasn't supposed to come out as an insult.

Jade lifted her head and raised an eyebrow. "Like you?"

"I'm not scared of you." Which wasn't entirely true, but why make a bad situation worse?

But Jade shook her head, her eyes right on his. "I mean, like you. Are there guys like you who want to go out with me?"

Dan couldn't free his gaze from hers. "Yeah. Sure. I'm sure there are plenty of guys like me who want to go out with you."

He finally managed to break the stare she'd had him trapped in and paged through his book.

Jade sighed. "You don't get it."

His first instinct was to ignore her. But she was so different today. So clearly hurting.

He closed the book and gave her his full attention. "What don't I get?"

She bit her lip, almost as if she were nervous. He threw a glance over his shoulder to make sure Brett hadn't come back to harass her. But there were only a few other students in the room, and none of them were paying attention to his conversation with Jade.

"I mean like *you*. Do *you* want to date me?"

Dan had to grab at the table to keep from falling off his lab stool. When she'd said she might surprise him, he definitely hadn't expected *that*.

"Well, I mean, I—" Why wasn't the bell ringing?

She didn't really expect him to answer that, did she? It was a hypothetical question, right?

Jade's face slid back into its typical hostile expression. "See? That's what I mean." She turned away but not before Dan read the hurt in her eyes.

He drew in a breath, as if he could suck courage straight from the air. This whole thing was likely a trap to make him look like a fool.

"Yeah, I'd go out with you." He forced himself to keep his eyes on her, so he caught the moment the creases in her forehead eased.

"But I'm pretty sure a girl like you wouldn't want to go out with me." There was no way she was serious about this. The two of them couldn't be more opposite.

"Try me."

"Try you, what?"

She rolled her eyes. "Try asking me out."

Don't do it. It's a trap.

But the words had come out anyway. "Would you like to go to a movie with me Friday night?"

Jade's reply had been immediate. "No."

Told you.

"But I would like to hang out with you at the beach."

"At the beach?" Dan's mind had barely been able to comprehend what was happening. Had he just made a date with Jade Falter?

She'd given him what may have been the first genuine smile he'd ever seen from her. "The beach."

Another jab in his side brought Dan back to the present.

"Sorry about that." Leah leaned forward, extending her leg between Dan and Jade as she stood so that Dan had no choice but to scoot closer to Grace. "I'm going to grab some popcorn. Anyone else want some?"

Dan frowned at Leah as Jade shook her head. Leah offered him an innocent smile and dropped a hand onto his shoulder, subtly pushing him away from Jade and toward Grace.

As he turned back to the fireworks, he saw that Jade had widened the distance between them even more. On his other side, Grace slid closer and sent him a sweet smile. It didn't make his heart flip the way Jade's smile did. But maybe sweet smiles—ones that didn't raise fireworks in his heart—were safer.

He returned her smile and clasped his hands in his lap, telling himself he could be happy in a world without fireworks.

Chapter 5

Jade stretched, the half-filled air mattress Violet had set up on her bedroom floor creaking beneath her. But she couldn't convince herself to get up.

Last night had only been a bad dream, hadn't it? A nightmare that she'd come face-to-face with the one man she'd ever had feelings for, and he was with another woman. A woman who looked exactly like the kind of wholesome, virtuous woman he should be with.

She peeled her back off the mattress and swung her legs over the side.

You had your chance. What she needed was a stern talking to. *And you messed it up.*

The same way she always did.

It was just, did he have to look so good? Like *good* good. The once lanky and somewhat gangly teen had filled out into a broad-shouldered yet trim man. But his smile. That was the same as always. Still warm and easy—though maybe a bit guarded with her. Not that she blamed him for that.

And his smell. She'd had to stop herself from leaning closer to soak up the light, sporty scent she'd recognized from high school.

It had made her think of that first night they'd hung out at the beach. They'd spent hours together, first walking, then settling into a cozy spot in the sand between two dunes.

That night was the first time Jade had ever felt like the guy she was with was listening to her with his full attention, not nodding along while wondering how long it would be before she'd stop talking and he could feel her up.

In fact, Dan kept a healthy couple of feet between them all night. Even when she moved closer, complaining of the chill, he pulled off his sweater and passed it to her but didn't make a move toward her. At first, she found it strange. Maybe he wasn't attracted to her. But then she'd realized he was being respectful.

The realization had filled her in a way she'd never expected. It had made her feel precious and protected.

It was a feeling she hadn't experienced again in the eight years since she'd left Hope Springs. She shook herself out of the memories and stood. She didn't need to feel precious and protected. She needed to be strong and independent.

She *was* strong and independent.

The bedroom door opened a crack, and Vi poked her head through slowly. "Oh, good, you're up. I didn't want to wake you since you had a long day yesterday. But if you're up for it, I'll be leaving for church in about an hour."

Jade startled. Was today Sunday? Despite Keira's constant nagging, Jade hadn't set foot in a church in eight years.

But for some reason, the idea of going to Hope Church appealed to her today.

Maybe it was the nostalgia of being home.

Maybe it was guilt for all the things that had driven her from Hope Springs in the first place.

Or maybe it was the desire to see a certain dark-eyed preacher—even though she knew how much it would hurt.

At any rate, she could tell by Vi's hopeful expression that nothing would make her sister happier than Jade agreeing to go to church with her.

"Let me just grab a quick shower."

The light in Vi's eyes chased away any lingering doubts. Jade had a lot to make up to her sister.

Someone knocked on the apartment door, and Vi broke into a huge smile. "That's Nate. He always comes over for breakfast before church. He'll have to eat right away, so he can get to church to warm up the band, but we'll save you some pancakes if you want to shower first."

Jade eyed her sister. She and her fiancé had the oddest living arrangements Jade had ever heard of, living in apartments across the hall from each other, even though Vi had told her they'd closed on a house they planned to move into after the wedding.

"Wouldn't it be easier if you two moved in together right away? Your wedding is in a couple months, anyway."

Vi hit Jade with a penetrating gaze that made her squirm. "Easier isn't always right. We want to honor God with every part of our marriage. Living together now would open the possibility for too many temptations."

Jade rolled her eyes. That was so old-fashioned. Didn't her sister know that times changed? She shoved aside the twinge of conscience that said her own life hadn't exactly been God-honoring and padded down the hall to get ready for church.

The low buzz of voices didn't let up as Jade followed Vi through the lobby of Hope Church. But she felt as if every eye in the building had zeroed in on her. She could practically hear their thoughts:

Isn't that Jade Falter?

What's she doing here?

Jade Falter in a church? You've got to be kidding me.

She ducked her head and kept walking.

Anyone who wasn't trying to figure out what she was doing in church was probably wondering how she'd turned out so bad when she had such a perfect mother and sister.

Well, let them wonder.

Hadn't she wondered the same thing a thousand times herself?

Maybe someone here could figure it out. She sure never could.

Vi passed the pews at the back of the church, where Jade would have preferred to hide out, and stopped at a pew nearly at the front. Several of the people Vi had introduced her to last night were already seated. Jade fiddled with the edges of her cutoff shorts as she eyed Grace in a light floral print dress. Vi gestured for her to enter the pew first, so she slid in and settled next to Grace with a half smile.

But Grace leaned over and gave her a one-armed hug. "It's so nice to see you again. I take it you and Dan go back a long time."

Jade eyed her warily. "We went to high school together." Best to leave it at that. No one had known they were seeing each other in high school, so no reason to bring it up now.

"That's so neat." Grace patted her hand as if they were old friends. "I bet y'all have a lot of catching up to do."

Jade moved her head noncommittally. She was pretty sure she and Dan wouldn't be doing any catching up. In fact, he probably wished she'd never come back.

Not that knowing that kept her stomach from dipping as he stepped to the front of the church and offered his warm smile to everyone seated there. Nor did it keep her from remembering the days when that smile was reserved for her.

But at least she didn't long for those days again.

Much.

33

Chapter 6

"*H*idden Cafe?" Dan flipped off the last bank of sanctuary lights and turned to the dozen or so friends waiting for him in the lobby. His eyes automatically went to Jade, standing with Violet and Nate, looking completely uncomfortable and as if she'd rather be far from here.

"Where else?" Spencer clapped a hand on his back. "Good sermon today, Pastor."

"Thanks." Dan still hadn't gotten used to being called by that title. For as long as he could remember, that's what people called his dad. Thankfully, his friends generally called him by his first name—although Spencer preferred to address him as pastor when they were talking church things.

He followed his friends to the parking lot, where they all got in their own cars for the short drive to the cafe.

While he waited for everyone else to leave, he loosened his tie and tugged it off, then slipped out of his suit coat.

Much better.

If he could get away with preaching in jeans, he'd be perfectly content. But that probably wouldn't go over very well with his congregation.

He reached into the backseat to dig for one of the water bottles he kept stocked there. By the time he turned around, only Grace's car was left, but she appeared to be talking on the phone.

He debated—should he pull out ahead of her or be a gentleman and wait?

Before he'd made a decision, she hung up, then looked over and smiled at him. He waved for her to go ahead. But when she tried to start the ignition, the engine only coughed. She tried twice more with no result.

Dan groaned. Fixing a car wasn't really on his agenda for today. But he couldn't leave her stranded here.

He started his own engine and eased his car into place across from hers. It probably needed a jump start. At least that would only take a couple minutes. He was starving.

Grace slid out of her car and approached with a sheepish look.

He closed his car door. "Car trouble?"

She nodded. "I meant to fill up with gas on my way to church this morning."

Dan stared at her. "It's out of gas?" He resisted the urge to rub his temples. The nearest gas station was across town. And he'd used up the last of the gas in his gas can when he'd mowed the lawn yesterday.

"Don't worry about it. Grandpa was doing pretty well this morning. I'll call him and ask if he can fill up a gas can and bring me some. Y'all go ahead and eat without me."

Dan sighed. He couldn't do that. "Tell you what, why don't you ride with me to lunch and then afterward we'll get you some gas and get your car going again."

Grace looked uncertain. "You're sure?"

A loud growl from his stomach sealed the deal. "I'm sure."

Grace's smile was sweet, and again Dan tried to feel something for her. But it didn't spark anything.

"I talked to your friend Jade this morning," Grace said as he drove out of the parking lot.

"Yeah?" He hated the way his heart gave that jolt every time he heard her name.

He thought about correcting Grace and telling her Jade wasn't his friend. Once upon a time, he'd thought she was more than that. But he'd been wrong.

He should have realized when she never wanted to be seen with him in public that she wasn't serious about him. He finally got the message when she left—what she'd claimed to feel for him had never been real. And it never would be.

"She seemed nice," Grace continued, and Dan had to bite his tongue to keep from asking if they could talk about something else.

Anything else.

"A little aloof, though." Grace looked at him, as if to confirm whether he agreed.

He raised a lip. Aloof was putting it mildly.

"I wonder what happened to make her that way?" Grace tapped a finger to her chin. "Some kind of hurt early in life, I'd bet."

When Dan didn't say anything, she laughed at herself. "Don't mind me. I've been watching way too many daytime talk shows with Grandpa."

He laughed too and shifted the conversation to the grandfather Grace had moved here to take care of.

Unlike Jade, who'd fled from everyone who loved her, Grace had upended her whole life to be there for those she loved.

If that wasn't something he should be looking for in a woman, he didn't know what was.

So why did his eyes track to Jade the moment they entered the Hidden Cafe?

You were just looking for the right table. It's not your fault she's the first one you saw there.

Dan wanted to believe his own excuses.

Violet was on one side of Jade, Leah on the other. The moment his sister noticed him, standing in the doorway with Grace, a ginormous smile tipped her lips.

Great. Now she was going to assume her matchmaking had worked.

Dan followed Grace to the table and sat next to her in the only two chairs that were empty. He took a quick survey of the restaurant. It was a popular after-church destination, and he recognized at least six or seven families from his congregation. He waved to them.

He loved to see the members of his flock out and about, but sometimes he felt like he was always on display. Were they just waiting for him to say or do something that would prove he wasn't ready to be head pastor?

He picked up his menu, but his gaze flicked to Jade as he opened it. She was staring intently at her own menu, even though she must have had ten minutes to read it already.

By the time they'd ordered, she hadn't glanced toward him once.

So that was how she wanted to play this? They'd ignore each other? That was completely fine with him.

Better than fine. It was ideal. Now he wouldn't have to keep rehashing the past—all their moonlit walks on the beach, talking about everything and nothing in their special spot between the dunes, feeling like she knew him better than anyone besides God.

None of that would have to cloud his mind for even a second.

Dan gave his attention to a conversation with Grace and Tyler, who were both serving as chaperones on the trip to Camp Oswego in two weeks. By the time his omelet was almost gone, they'd worked out most of the details of who needed to bring which supplies.

"Who's going to watch the boys?" Grace turned to Tyler, whose twin five-year-old boys had gone home with their grandparents after church.

"Only their coolest aunt and uncle," Sophie called from the other end of the table.

Dan smiled. He loved the moments when they all felt like one big happy family. Well, one big happy family, plus Jade now. She hadn't lost any of the tension Dan had noticed in her face last night. It was as if she expected someone to jump out and ambush her at any moment.

A heavy hand fell on Dan's shoulder, and he nearly jumped. Talk about ambush.

He hadn't noticed Terrence Malone, president of Hope Church's board, walking over.

"Pretty good sermon this morning, Danny. I remember the last time your dad preached on those verses. He had a slightly different take." He coughed. "But you're still young. You'll get there."

"Thank you." Dan forced himself not to grit his teeth. Terrence was only making small talk, not trying to insult him. Since he'd taken over his dad's role as head pastor, he'd come to recognize that there were two types of people in his congregation, at least when it came to how they saw him: There were those who put him on a pedestal, and those who saw him as a little boy playing church. He wasn't sure which group he was more afraid of disappointing.

Terrence patted him on the back. "Your father left some pretty big shoes to fill. But you know that already." With one more shoulder clap, Terrence left. Across the table, Jade looked from Terrence to Dan. For some reason, it unnerved him that he couldn't read what she was thinking.

Next to him, Grace set her napkin on her plate. "I didn't know your daddy, but I do know you'll fill his shoes well."

Dan nodded, wishing he could be as sure.

Chapter 7

*J*ade clicked on her phone to check the date. It was Friday, which meant she'd been in Hope Springs one day short of a week. Why did it feel so much longer?

The familiar claustrophobia this town had always given her was creeping up on her already.

It didn't help that she'd spent all week holed up in Vi's apartment. But there wasn't anything she wanted to do or anyone she wanted to see.

And there was one person she very much *did not* want to see.

She raised her hands to her face and rubbed it. Why was it in the six days she'd been home she'd thought about Dan at least six million times? Over the past eight years, she'd managed to leave thoughts of him behind, but now that she was here, it was like he'd invaded her head.

The head is fine. Just don't let him get to your heart again.

Jade pulled her hands down, firming her resolve. Of course Dan wouldn't get to her heart again.

Anyway, he was with another woman now. When he'd walked into the Hidden Cafe with Grace after church on Sunday, she'd told herself she was fine with it. But the longer the meal had gone on, the more painful it had been to watch him with her, laughing and planning their trip. And when that guy from church had come over to tell Dan what big shoes he had to fill, it had hit her.

Even if he weren't with Grace, he would never consider a relationship with her. He had a role to fill here, a reputation to maintain. And being with her wasn't the kind of reputation he needed.

Not that she'd wanted to get back together with him. That wasn't the point. The point was, she'd burned any hope of a future here before she'd left in the first place.

She shook her head at herself. It wasn't like she wanted a future here anyway. All she had to do was make it through the summer, and then she could get back to her real life in LA.

The real life with the dead-end job, string of meaningless men, and, oh, don't forget the generous helping of self-loathing.

Jade shut off the voice and grabbed her phone again, swiping at her contact list. She needed someone to help her get her head on straight.

Keira answered before the phone had even rung.

"Wow. Were you waiting for me to call?"

"Yep." Keira's voice was reassuringly familiar. "I figured you were due to be going crazy right about now."

Jade snorted. "You could say that."

"So those wholesome Hope Springs guys aren't enticing you, huh?"

Jade closed her eyes. She'd had a wholesome Hope Springs guy once. "I already told you I wasn't coming here to date."

"Ah, well, the summer is young. Don't give up yet."

"Actually—" Jade fiddled with the small turquoise ring her mother had given her for her sixteenth birthday. It was the one piece of jewelry she never took off. "I'm not sure I can make it the whole summer. I might just come back to LA. I'll tell Vi I have an audition." No need for Vi to know she'd quit going on auditions two years ago when she'd realized that even if she ever got a decent part, she actually hated acting.

"What about the shower and the wedding?"

"I don't have to be here all summer for those. I can just fly here for those weekends." The more she talked about it, the better the plan sounded.

40

"Jade Lynn Falter."

Jade winced at her roommate's use of her middle name.

"Do you remember how many nights you spent crying to me about what an awful sister you've been?" Keira's voice was sharp and sympathetic at the same time.

"It wasn't that many nights," Jade muttered.

"It *was* that many. And if you come back now, it's going to be that many more. And I can't take that—my tissue budget is empty for the year."

Jade let herself laugh a little. She pushed out an exaggerated sigh. "Fine. I'll stay."

"Good girl." Keira's voice gentled. "It can't be that bad there, can it?"

This time Jade's sigh was too real, pulling with it all the mistakes from her past. She'd never told Keira about Dan, and she didn't feel like getting into it now. Next thing she knew, Keira would be telling her God had brought her back into Dan's path for a reason. And unless that reason was to torture her, Jade couldn't agree.

"There's just not much to do, I guess."

"What did you used to do?"

The question was innocent enough, but Jade flinched. "Nothing I'm proud of or want to repeat."

Keira paused. "Okay, what does your sister do?"

"Works in her antique store."

"There you go then."

Jade wrinkled her nose. She'd popped down to the store below Vi's apartment a couple times during the week to ask her sister where things were, but she hadn't hung around long. Too dull for her taste.

"I'm not sure that would be much more fun than sitting around staring at the walls," she told Keira.

"Jade." For a single woman with no children, Keira sure had a good mom voice. "You're supposed to be spending the summer there to catch up with your sister. Wouldn't it be easier to do that if you actually spent some time with her? I'm sure it'd mean a lot to her."

"Well—" But she had no counterarguments. "Ugh. I hate when you're right."

"But I always am. Gotta fly, but call me soon and let me know how antiquing goes."

Jade sighed again as she hung up the phone, but she dutifully got dressed and made her way downstairs to her sister's antique shop.

It may not be fun, but at least it should help get her mind off Dan.

Chapter 8

"Thanks, Pastor Dan."

"Anytime." Dan ushered the young newlyweds he'd been counseling to the door of his office. When he'd married Colton and Sierra two weeks ago, both had been radiating happiness. So he'd been more than a little surprised when they'd knocked on his office door this afternoon, both near tears, asking if he had time to talk.

Thankfully, the issue hadn't been anything serious. Just some difficulties in adjusting to married life and setting realistic expectations of each other.

"Why don't you two go out and get a nice dinner together and keep talking?"

"We will." Colton shook his hand, but Sierra gave Dan a hug.

"I know you told us before the wedding that marriage would be hard, but I didn't know you meant *this* hard," she said.

Dan laughed as he released her. He may not have any personal experience with marriage, but he'd done enough couple's counseling to know marriage took work.

"It's worth it though." Colton draped an arm over his wife's shoulders and dropped a kiss onto the top of her head.

"Stay in the Word together and pray together," Dan reminded them as they started down the hall. He watched them until they turned the corner into the church lobby, a deep sense of satisfaction filling his soul. The impromptu counseling session had been an interruption to his plans for the day, no doubt about that. But for him, one of the most rewarding parts of ministry was moments like this, when he could sit down with people one-on-one and help them work through their problems. Most importantly, he could point them to God's Word.

Help them to keep you at the center of their relationship always. He offered a silent prayer for the couple, then checked the time.

Four-thirty. Which meant he had just enough time for a short run before dinner at Violet's.

He switched off the lights in his office and pulled the door closed. But as he came to the end of the hallway, he heard the church's door open, followed by footsteps.

He paused, undecided.

He could backtrack and take the side exit, so he wouldn't run into whoever had just come in. But he dismissed the thought. What if it was Colton and Sierra with more questions?

He continued toward the lobby, promising himself he'd give whoever was there the time and attention they needed, even if it meant missing his run.

But the only one in the lobby was Leah.

"Oh, it's just you." He moved toward the door, gesturing for her to follow him.

She slapped his shoulder as he passed. "That's a nice way to greet the sister who brings you good news."

Dan held the door open for her, then stepped outside, locking it behind him. "What good news?" He took a deep breath of the lake-scented air. The day was warm, but the usual humidity of late June hadn't hit yet, and the light breeze off the water was refreshing. Perfect running weather.

"I was just talking to a certain someone, and I get the impression she'd be more than happy to go on another date with you."

Dan's thoughts jumped to Jade, before he realized his sister was talking about Grace.

He rolled his eyes. "It's tough to go on *another* date with her since we haven't gone on *one* date."

"Yes you have. Dinner last week. And the fireworks."

"Those were not dates. They were setups. By you."

Leah shrugged. "Same difference. Anyway, I'm not the one who made you bring her to the Hidden Cafe after church on Sunday. That was all you."

Dan threw his hands in the air and walked across the parking lot toward his house next door. "Her car was out of gas. What was I supposed to do, leave her?"

Leah fell into step next to him. "Still, it was pretty chivalrous, especially the way you insisted on filling her car up afterward, at least the way she tells it."

Dan scrubbed a hand down his face. "I told you, I just don't see it going anywhere, Leah."

"Why not?"

But he didn't have a good answer. Grace was a nice woman, and he appreciated all her help at church. But that was the extent of his feelings for her.

When he didn't answer, Leah's hand went to her hip. "Dan, if she's not perfect for you, I don't know who is. She's a pastor's daughter, she jumped right into volunteering at church, she has all kinds of ideas for ministry and the ability to carry them out. Oh, and she was helping me out in the kitchen the other day—she knows her way around in there."

All of that was true—Dan knew that. On paper, Grace would make a perfect pastor's wife.

"This is about her coming back, isn't it?" His sister's sharp stare made him look away.

"Her who?"

Leah whacked his arm. "You know who."

He shook his head. "It's not about Jade, if that's what you're implying."

"Good." Leah was still watching him too closely. "Because that is a high school dream that's over. You know that."

"Yeah." Dan kicked at a rock in front of him. "I do."

He wished, not for the first time, that he'd never told her about his short-lived relationship with Jade.

Leah stopped as they reached the front of his house. "I'm serious, Dan. Grace is a great woman. Promise me you won't get so blinded by what was that you don't notice what's in front of you. Give Grace a chance, at least."

"Yeah, fine. I promise." He jogged up the porch steps. "Now get out of here. I want to go for a run before we have to be at Violet's."

"Fine." Leah backed toward the church parking lot, where she'd left her car. "But just so you know, I invited Grace tonight. So you can start keeping your promise right away." With a wave and a laugh, she skipped off.

Dan closed the door harder than necessary behind her. His sister's meddling got worse every year. For some reason, she couldn't bear to see Dan single, even though she herself rarely dated and claimed she'd be perfectly content to end up alone.

As he was changing into his running clothes, Dan's thoughts wandered to Leah's accusation that his lack of interest in Grace had something to do with Jade's return.

That was ridiculous. What he'd had with Jade—if it had ever been anything—was long over.

He tied his running shoes and headed out the back door, jogging across his yard to the wooden staircase next to church that led down to the beach.

Telling himself it was the better workout, he turned to the south, images of Jade chasing him all the way. When he reached their special spot between the dunes, he stopped short, sucking in sharp breaths. He'd avoided this place for the past eight years, but in the last week, he'd found his runs ending up here every day.

He moved closer and squinted, as if that would make it possible to see into the past. To figure out what had gone wrong.

For two months, everything had been as close to perfect as possible. The beach had become their refuge, the spot where they sat close and talked about everything from school to his plans to enter seminary to her mom's cancer. He'd even worked up the courage to hold her hand.

He'd tried for weeks to find exactly the right moment to kiss her, but every time he thought he might go for it, he chickened out.

A couple weeks before graduation, Jade's mom died. He ached to be there for her, but the more he tried, the further she pulled away. She didn't want him to sit with her at the funeral. She shut down all his requests to meet at the beach. Eventually, she quit coming to chemistry class too, although he saw her in the halls at school, always with some guy or another. The same guys who'd treated her so badly at the beginning of the year.

Dan had tried to be understanding, tried to tell himself she was going through a lot. That she just needed time.

Finally, on graduation day, she slipped him a note as they rehearsed the recessional.

Meet me at our spot tonight after graduation?

He looked up to meet her eyes, not caring who saw his grin. Giving her time had worked. Now things could get back to normal.

Looking back later, Dan realized that her return smile had held a trace of sadness behind it, but at the time, he'd been too ecstatic to notice.

He barely paid attention to the graduation ceremony. He couldn't wait to get out of there and get to Jade. When he finally made it to the beach after his family had given him about a gazillion hugs, she was already there.

The night was dark, clouds completely obscuring the moon, but as his eyes fell on her silhouette, the clouds slid aside, letting a slice of moonlight illuminate her face.

Dan's breath caught as it hit him: He was in love with Jade Falter, and he would be for the rest of his life.

"Hi." Jade's voice was thick with emotion, and he wondered if she'd had the same realization as he had.

He stepped closer, all the fears that had held him back so many times falling away.

He knew it then.

This was it. Exactly the right moment.

As he'd leaned toward her, he'd never been so uncertain and so sure of something all at once.

The kiss had been . . . awkward. But also sort of magical.

Dan hadn't had much practice in the kissing department, and his lips had fumbled against hers. He didn't remember doing it, but somehow he'd lifted his hands to her shoulders, and he still remembered the simultaneous warmth of her skin with the chill of the night air.

Jade had sighed against his lips, and it was the most beautiful sound he'd ever heard.

When she'd pulled away, she'd given him a smile he'd never seen on her. Sort of happy and scared and overwhelmed all at once.

For some reason, it had made him self-conscious. "Sorry if that wasn't very good. I don't—"

But her hand had brushed against his cheek. "That was perfect."

"Hey, man, can you get that?" The guy's voice yanked Dan out of his memories, and he shook himself, eyes tracking to a Frisbee that lay a few feet from where he stood. He stooped to pick it up, then tossed it to the guy.

As the guy called out a "thank you," Dan lifted a hand to wave, then started toward home at a slower jog.

Apparently the kiss wasn't as good as Jade had let him believe.

The next day when he went to meet her again, all he'd found was a note.

And, until last weekend, that was the only word he'd heard from her in eight years.

Leah was right.

He should give Grace a chance.

Jade was a dream who had walked out of his life.

He'd be a fool to let her back in.

Chapter 9

*J*ade took a second to survey her handiwork.

"That's looking pretty good." Vi stepped over to examine the dining table Jade had been sanding down for her. "Tomorrow I'll teach you how to refinish it."

Jade groaned, but she couldn't help smiling. When she'd taken Keira's advice to come down here, she'd planned on talking with Vi for an hour or so and then making her escape. When Vi had asked if she wanted to help, she'd said yes only out of a sense of obligation.

But she had to admit that she'd enjoyed working with her hands. And seeing the fruits of her labor left her feeling more satisfied than she'd been in a long time.

Satisfied and exhausted.

She lifted her arms in front of her to stretch them. "How do you do this every day?"

As she'd watched her sister move from helping customers to repairing broken table legs to taking care of the accounts, Jade had been amazed.

Vi shrugged. "I love what I do. Just like you love acting."

Jade turned away. She'd wanted to love acting, so maybe that counted for something. Truth be told, she'd never found anything that she really loved. Or that she was good at.

"I flipped the sign out front to closed," Vi said, "so as soon as we get this all cleaned up, we can head upstairs for dinner."

"Already?"

"Yep." Vi held out what looked like a piece of netting.

"Fishnet stockings?"

Violet burst into laughter. "Cheesecloth."

Jade wrinkled her nose as the fabric hit her fingertips. Instead of the smooth silkiness she'd anticipated, it was gummy.

"You use it to wipe off the dust from sanding." Vi pantomimed wiping the cloth over the table.

Jade followed her sister's instructions as Vi put away her tools. Ten minutes later, the workshop looked just as it had this morning, with the exception of a couple items she and Vi had managed to maneuver onto the sales floor.

"This was nice." Vi flipped off the light and pulled the door closed.

"It was." To her surprise, Jade meant it.

One of the things she'd worried about most when she'd agreed to come to Hope Springs for the summer was that things would be awkward between her and her sister after not seeing each other for so long. But thankfully they'd been able to pick up right where they'd left off—better than they'd left off, actually, since they'd never been terribly close as kids.

She followed Vi up the stairs at the back of the building.

"We should have just enough time to get ready before everyone gets here," Vi said over her shoulder.

Jade glanced up. "Get ready for what?" She'd been looking forward to slipping into some pajamas and spending the night binging Netflix.

But before Vi could answer, the door at the bottom of the stairs opened. They both glanced over their shoulders.

"Hey! I didn't expect you to be home yet." Instantly, Vi turned and skipped down the steps to greet her fiancé. Jade smiled at the clear adoration on Nate's face as he looked up at his future bride.

But her smile wilted as Dan stepped through the doorway behind Nate. His eyes met hers for half a second before he looked away, his jaw tight.

"Sorry I'm early," he said to Vi, who had already pulled him into a quick hug.

"Don't be silly. Come on up. Jade helped me in the shop today, and we were just heading up ourselves."

"Yeah?" Nate smiled up at Jade. "How'd you like it?"

"It was good." If they wanted more intelligent conversation from her, she was going to need to know what was going on. Why Dan was here. "So what are you guys up to tonight?"

Vi slapped a palm to her forehead. "I can't believe I forgot to tell you. Everyone's coming over for dinner tonight. I hope that's okay?"

"Of course." It was Vi's place, after all. Jade only wished she'd known ahead of time so she could have made plans to escape.

Maybe it wasn't too late.

But no matter how much she wracked her brain, she couldn't come up with somewhere to go by herself on a Friday night around here.

She let Nate and Vi pass her on the stairs. Dan was still at the bottom, though, busy with his phone, so she turned to follow them up. After a second, Dan's footsteps sounded below her, but she refused to let herself look back. The same way she'd done when she'd left that note on the beach years ago.

In the apartment, Vi and Nate were already bustling around the kitchen, gathering the taco fixings Jade had smelled Vi making before she'd left for work this morning. The way they moved together, handing each other plates, sidestepping to move out of the way, occasionally pausing for a smile or a quick kiss, made them seem like a married couple already.

Jade had pretty much always been sure she didn't want anything like that, but watching them now almost made her change her mind.

She crossed through the apartment to take refuge in the bedroom. She didn't really need anything in there—aside from a minute to compose herself.

After spending all week fighting to get Dan out of her head, having him in the next room wasn't helping.

She pulled her hair into a ponytail, just so it would look like she'd come in here for a reason, then forced herself to rejoin the others. In the few minutes she'd been in the bedroom, the small apartment had filled up. Emma, Leah, Grace, and Sophie had joined Vi and Nate in the kitchen. Sophie's husband—Jade thought she remembered his name was Spencer—and his brother—Tyler, maybe—were talking to Dan in the living room.

And there was Jade, all by herself between the two, not belonging anywhere. Story of her life.

She took a tentative step toward the kitchen, but the apartment door swung open, and before she knew what was happening, everyone was oohing and swarming the couple who had just come in. It wasn't until the group shifted positions that she saw why. The woman was holding a small, squirming bundle.

Jade retreated to the kitchen to busy herself with something. Anything. She couldn't coo over the baby. Not with this terrible ache in her throat.

"She's getting so big already." Vi stroked the baby's cheek as she led the couple to the living room.

"She's a month old today," the woman said, never taking her eyes off the baby.

Vi moved toward the kitchen. "Jade, you haven't met Ethan and Ariana yet, have you? They weren't at the fireworks the other night because of the baby." Vi grabbed Jade's arm and dragged her to the living room, not stopping until they were right in front of the happy family. "Ethan. Ariana. This is my sister Jade."

They both smiled and said hello.

53

"And this is little Joy." Vi leaned down to touch the baby's hand, and instantly Joy grasped her finger. Vi looked like she was in heaven. "Isn't she just the most precious thing?"

Everyone was watching her expectantly. Waiting for her to—what? Play with the baby?

She nodded mutely and turned toward the kitchen.

The apartment door opened again, and the woman Vi had introduced as Peyton at the fireworks held up a pink box. "Sorry we're late. But I brought cake, so you can't be mad."

Her husband followed her through the door. "It's my fault. I was on a call."

"Ask him what it was." Peyton laughed as she opened the box, revealing a beautifully decorated cake covered in swirls of flowers.

Jared groaned. "It was a first for me. Some kid got stuck in a laundry chute."

A mixture of laughs and gasps went up from the group.

"Did you get him out?" Grace asked.

"Her," Jared corrected. "And yes. But it took several hours, and I'm afraid the parents are going to be facing some pretty costly repairs."

"Great." Ariana sighed. "Add one more thing to worry about as a new mom."

Ethan kissed her forehead and took Joy from her, snuggling the baby against his shoulder. "We don't even have a laundry chute."

Ariana laughed along as the others giggled. When they stopped, she stood, grabbing a diaper bag from the floor. "I know, but seriously you guys, I had no idea how much there was to worry about as a parent. I pray for this little one constantly."

"And that's the best thing you can do for her," Dan said.

Jade glanced at him, then at the others, who were nodding in agreement. Did they really believe it was that easy? Just pray and everything would be fine?

"Dinner's ready," Vi called from the kitchen.

The noise swelled as there was a mass surge for the food. Jade watched everyone for a minute. They were all comfortable together. Relaxed. Like a family.

One she didn't belong to.

But as dinner wore on, Jade had to admit that the others were striving to include her—everyone except Dan, who'd chosen a spot as far from her as possible in the small quarters.

Sophie had asked about life in LA. Ariana had complimented her earrings. And Grace had been interested in knowing what it was like on a film set—which Jade could only answer with details she'd picked up from friends since the closest she'd come to an actual film set was the training video she'd starred in for an insurance company.

When the dishes were cleared and washed—by the men, since they apparently traded off turns between the sexes—they all settled on various pieces of furniture or the floor of the living room. Jade took a spot on the floor with her back against the wall. To her surprise, she had to admit she enjoyed listening to the flow of their conversation.

There was no talk of parties or clubs or who wore what when. But they all seemed to care about the mundane details of each other's lives, like Ariana and Ethan's sleepless nights with the baby and Peyton's plan to expand her bakery and Tyler's tales about the twins' latest mischief.

Jade let herself wonder briefly what it would be like to have a group of friends like this—people she was one hundred percent comfortable around and never worried would judge her. But she dismissed the thought. She'd never needed a close friend group like this before—and she didn't need one now. Besides, she wasn't hanging around long enough to form friendships.

"I know!" Grace chirped during a lull in the conversation.

Jade had tried not to notice that Grace had chosen a spot next to Dan on the couch, along with Vi and Nate. The four of them were crammed on there so tightly that Grace's shoulder was pressed up against Dan's.

"Let's play Bible Pictionary." Grace's enthusiasm was almost alarming.

Jade made a face. She had to be kidding, right?

But apparently Jade was in the minority with her opinion, as Vi was soon pulling out a large pad of paper and some markers.

Tyler did a quick count of the room. "It'll be uneven teams, unless baby Joy plays."

As if she'd heard her name, the baby cooed in her sleep, and everyone aahed over her again.

Jade stretched her cramped legs and pushed to her feet. "That's okay. You guys play without me. I'm going to get a little air."

She ducked her head so she wouldn't have to see Vi's disappointed look. But her sister followed her to the landing outside the door.

"Everything okay?" Vi asked in a low voice.

"Of course." Jade lifted her lips into a smile. "Your friends are great. I just need a little break."

Vi laughed. "That's understandable. They are pretty great, but they can be a bit much to get used to." She squeezed Jade's arm. "Be careful out there."

Jade resisted rolling her eyes. She'd lived in LA for eight years. There wasn't much about Hope Springs that could scare her. But she dutifully answered, "I will," before trundling down the steps.

She paused outside the exterior door. Where was she going to go?

The sound of the waves reached up the long hill behind the apartment building. She'd been working to avoid the beach all week. It held too many memories of what could have been.

So she absolutely shouldn't go there now.

But apparently her feet hadn't gotten the memo, as she was already halfway there.

Chapter 10

"Samson and Delilah," Grace shouted, and Dan pumped a fist in the air.

"See," he said to the rest of the group. "I can draw."

"I have no idea how she got that." Spencer tilted his head to the side. "It looks like a potato to me."

"You two must have some kind of connection," Leah piped up.

Dan shot his sister a look as Grace beamed at him.

"It was the scissors that did it." Grace pointed to an X on Dan's drawing.

"That was supposed to be a braid." Dan held his hand up to her for a high five. "But whatever works."

He deliberately ignored his sister, who was probably exploding with googly eyes right now.

"And on that triumphant note, I must bid you all adieu."

They all protested, telling him to stay, but he held up a hand. "Some of us have a sermon to finish preparing for Sunday." Not to mention, some of them wanted to escape before Jade came back inside.

She'd been gone at least half an hour already, and if he didn't get out of here soon, he was going to have to see her again. And if he saw her again, he was going to have to remind himself all over again of all the reasons he should avoid her, same as he'd been doing all night. It was getting exhausting.

He said goodnight, then jogged down the stairs and out the door, savoring the cool night air after Violet's warm apartment.

"Oh, hey." He stopped short as his feet hit the parking lot.

Great plan. Not only was Jade standing right here in front of him, but now they were alone together.

"Hey." Jade ran a hand through her hair, which she'd pulled out of its ponytail. It was now dancing in the lake breeze.

"Were you down by the beach?" He didn't intend to ask, but the words slipped out right past the wall he'd meant to erect around his heart.

She nodded wordlessly.

"Oh." Was that really all he had to say? *Oh?*

But what else was he going to do? Ask her if being down there made her think of him? Ask if she remembered the time they'd kissed down there?

If she could tell him why she'd left?

"I was just heading out." He pointed to his car behind her as if his words weren't clear enough to explain what he was doing.

She nodded again but looked away, biting her lip.

The gesture was so familiar that he had to remind himself that it was eight years since the last time he'd seen her do that.

But he still knew what it meant. "What is it?"

"Can we get something in the open?" Jade gave him a direct look, and he forced himself to return it.

"Of course," he said evenly. Maybe she was finally going to tell him why she'd left. Not that he was sure he actually wanted to know anymore. Some things were better left buried.

"I understand if you don't want me to hang out with you all anymore." She gestured toward the upper floor of the apartment building behind him just as a burst of laughter sounded through Violet's open apartment window. "You have every right to hate me."

Dan scrubbed a hand against his jaw, staring past her toward the lake. Moonlight reflected from the foamy tops of the waves. She didn't really think he hated her, did she?

"I don't hate you." He couldn't look at her as he said it. Otherwise, he might be tempted to tell her that far from hating her, he was beginning to fear that he was as taken by her as ever. Even though he very much shouldn't be.

"Of course not. You're a pastor. You don't hate anyone."

Dan laughed and brought his eyes to her face. But she was staring at her feet. "I'm human, Jade. I struggle with emotions just like everyone else. But I don't hate you. I never did."

She looked at him then, skepticism written all over her face. "Why not?"

He lifted his shoulders. How could he tell her that no matter what happened in this world, he was pretty sure he could never hate her?

"You did what you thought you had to do." His gaze swung back to the lake. Much as he hadn't wanted to see it then, it was probably for the best that she'd left. "Anyway, I'm here doing what I'm supposed to be doing. You're in LA doing what you're supposed to be doing. So it all worked out." He forced a tight smile, and she half returned it.

"So you weren't angry with me for leaving?"

Dan pondered the question. She deserved an honest answer. "I was maybe a little angry at first. But mostly I was confused."

He waited, hope and dread colliding over the possibility that she might take the hint and fill him in on what had driven her away.

When she remained silent, he stepped past her to his car. "But then, you always were the most confusing girl I knew."

Jade's soft laugh followed him.

"Anyway—" He paused with his hand on the car door. "I don't want you to stop hanging out with everyone. You should feel comfortable with your sister and her friends. And if me being around makes you uncomfortable, I'll step back for the summer." He had plenty to keep him busy at church, although the thought of not spending time with his friends left him empty.

Jade shook her head. "You don't make me uncomfortable."

"Good." He pulled the car door open. "Then you should join us all for dinner again next Friday. My place."

He dropped into his seat and closed the door. It'd been a dumb thing to say, and he didn't want to hear her answer, whether it was yes or no.

Chapter 11

"Here we are." Vi parked the car in the driveway of a cute little house after church on Sunday. "What do you think?" Vi was clearly enchanted with the place.

"It's sweet." Jade could easily picture her sister and Nate starting a family here. She unclicked her seatbelt and followed Vi onto the front porch, with its white railing, decorative pillars, and cozy swing.

Vi paused with her hand on the front door. "The house needs some work on the inside, but we'll get to that eventually. When we have time."

Jade gave her sister's arm a reassuring pat. Vi didn't have to worry about impressing her.

"I'm sure it's— Whoa." She stopped as she entered the house. She didn't know where to look first. Wallpaper in every pattern imaginable covered every wall—and even some doors. The entryway was a checkered red plaid, while the living room walls boasted a pink floral print. Jade made her way slowly through the first floor, taking in the jungle print on the dining room walls and the fruit basket border in the kitchen.

"There's more upstairs." Vi laughed at Jade, who struggled to ease her features into an expression somewhere short of horror.

"More?"

"It's no big deal. We'll take it one room at a time after we move in, and eventually it'll get done."

"And in the meantime, you'll be happy living here?"

"Of course." Vi rubbed a hand over the kitchen wall. "I don't care what our home looks like. Nate and I will be here together. That's what matters."

Jade nodded, even though she'd have no idea about any of that. She walked to the French doors that looked out onto the backyard.

"It's an amazing view, though." The house overlooked an empty section of beach below the town.

"Yep." Vi pulled the doors open and led the way onto the patio. "That's what drew us here."

Jade shielded her eyes against the morning sun as she watched the water. It was completely still today. Completely peaceful.

"So—" Vi poked her shoulder. "What's up with you and Dan?"

Jade wrinkled her nose at her sister. "What are you talking about?"

"I saw the way he looked at you the other night at the fireworks and the way you kept staring at him Friday night when everyone was over."

"He wasn't looking at me any way." Jade tried to keep her voice disinterested. "He was probably trying to remember who I was. We didn't exactly run in the same circles in high school." Which wasn't a complete lie. Aside from each other, they'd had no mutual friends— something she'd worked hard to maintain since the kind of people she called friends would have had a field day picking on the preacher's son if they'd known she was seeing him. Dan would have beat his own school record in the one hundred meter dash running away from her if he'd spent any time with them.

"What about you, then?" Vi tipped her head to the side, scrutinizing her. "You can't deny you were staring at him. A lot."

"I can deny it." Jade took a few steps toward the edge of the patio. "And anyway, if I *was* staring at him, it's because I was thinking about his sermon from last week." She didn't know why she was so determined to keep her feelings about Dan from her sister. Probably because she didn't have any feelings for him. Just silly memories that were better left in the past.

"Oh." Vi seemed to take her at her word. "I'm glad you came to church with us again today."

Jade offered a noncommittal nod.

Vi's brow creased. Not for the first time since she'd been home, Jade felt Vi studying her. She wasn't sure what her sister was looking for, but she clearly wasn't finding it. Big surprise there. Jade rarely had what people wanted.

"Did you not like the service?" Vi finally asked.

"The service was fine." In fact, a couple of the songs had reminded her of going to church with Mom and Vi as a kid, and she'd been surprised to find their familiarity comforting. And Dan's sermon about God's grace had actually pulled her in. Even if she remained skeptical about the message, she had to admit that Dan was an engaging speaker. His love for what he did came through so clearly as he preached, and she couldn't help but admire his passion.

"What is it, then?" Vi sat in one of the chipped Adirondack chairs and gestured for Jade to sit in the other.

Instead, Jade leaned against its back. "I guess I don't feel like I belong there. I can feel everyone wondering what I'm doing there."

Vi turned in her seat to stare up at her. "You know no one thinks that, right? Everyone at Hope Church is very warm and welcoming."

"Easy for you to say," Jade muttered.

"What do you mean by that?" Vi's eyes were wide, as if she had no idea what Jade was talking about.

"Oh, come on, Vi." Jade threw her hands in the air. "You know you were always the good one. Of course everyone at church loves you." She paced to the other side of the patio. "I know you were away at college my last couple years of high school, but even you must know that I didn't exactly have—" She cut off, suddenly not wanting to continue. If by some miracle her sister had lived in Hope Springs all these years without hearing rumors of Jade's less than savory past, she didn't want to be the one to shatter her sister's image of her.

"Have what?" Vi's voice was gentle, her eyes searching, although Jade had a feeling Vi knew exactly what she had been about to say.

"Never mind." Jade strode toward the door. "We should get going. You and Nate promised to be at Peyton's by two for the cake testing."

Vi pressed her lips together but got up and crossed toward the door. Jade didn't wait for her.

It wasn't until they were almost home that Vi turned to her. "Whatever happened in the past is in the past. You're forgiven for all of it. And no one here is thinking about it." She squeezed Jade's arm. "Got it?"

Jade kept her gaze directed out the window and made herself nod to placate her sister. It was a nice sentiment.

And Vi probably really did believe it was true.

But Jade had seen enough of the world to know it wasn't.

Not for girls like her.

Chapter 12

S he shouldn't be here. It was all Jade could think as she followed Nate and Vi to the front door of Dan's house Friday night. Dan's invitation last week had been made out of pity—not a desire that she'd actually show up. But Vi had insisted that if she wanted dinner she'd have to come, since there was no food left in the apartment.

Plus, as Jade had joined Vi in the antique shop all week, a brilliant plan had occurred to her. But she was going to need the help of Vi's friends to pull it off. And this was the only way she could think of to talk to all of them without raising Vi's suspicions.

Now that she was here, though, she wished she had tried harder to come up with another way.

She paused at the bottom of the steps leading up to Dan's front door, waiting for Vi to ring the doorbell. At least she'd have a few more seconds to come to grips with being here before Dan answered the door. But Vi grabbed the knob and let herself in.

Jade shot Nate an alarmed look, and he shrugged. "That's how we do things around here."

Jade pushed down the swirl trying to flutter from her belly toward her heart and followed Nate into the house. There was nothing to be nervous about, now that she and Dan had cleared the air and she knew that at least he didn't hate her.

But instead of reassuring her, the conversation in the apartment parking lot last week had left her shaken. Probably because Dan had incomplete information about why she'd left. If he knew the real reason, he would hate her, pastor or not.

But he would never know the real reason, she reminded herself. She didn't understand why that didn't make her feel better.

Inside, the house was bigger than Jade had expected. Though the furniture was worn, it was tasteful and gave off a homey vibe. Not exactly what she'd expected in a bachelor pad. But then, she supposed Dan wasn't your typical bachelor. Aside from her, she didn't know of anyone else he'd dated in high school. Of course, that was a long time ago. He could have dated a whole slew of women since then. But somehow Jade knew he hadn't. Probably no one besides Grace.

Jade's gaze traveled to the kitchen, where Grace and Leah were chatting and cutting up vegetables while Dan rolled out dough.

He lifted his head as Jade closed the door behind her.

"Glad you could make it," he called in the general direction of the door, keeping his eyes off hers. He could as easily have been talking to Vi and Nate as to her. In fact, she was sure he was.

"Hope you guys don't mind pizza." He slid the crust onto a pizza stone, his movements deft and sure. "We have an early morning. The bus for Camp Oswego leaves when the sun comes up."

"Oh, I almost forgot." Grace laid a hand on Dan's arm. "I picked up some snacks for the ride."

Dan smiled at her, and Jade looked away. Listen to those two throwing around that word, "we."

That's what couples do.

Of course it was. That was why Jade had been so careful not to use that word with Dan in high school. It was always, "Meet me at the beach." Or "I'll grab some sandwiches." Never "We should go to the beach" or "we" anything.

We meant attachment. It meant opening yourself up to hurt when there was no longer a *we*.

Nate and Vi moved to talk to Dan, but Jade took a seat next to Sophie and Spencer, with her back to the kitchen.

"Hey, Jade." Sophie offered her a kind smile. "Vi said you were a lot of help in the store this week."

"I'm not sure help is the right word. I'm pretty sure I slowed her down more than anything. But I was there, anyway."

"I'm glad." Sophie patted her leg. "Vi works way too hard and never knows when to ask for help."

Jade couldn't have hoped for a more perfect opening. "I've noticed." She lowered her voice, not enough to draw suspicion, but low enough that no one would be able to hear from the kitchen, especially over the rest of the chatter. "I was thinking, maybe we could all get together and take down that hideous wallpaper in their new house and paint for them. You know, as part of their wedding gift or something."

Sophie's grin grew as Jade talked, and she reached one arm to give Jade a quick squeeze.

"That's a great idea." In her enthusiasm, Sophie practically shouted, and her eyes widened.

"Sorry," she whispered. "That's a great idea."

"What's a great idea?" Peyton asked from the chair across from them.

Jade peeked over her shoulder, but Vi and Nate were deep in conversation with Dan and Grace and didn't even glance toward the living room.

As stealthily as she could, Jade made her way around the room to the others as they ate, cleared the dishes, and talked.

Finally, the only ones she hadn't talked to were Dan, Grace, and Leah. She figured if she talked with any one of them, they could tell the other two. So now it was a matter of who she saw first. If she were a praying woman, she'd pray that it was Leah or Grace.

Chapter 13

The clamor of his friends eating and talking and laughing at his house always filled Dan's heart with a special kind of contentment. As the kid who was always picked on, he'd never imagined this would be his life.

In the short time he'd been back in Hope Springs, this small group of people had become a second family to him.

If she let them, they could be a second family to Jade too. Hard as he'd tried not to watch her, he had noticed how she spent time talking to everyone here tonight. Well, everyone except him. She hadn't so much as been in the same room as him all night. He'd told himself it was a coincidence at first, but as he moved into the living room now, she got up and headed for the kitchen.

He briefly considered doubling back to see what she would do but decided against it. He'd respect her wishes. If she didn't want to be near him, he wouldn't push it.

Grace offered him an open smile as he sat on the couch next to her. "That was the most delicious pizza I've ever had. And I'm Italian, so that's saying something." She leaned closer and nudged him with her shoulder.

"Thanks." Dan returned her smile. Much as he hated to admit his sister was right about anything, he had to agree that Grace was sweet and easy to be with. "Did everyone get enough?"

"Ugh. Too much." Sophie rubbed her stomach. "Not that I'm complaining. It was all delicious."

"That's good." Spencer wrapped an arm around his wife and snuggled her close. "Since you're eating for two now."

"Spencer!" Sophie slapped at his thigh. "We agreed to wait another month to tell everyone."

But the whole group had already gotten to their feet to take turns engulfing the couple in hugs. When it was Ariana's turn, she held Joy out toward Sophie's tummy.

"That's either your future best friend or future husband in there," she cooed to the baby, and everyone laughed.

Dan jumped to his feet and headed for the kitchen to grab some celebratory apple juice, since he had no wine in the house—and Sophie couldn't drink it even if he did. He counted out enough paper cups, since he had nowhere near enough wine glasses for everyone either, then passed the juice around.

But when he was done, he had an extra left. He scanned the room, trying to figure out who he'd missed. But everyone had a cup—even Ariana, who was struggling to keep hers out of Joy's grabbing fingers.

Maybe he'd miscounted. But then he realized one person was missing.

Jade.

A clunk from down the hallway caught his ear.

Oh no. Please tell him she hadn't found—

He strode down the hallway.

Sure enough, there she was, right in the middle of his Star Wars room, bending to pick up a storm trooper mask. As she straightened, her eyes fell on him, and she jumped as if she'd been caught toilet papering the principal's office again.

"Sorry." She set the mask on its stand and stepped away from it. "I don't think I broke it."

Dan shrugged. He was more worried about the fact that Jade Falter was standing here in the middle of his Star Wars collection. It was the one thing he'd kept hidden from her in high school—because if there was anything that proved they didn't belong together, it was this. She was the too-cool-to-care girl, and he was the nerdy guy who collected Star Wars toys.

"I'm sure it's fine," he finally said. "What are you doing in here?" He didn't mean for it to come out so harsh, so he passed her the juice to soften the words.

She raised an eyebrow and took a sip. "Apple juice?"

"Yeah." He toed the edge of the Millennium Falcon-shaped rug that had seemed like such a find when he'd picked it up at a garage sale. "Sophie and Spencer announced they're expecting."

"I heard." Jade's voice was quiet, and he almost thought he detected a wistful note in it.

"It's crazy, isn't it? Everyone getting married and having babies?" A pang he'd never felt before tugged at his gut. A pang that said maybe he'd like that too—someday.

"Yeah." This time he definitely heard a layer of sadness in her voice.

He took a step closer. "You okay?"

"Of course." She walked over to the set of shelves where his Star Wars action figures were lined up. "So, you like Star Wars, huh?"

Dan laughed. There was no point in denying it. "You could say that. I watched the movies with my dad all the time growing up." He cleared his throat. He hadn't been able to watch them since Dad died.

"You never told me." Her words were soft, but the look she gave him was searching.

He found that he had to look away. "It didn't exactly seem like the kind of thing that would impress you. I figured it'd ruin any chance I had with you." A half laugh slipped past his lips. "Not that I had much of a chance in the first place."

When she didn't answer, he made himself look at her. She'd picked up a Luke Skywalker action figure and was bending its arms and legs.

"Maybe I didn't want to be impressed. Maybe I just wanted to know the real you."

Dan nodded slowly. That's what he'd wanted—to know the real Jade. And he'd thought he was starting to—until she left.

"Jade." He didn't know what he was going to say, but she shook her head and cut him off.

"So, who is this guy?"

He studied her. He didn't believe for a second that she cared about any of the Star Wars characters. But this was probably the safest topic to stick to. He took a few steps closer—close enough to point out the figures but far enough to fit at least three people between them—and started telling her about the various items.

She did a good job of feigning interest. So good she almost had him convinced. Until he remembered that she'd spent the past eight years in Hollywood, pursuing an acting career. Feigning was what she did for a living.

He was in the middle of telling her about the difference between the first trilogy and the second trilogy when his phone rang. He pulled it out of his pocket, frowning at the number. He didn't recognize it, but he didn't have every one of his congregants' numbers in his phone. And if someone was calling after nine on a Friday night, it could be an emergency.

"Sorry, I have to take this."

Jade nodded and slipped out of the room.

As Dan answered, his mind was still on her. He couldn't help wondering, if she hadn't left, would they be planning their own wedding or preparing for the arrival of their baby?

He shook his head at himself. The idea was ridiculous.

He and Jade Falter had never been intended for each other.

And they never would be.

Chapter 14

Jade wandered toward Dan's living room, her thoughts still on the Star Wars collectibles he'd been showing her. Much as she could tell he was trying to downplay it, it was clear that he loved everything having to do with the movies. But before today she'd never heard him utter the words Star Wars. Had he really been afraid to let her know that side of him in high school? Had he really thought that would impact how she felt about him?

"There you are." Vi glanced up as Jade entered the room. "We were just figuring out a date for Sophie's baby shower. She and Spencer are expecting!"

"I heard." Jade took half an awkward step forward, wondering if she was supposed to hug Sophie. But she pulled back, settling for a feeble "congratulations" and a low wave to the expectant parents.

"So where'd you wander off to?" Vi slid over on the couch, gesturing for Jade to sit next to her.

Jade took the seat, wedging herself between Vi and Grace. "I was looking for the bathroom, but then I ended up in this room with all kinds of Star Wars memorabilia."

"Oh no." Vi patted Jade's leg. "I'm sorry. I completely forgot to warn you about the Star Wars room. At least Dan must not have known you were in there, or you'd be stuck listening to him talk about all that stuff for a few hours."

Everyone else joined in the laughter—all except for Grace, who looked confused.

"The what now?" Grace asked.

"Oh, the Star Wars room." Spencer leaned forward. "Dan has spent his whole life collecting Star Wars stuff, and once he gets someone in there, he doesn't let them go until he's told them every last detail of every last item."

"Oh, it's not that bad." Nate defended Dan from the other side of Vi.

"No, it's worse," Emma chimed in.

Jade laughed along with them. "Actually, I think it's kind of neat that he has something he's so interested in." To her surprise, she'd enjoyed listening to him, not so much because she cared about the movies but because he was fun to listen to.

"Yeah," Grace spoke up from beside her. "It sounds neat. I'd like to see it."

Jade cut a look at her. Dan hadn't shown her the Star Wars room? Surely he wasn't afraid this perfect woman would judge him for it. Or maybe they weren't as serious as she'd assumed. An unnamed hope spread through her at the possibility, but she pushed it away. It didn't matter how serious Dan and Grace were. They could be about to announce their engagement for all Jade knew—and for all it mattered to her.

Grace got to her feet, but before she made it out of the living room, Dan rushed in, his face drawn.

"That was Cassandra." He held up his phone. "She tripped on her kids' toys and fell down the steps. Her leg is broken pretty badly."

Everyone gasped.

"Is she okay?" Grace moved to Dan's side lickety-split and laid a hand on his arm.

Jade ignored the unpleasant flash of feelings in her stomach. The fact that this was the seventh time Grace had touched Dan tonight didn't affect Jade in the least.

"She's going to be fine." But Dan's face remained grim. "But she can't chaperone for camp tomorrow. Which means we have to cancel the trip."

Grace's hand flew to cover her mouth, and Jade almost rolled her eyes.

Talk about overreacting. It wasn't the end of the world. In fact, if she were scheduled to go on the trip, she'd be relieved. Who wanted to spend the weekend in the middle of nowhere, with a bunch of bratty kids?

"But it's all the kids have been talking about for weeks." Grace looked near tears. "They'll all be crushed."

"I know." Dan seemed pretty crushed himself. "I really wanted this to happen."

A twinge of regret went through Jade for his sake.

"I know you did." Grace patted his shoulder. Make that eight times she'd touched him tonight.

"Unless—" Dan scanned the room, a gleam in his eyes as if he'd had a brilliant idea. "One of you wonderful ladies wants to save my life by filling in." He folded his hands in front of him, as if praying. "Sis?"

Leah raised her shoulders. "You know I would have been the first to sign up, but I'm catering a wedding tomorrow and then I'm slammed all week."

"And I'm doing the cake for the wedding. Sorry." Peyton gave him a sympathetic look.

"I don't think you want Joy keeping your campers up all night with her crying," Ariana added.

"Violet?" Dan turned to Jade's sister, eyes pleading.

Vi chewed her lip. "You know I would, but between the store and the wedding plans and . . ."

"I know." Dan waved her off. "Forget I asked."

His gaze moved to the chair across the room. "Emma? Pretty please? You're my last hope."

Emma shook her head. "I'm sorry. Any other time, I would. But I have a new horse arriving tomorrow, and I've been told he's a handful."

Dan's shoulders fell, and he slumped into a chair. "I guess that's it then." He pulled out his phone, his voice sharp with defeat. "I hate to call everyone so late, but I don't want the kids to show up bright and early tomorrow only to find out we're not going."

"Wait!" Vi shouted, making everyone jump. "What about Jade?"

Jade felt all the eyes in the room shift to her.

She gave an uncomfortable laugh. "What about Jade?"

"You could do it." Vi said it as if it was the most obvious thing in the world.

Jade was pretty sure this time her laugh came out as more of a desperate gulp for air. "Do what?"

"Chaperone." Vi nudged her.

"Oh— I— Well—" Jade could feel the heat climbing up her neck to her cheeks, and she resisted the temptation to give her sister a quick elbow to the ribs.

"Oh, that's so perfect." Grace beamed at Jade as if she'd agreed to do it.

"No. I mean, wait. I mean—" Jade stopped to sort out her flustered thoughts. "Camp isn't really my thing. I don't know the first thing about the outdoors or survival or kids."

"We can help you with that." Dan spoke for the first time since Vi had volunteered her, and Jade let herself meet his eyes.

Which was a mistake. The look he gave her—head tilted to the side as if waiting for her to say yes—almost made her lose her resolve.

She contemplated the front door. Too bad it was too far across the room to make a quick, unobtrusive escape, especially with everyone watching her.

"I'm supposed to be here to spend time with Vi. I can't just up and leave for a weekend." There. That tactic had to work.

"Of course you can." Vi patted Jade's knee. "I have you all summer. I can spare you for five days for a good cause."

Five days?

Jade almost choked. She'd been unsure when she'd thought the camp was only for a weekend. But five days? She'd never survive.

"But—" More arguments spun through Jade's brain, but the way Dan was looking at her made her forget every single one.

His eyes pleaded with her. But more than that, his look said he believed she could do it. That he was counting on her.

She took a deep breath. For once it would be nice to live up to someone's belief in her.

"Okay," she finally said. "What time do we leave?"

The whole room erupted in cheers, and Jade had to admit to herself that it felt good to be the reason.

But it felt even better to be the recipient of Dan's quiet smile and mouthed "thank you."

Chapter 15

When Jade's alarm went off at four o'clock the next morning, she asked herself for the thousandth time what she'd gotten herself into.

It didn't help that she'd spent half the night dreaming about all the creepy crawly critters she might encounter at the camp. Twice, she'd woken up and had to turn on the flashlight on her phone to make sure there were no bugs in her bed. And that was here in Vi's apartment. How much worse would it be in a cabin tonight?

She picked up the small bag she'd packed last night and stepped silently into the bathroom to get ready without waking Vi.

If she was honest with herself, it wasn't the bugs that scared her most about camp. It was that this was a Jesus camp—not exactly somewhere she'd fit in. Even though she'd been going to church with Vi since she'd come back, that didn't exactly make her an expert in all things Jesus. What if one of the kids called her out on her lack of Bible knowledge? Or, worse, what if they asked if she believed in God? It'd be wrong to lie to them, wouldn't it? But in this case, she was pretty sure it'd be worse to tell them the truth: that she hadn't been sure there was a God for many years now. And even if there was, she wasn't sure she wanted anything to do with him.

She sighed as she applied a light layer of makeup. Faith seemed to come so easily to Vi and her friends—it was something they simply talked about in the course of regular conversation, as if it were as natural as talking about the weather.

Even when she was little, Jade had never been completely comfortable talking about God. But now, after everything she'd done, she was the last person who should be taking a group of kids to church camp.

You're just there to chaperone, she reminded herself. *It's not like you have to preach.*

Besides, she was an actor. How hard could it be to play the role of Miss Holy Camp Leader?

She fixed her hair in a loose ponytail. At least she looked the part, in a cutoff pair of khaki shorts and a short-sleeved white blouse.

She was as ready as she'd ever be. She grabbed her bag and padded out of the bathroom, stopping to pull Vi's blankets up over her shoulders. She kissed her fingertips and pressed them to the top of Vi's head. All those years in LA, she'd told herself she didn't need her sister, even if she was her last remaining family, but she'd been wrong. Being home with Vi had filled spots in her heart she hadn't realized were empty.

With one last glance at her sleeping sister, Jade tiptoed out of the apartment. The door across the hall opened at the same time as she stepped onto the landing, and Jade pressed a hand to her heart.

"Good morning." Nate grinned at her, his dog Tony straining at the leash to get a sniff of her legs.

"Ugh. Violet warned me you were a morning person." But she smiled at him. The truth was, she liked Vi's fiancé.

Nate laughed. "Guilty as charged. But you look pretty chipper yourself. All ready for camp?"

Jade shrugged. "Honestly? I have no idea what I'm doing."

Nate let the dog tug him down the steps, and Jade followed.

"Thanks for doing this," Nate said over his shoulder. "It means a lot. To all of us."

Jade nodded as he opened the door for her. She got the impression that their church was more important to Vi and her friends than pretty much anything else.

"Wish me luck." She passed through the door and headed to Vi's car, which her sister had said she should take and leave in the church parking lot.

"You won't need luck." Nate's voice followed her. "You've got God on your side."

Jade closed the car door without responding. She wasn't so sure of that.

A soft spray of light was just creeping over the lake as Jade turned onto Hope Street. She couldn't remember the last time she'd seen the sun rise because she'd gotten up so early instead of because she'd stayed up so late.

Something about the muted light and the quiet of the morning stirred a longing in her soul, but she couldn't place what it was she longed for.

Peace, maybe.

But as she drove into the church parking lot, she suppressed a groan. Peace was the last thing she was going to find today.

Dozens of kids surrounded an old school bus that had been repainted green and gold. Some of the kids looked sleepy, but others had already started a game of tag.

Jade sucked in a deep breath and let it out. She could do this.

She opened the car door and grabbed her bag out of the backseat, the early morning humidity clinging to her skin. She made her way toward the bus, thankful that other than a few curious glances, most of the kids ignored her.

As she came around the side of the bus, her eyes fell on Dan, who was squatting next to a boy with red hair and two missing front teeth.

"All right, bud, you're all set. Why don't you go grab a seat?" Dan rumpled the kid's hair and straightened as the boy scampered toward the bus door.

"Thanks for coming." His smile was warm but guarded.

"Did you think I wouldn't show?"

He looked away, and she could almost hear the unspoken words. *It wouldn't be the first time.*

"So how does this work?" She jumped to fill the silence.

"Well, we get on the bus and we sit down, and the driver drives us there." Dan gave her a lazy grin.

"You know what I mean." She resisted the playful push she was tempted to give him. Grace may feel free to touch him whenever she wanted, but Jade most definitely did not.

"For now, we'll just be one big group. But when we get there, I'll give out cabin assignments. Each chaperone will lead a cabin of about a dozen kids. You'll take your cabin to their activities, oversee meals, make sure they go to bed on time, that sort of thing."

Jade gaped at him. That sort of thing?

She'd figured she was along as an extra pair of hands and eyes. Not as a leader.

"Is that all you brought?" Dan gestured to the gym bag slung over her shoulder.

"Yeah. Why? Is it not enough?" Leave it to her to forget all the important things.

"No, it's good." Dan rubbed a hand over his hair. "I'm just surprised."

"Why?" She slid the bag off her shoulder and looked at it. It was just an ordinary bag.

"To be honest, I had these visions of you showing up with three suitcases." He cringed. "Sorry."

She let herself laugh. "I guess I'm full of surprises."

He studied her, as if trying to solve a riddle. "Yes. I guess you are." After a second, he seemed to shake himself. "If you want to get on the bus, we'll be leaving soon. We're just waiting for a couple more kids."

Jade nodded, but as she turned toward the bus door, a woman about her age approached, pulling a crying little girl behind her.

"Sorry we're late, Pastor Dan." The woman stopped in front of them, the little girl cowering behind her. "Penelope got cold feet right as we were leaving, but I told her—" She broke off as she noticed Jade. "What are you doing here?" The woman's voice was filled with resentment.

"I'm sorry?" Jade's back stiffened, and every muscle in her shoulders tightened. Did she know this woman?

"Oh, I'm sorry." Dan stepped in smoothly. "Brianna, this is Jade Falter. She grew up in Hope Springs and is visiting for the summer. Jade, this is Brianna Miller. She was a few years ahead of us in high school."

Jade tried to smile, but her face had gone numb.

"I believe you knew my ex-husband Derrick." Brianna's stony look could have rivaled the boulders that littered much of the shoreline.

Jade could feel the color slip right off her cheeks. Of course it was Brianna. President of the senior class the year Jade was a freshman. Head cheerleader. All-around popular girl.

"I'd heard you were home. You're helping with this?"

Jade heard the implication, the subtle suggestion that she, of all people, wasn't fit to be chaperoning a church camp.

More to escape the look Dan was directing between her and Brianna than for any other reason, Jade crouched at the still-crying girl's side.

"Do you want to know a secret?" Jade cupped a hand around her mouth, then mock whispered, "I'm nervous about camp too."

The girl's eyes widened, but she let out a small giggle.

Jade held out her hand. "Maybe if we stick together, we'll both be braver."

After a second, the girl reached out a tentative hand and set it in Jade's.

The warmth of her fingers sent a jolt right to Jade's heart.

She swallowed down the sudden lump of emotion and stood up, leading the girl to the bus door.

"What's your name?"

"Penelope." The girl had a slight speech impediment, which only endeared her to Jade more.

"Nice to meet you, Penelope." Jade stopped with one foot posed on the bus step. "Better say goodbye to your mommy."

Penelope waved toward Brianna and called out a goodbye, then bounded up the bus steps.

As Jade followed, she pretended not to notice the sharp glare Brianna hit her with. Someday, she owed Brianna a proper apology. But for now, she'd have to settle for taking good care of her daughter. She only hoped she didn't mess that up.

Dan stared after Jade, completely dumbfounded. He was eternally grateful she'd agreed to chaperone, of course, but he had to admit he'd had his doubts about the whole plan. First, that she'd show up at all, and second, that she'd be prepared for what camp involved. But she'd shown up—on time and without a heap of luggage—and now she'd helped calm poor Penelope, who'd been going through such a rough time since her dad had split a few months ago.

"Can I talk to you for a minute?" Brianna shuffled next to him, and Dan turned to her. She was frowning at the spot where her daughter had disappeared onto the bus.

"Of course." From the few times Brianna had come to him for counseling, he knew the divorce had been messy, so it was understandable that she was apprehensive about Penelope.

She led him a few steps away from the bus, looking around as if she didn't want to be overheard.

"Don't worry about anything." Dan gave her a confident smile. "Take some time for yourself this week to relax. Penelope is in good hands."

Instead of seeming reassured, Brianna crossed her arms in front of her. "Jade Falter's hands?"

Dan tensed. "Yes. Jade and Grace and Tyler and I."

"Pastor, maybe you don't remember Jade's reputation, but I do. She was the first one Derrick cheated on me with. Under the bleachers. At homecoming."

Dan fought the urge to cover his ears. He'd known of Jade's reputation, of course, but he'd always tried to avoid learning any specifics.

"That was a long time ago, Brianna." He worked to keep his tone gentle. "I'm sure you don't still hold that against her."

Brianna grimaced. "Girls like her don't change."

Dan clamped his jaw against his instinct to jump to Jade's defense. Brianna's father was Terrence, the church president, and Dan couldn't afford to get into an argument with his daughter.

"The fact of the matter is, we have no one else who can chaperone, since Cassandra broke her leg. If Jade hadn't stepped up at the last minute and volunteered, we'd have had to cancel the whole trip." Not exactly the glowing defense he owed Jade for saving the trip, but maybe it was a neutral enough middle ground to diffuse Brianna's anger.

"Canceling might have been the smarter option." Brianna smoothed her hair. "Trust me, *she* is not the kind of woman you want influencing young people."

Dan kneaded at a kink in his neck. "Penelope seems to like her."

Brianna's cheeks reddened. "She likes chocolate cake too. But that doesn't mean it's the best thing for her."

The bus driver honked, and Dan peered at the vehicle. It was loaded with rambunctious kids eager to be on their way to camp.

"We need to get going." Dan sought his most mollifying tone. "Thanks for sharing your concerns. If you'd prefer for Penelope to stay home, we can get her off the bus. Otherwise—" He gestured toward the bus, indicating that he needed to go.

Brianna threw her hands in the air. "I'm cleaning out the rest of Derrick's stuff this week, and I don't want her there for that. Take her. But—" She flailed a wild arm toward the bus. "I don't want her anywhere near Jade. Put her in someone else's cabin." She strode toward her car without a backward glance.

The tension in Dan's jaw shot up through his forehead, but he jogged to the bus. He couldn't worry about what Brianna thought right now. He had fifty excited kids to keep happy.

And one chaperone he was going to have to avoid.

Chapter 16

"We're here." Penelope's squeal nearly burst Jade's eardrums. The little girl pointed to a wooden sign with the name Camp Oswego carved into it.

Jade picked up on the girl's contagious grin. In the two hours they'd been on the bus, Penelope had talked nonstop, and her childish enthusiasm had captured Jade's heart.

She had learned that Penelope was seven, that she loved unicorns, and that she absolutely did not like the dark. Jade tried not to think about what that last one meant for tonight.

The bus bumped down the long gravel driveway, and Jade watched as the trees on either side of them closed in, shutting out the rest of the world.

"Look." She pointed to a stand of trees, where a buck stood staring at the bus, his tail quivering.

Penelope turned her head toward the spot. "That's a daddy deer." Her know-it-all voice made Jade smile. A second later, the deer sprang into the forest and was gone.

Penelope turned away from the window. "Do you think that deer has any babies?"

"I don't know. Maybe."

"But it's not with them. Maybe it left them like my daddy left me."

Jade's smile shriveled. "Oh, I'm—" But she had no idea what to say to that.

Penelope's lip quivered, but she shook her head. "Mommy said not to think about it this week."

"That's a good idea." Not that Jade had ever succeeded in trying not to think about something. Just look at the way her eyes had been glued to Dan during the entire bus ride.

The bus stopped in front of a dilapidated building of weathered gray boards.

"Is that where we sleep?" Penelope's eyes were wide.

"I sure hope not," Jade muttered.

"I can be with you, though, right, wherever we sleep?" Penelope grabbed Jade's hand in her sweaty palm, and Jade squeezed.

"I don't see why not."

Dan stood in the aisle at the front of the bus, holding up a hand until the kids quieted. "Grab your things and let's gather right over there in front of the lodge—" He pointed to the tumbledown building, and Jade almost fell off the bus seat. If that was a lodge, she was a princess. But she dutifully helped shepherd the children to the spot he'd indicated.

Once everyone was there, Dan pointed down a narrow footpath. "The cabins we'll be staying in are a little hike down this trail. Once I've called out your assigned cabin, you can follow your leader to it and get settled in."

He first called off the campers in Tyler's cabin, then in his own, putting one of the older boys in charge of getting the others settled while he gave out the girls' cabin assignments.

Jade watched with interest. Maybe she could have an older girl in her group take on some of the responsibility.

"For those of you who don't know, this is Miss Jade. She'll have Melody, Dakota, Sarah, Libby, Lily, Andrea, Abby, Brooklyn, and Madison."

A group of girls moved to surround her. A couple looked about Penelope's age, but most looked to be about nine or ten and two of the girls were probably closer to their early teens.

"Miss Jade." Someone shook her arm, and Jade looked down as Dan read off Grace's campers. "He didn't say me."

"Oh." Jade listened as Dan called Penelope's name for Grace's cabin. "I'm sure we can get that switched."

She surveyed the other girls in her group. "Hang tight a second. We just need to talk to Pastor Dan."

Dan was making a few scribbles on his list, but he looked up with a smile as they approached. "You got the best cabin. It's the shortest walk too."

"Oh, thanks. Just real quick, is there any way to put Penelope in my cabin instead of Miss Grace's? We kind of became BFFs on the bus." She held up their linked hands as proof, and Penelope giggled.

Dan's smile dimmed, and he avoided her eyes. "Actually, we can't change up the cabin assignments." He held up his list as if that were all the evidence he needed, and she grabbed it out of his hand. How difficult was it to swap Penelope's name from one list to another?

"Why not?" Her finger slid down the list of names until it landed on her own. "Oh."

Penelope's name had been printed under hers, but it had been crossed out and added in pencil under Grace's. Her memory cut to watching Dan talking with Brianna outside the bus this morning. She'd wondered what that was about. Guess she didn't have to wonder anymore.

Dan scrubbed a hand down his face. "I'm sorry. I—"

Jade thrust the clipboard back at him. "It's no problem."

She crouched to be at eye level with Penelope, whose cheeks were streaked with tears. "Here's the deal. We'll still see each other lots, but you'll sleep in Miss Grace's cabin. If you want to know the truth, Miss Grace is much better at camping than I am, so you'll be in good hands."

But Penelope threw her arms around Jade. "You said we'd make each other brave. I can't be brave without you."

Jade's heart cracked, but she kept her voice soothing. "You've already been so brave. And you've made me brave. If you can do this, you'll be the bravest person I've ever met."

Penelope let out a hiccupping cry. "I want to go home." Her hiccups soon escalated to deep sobs, and Jade clutched her close. She had no idea what else to do.

"Oh, sweetie, you're going to have so much fun with Miss Grace. She—"

"Take her to your cabin." Dan's voice cut through her own.

Jade looked up at him. "But—"

Dan shook his head. "Don't worry about it."

"You're sure?"

Dan reached a hand to help her up and nodded. "I'm sure."

She eyed his hand but stood without taking it—which was a challenge with Penelope wrapped around her. Still, she'd take the risk of falling flat on her back over the risk of one simple touch of his hand. "Thank you."

Dan's eyes searched hers, and she forced herself to look away.

"Come on." She pulled Penelope away from Dan toward the rest of their group. "Let's go check out our cabin."

He'd done the right thing. Hadn't he? Letting Penelope switch to Jade's cabin.

He wasn't sure if it was Penelope's tears or the look of hurt on Jade's face when she realized why he had assigned Penelope to Grace's cabin that had made him change his mind.

There would likely be consequences when they got home. There was no way Penelope wouldn't tell Brianna about all the fun she'd had with Jade. But hopefully by then Brianna would realize that Jade hadn't been a bad influence and would rethink her judgment.

He plopped his small bag onto the bottom of one of the bunks and broke up a fight between two boys who each wanted the top bunk.

"Why don't we—"

But his words were cut off as a sharp scream ripped through the open door of their cabin. Dan's head jerked up. That was a woman's scream. Jade?

He was already tearing out of his cabin, his feet pounding over the packed dirt trail that led to the girls' cabins on the other side of the small clearing.

As he ran, he realized he should have grabbed the first aid kit. Or maybe a weapon. Who knew what was going on over there?

He burst in the door of Jade's cabin without knocking. "What's wrong?"

He pulled up short, a dozen girls gaping at him as he stood in the doorway gasping for air. "I thought I heard a scream."

Everyone appeared to be in one piece, and there were no apparent signs of danger.

Until he spotted Jade standing on a rickety old chair in the far corner of the room.

"There are ladybugs." She pointed to the opposite corner.

"Ladybugs?" Dan repeated dully. What did ladybugs have to do with anything?

"Miss Jade doesn't like ladybugs." Penelope let out a giggle, and the other girls joined in.

"Oh." Dan raised an eyebrow at Jade, and she gave him a chagrined look.

"I got bit by one once."

"By a ladybug? I don't think they bite."

Jade gave him an indignant look. "They do when you accidentally lay on one that has crawled into your bed."

The girls laughed harder, and Dan pressed his lips together to keep from joining in.

"Who wants to help me save Miss Jade from the ladybugs?" He strode to the corner she had indicated. Sure enough, a dozen or so ladybugs were scattered across the wall and floor there. With the girls' help, he scooped them up and transplanted them outdoors.

"There." He crossed to the chair Jade was still perched on and held out a hand. "Now will you get down? I think that chair is more dangerous than all the ladybugs in the woods combined. It looks like it's about to fall apart."

She stared at his hand, as if afraid it was leprous. But he grabbed her arm as she wobbled. She might not want his help, but he didn't need a camp leader with a broken neck.

He ignored the zing that shot from his hand, up his arm, and right to his heart at the feel of her skin under his fingers. It had been a long time since he'd held her hand.

She pulled away the moment she was on the ground, and he backed toward the door. "We're going to do a devotion in ten minutes. Then how about a swim before lunch?"

The girls all cheered, but Jade looked panicked.

"Don't worry." He couldn't resist teasing her. "There shouldn't be any ladybugs in the water." He waited for the look of relief on her face, then added, "Just snakes."

The ladybug thing was embarrassing, Jade could admit that. But there was no way she was going in that lake if there was even a remote chance there were snakes in it. Dan, Tyler, and Grace had all reassured her repeatedly that Dan had only been teasing, but she wasn't taking any chances.

Besides, she and Penelope and a few of the other girls were making the most incredible sandcastle known to man. So far, they had three levels, plus a tower and a moat. And she was in the middle of constructing a drawbridge right now.

She'd probably have it done already if her eyes didn't keep drifting to the water, where Dan and Grace and Tyler had started a game of water volleyball with the kids. She worked hard not to notice the nicely defined muscles of Dan's chest and torso. Or the way he and Grace exchanged high fives every time their team scored a point—which seemed to be every five seconds.

"How about this for the bridge, Miss Jade?" Penelope held a piece of bark out to her, and Jade took it.

"Perfect, Penelope." She placed it in the opening of the castle wall. "There. I think it's done."

"Now what?" Penelope's eyes traveled to the water.

"You can swim, Penelope. I'll be right here watching you."

"No." Penelope's sigh held a trace of annoyance. "I want to stay by you."

Jade watched the little girl. Was she really going to let her own hang-ups keep Penelope from having fun?

"Tell you what, what if I come in a little way? Then will you swim?"

"Yes!" Penelope was already dragging her toward the water.

Jade cringed the moment she stepped into the shallows, but the water wasn't as cold as she'd anticipated. She always forgot how much warmer inland lakes got than Lake Michigan. And with no waves to speak of, at least she wouldn't get splashed.

She walked in until the water skimmed her knees, and Penelope seemed content to swim right in front of her.

She resisted as long as she could, but eventually her eyes were drawn back to the water volleyball game—just in time to see Dan laughing at something Grace was saying. Jade dropped her gaze to Penelope. There was no point in giving Dan another thought.

It wasn't like she could ever compete with a woman like Grace. And it wasn't like she wanted to anyway.

She'd known when she left Hope Springs that she'd never have a shot with Dan again. And she'd been fine with that.

"Watch this, Miss Jade."

Jade turned to watch Penelope as she porpoised up and down in the water.

"Wow, Penelope, that's very— Yikes!" A wave of water hit her square in the back.

She spun around, her mouth still open with shock. Which was how she ended up with a mouthful of water as another wave hit her.

"Sorry." But Dan was laughing too hard to be sincere. "*Now* you're in the water."

She stared at him, water still dripping from her face and hair.

"Why would you do that?" She infused her voice with as much anger as she could.

Dan's mouth fell open. "Oh, wow, Jade, I'm sorry." He stopped laughing and stepped closer. "I didn't mean—"

She waited, hands on her hips, keeping her lips in a straight line.

"I mean, I shouldn't have—" Two more steps closer. "I thought—" Another step.

Jade bent at the waist, slicing both hands into the water, then lifting them to send a huge splash cascading over him.

He froze as the wave hit him, eyes closing instinctively.

But when he opened them again, they were wide. All around them, the kids were laughing and clapping.

"I can't believe you did that." But he was grinning too.

"You totally deserved that," Grace called from behind him, and he laughed, sloughing the water off his face.

"I guess I did. Truce?" He held out a hand, and Jade eyed it. When he'd touched her arm in the cabin, the electricity had almost sent her sailing into the air.

But everyone was watching. Waiting.

Slowly, she placed her hand in his.

The moment his fingers wrapped around hers, she was yanked forward and off her feet. Water closed over her head, and she flailed to regain her footing.

When she came up spluttering, Dan smirked at her. "I can do this all day. Want to try again?"

But she shook her head and wrung out her hair. The offer to touch his hand again was too tempting.

"Smart decision. Truce for real this time?" Dan held out his hand, looking one hundred percent sincere. But Jade wasn't falling for that again. Just because the guy was a pastor didn't mean he was above tricking her a second time.

She dropped her hands into the water and sent a small splash toward him. "*Now* we can have a truce." She dashed out of the water and up the beach before he could retaliate.

When she reached the spot where their sandcastle stood, she chanced a glance at the water. Dan was still watching her, an expression she didn't recognize on his face. He took a couple steps toward the beach, and Jade's stomach tumbled. He was going to come up by her.

Out of the corner of her eye, she spotted something sailing through the air toward him.

"Watch—"

But her warning was too late. The volleyball smacked into the back of his head. He lifted one hand to his head and with the other scooped the ball out of the water.

"Sorry, Pastor Dan," an older boy with dark hair called.

"That's okay." Dan threw the ball back, then with one last look at Jade, rejoined the volleyball game.

Jade plopped into the sand to add a few decorative details to the castle, telling herself she was relieved.

It was like he'd said—he was where he belonged, and she was where she belonged.

And that was just the way she liked it.

Chapter 17

The campfire crackled in the growing dark, and Dan had to smile from his perch on the top of the picnic table. The first day of camp had gone even better than he'd hoped. The kids all seemed suitably worn out and happy. And other than one minor scrape and Jade's ladybug emergency, the day had been incident free.

As soon as the kids finished making their s'mores, they'd have a devotion, sing a few songs, and turn in for the night. His gaze drifted over the group. The older kids sat together on camp chairs, while Tyler had taken some of the younger kids to the other side of the clearing for a game of tag. Grace helped some kids make s'mores, while Jade led a group of chocolate and marshmallow covered kids to the bathroom to wash up.

He allowed himself a contented sigh. This was exactly what he'd wanted camp to be—a chance for the kids to get together and enjoy God's creation and time with each other. Maybe some of these kids would remain lifelong friends and encourage each other in their faith as they confronted all the things out there that were waiting to steal them from the truth. Dan had lost count of how many times he'd prayed for them, but if he had one hope as a pastor, that would be it.

"Pastor Dan, Pastor Dan." A little girl named Melody pulled Jade toward him, one hand clasped in front of her as if she were holding a precious treasure. His eyes traveled to Jade's face, and he almost laughed out loud at her repulsed expression. He wondered if Melody's treasure was a ladybug. But when she opened her hand, a big juicy nightcrawler wriggled there.

"It's a worm! Isn't it cute?" Melody sounded as if she'd found a puppy instead of a worm. "Do you want to hold it?"

She held the worm out toward Dan, and he opened his hand so she could drop it in. Jade took a large step backward.

"It *is* cute." He let the worm squirm in his hand a few seconds, then passed it back to Melody.

"Do you want to hold it, Miss Jade?" Melody asked.

Dan coughed to cover his laugh as Jade's face contorted. "That's okay, sweetie. I'm good just looking at it."

"Do you want to pet it at least?" Melody thrust her hand at Jade.

Dan was going to have to jump in and come to Jade's rescue.

But Jade poked out a tentative finger and inched it toward the worm, eyes squinted as if she couldn't bear to watch what she was about to do.

With a half gasp, she gave the worm the slightest brush of her finger, then snatched her hand back.

"Oh, it's slimy," she choked out.

Dan couldn't hold back his laugh any longer, and Jade shot him a look.

"What?" He held up his hands. "I'm actually impressed." Which was the truth. This had to be so far from Jade's normal life, but here she was, putting on a brave face and touching worms to make a little girl happy.

"What y'all got there?" Grace came up alongside them and peered into Melody's palm. "Oh, that's a good one." She held out her hand, and Melody dropped the worm into it.

"Miss Jade didn't want to hold it," Melody said. "I think she's scared of it." Her stage whisper made them all laugh.

"That's the great thing about God. He made us all unique. So not everyone likes the same things." Grace returned the worm to Melody.

"But I happen to love worms. They remind me of fishing with my daddy. Come on, let's go find it a nice home before it dries out."

Grace and Melody moved toward the cover of the trees, leaving Dan alone with Jade. He cleared his throat. Now what?

"She's made for this, isn't she?" Jade's gaze had followed Grace and Melody.

"Her dad was the resident pastor at a church camp for a few years, so it's in her blood."

"Ah." Jade sat on the very edge of the picnic table, leaving plenty of space between them.

"You're doing a great job too." He kept his eyes on his hands but looked up when she snorted.

"This isn't exactly my thing, if you hadn't noticed."

"I know." He looked her in the eye. "But you're doing it anyway. And the kids really like you. You have a gift for working with them."

Jade's lips parted, but she didn't say anything. The voices of the kids around them faded, and the quiet stretched between them, softer than the night.

"Okay. Worm is in a good home." Grace was all business as she returned to the picnic table. "Should we start the devotion?"

Dan jumped. Why did he feel as if he'd been caught doing something wrong? He pulled out his phone, scrolling to his Bible app.

Nothing like a good devotion to clear his head of the unwanted thoughts that had crept in. Thoughts about how Jade's lips shone in the firelight. Thoughts about what it might be like to feel those lips on his again. Thoughts that maybe, just maybe, God had brought her back to Hope Springs to give them a second chance.

He pushed every last one of those thoughts aside.

They were all ridiculous and unrealistic.

But when he let himself chance another glance at her, he couldn't help it: They all came rushing back in.

"Sleep well, girls." Jade clicked off the cabin light. She had never been more exhausted in her life, but somehow she knew she wouldn't be able to sleep yet, so she slid out the cabin door, zipping up the sweatshirt she'd put on over her blouse—which was now covered in dirt stains and chocolate from little fingers.

"Miss Jade?" Penelope's voice followed her out the door, and Jade turned to find the nightgowned girl standing in the doorway behind her.

"What is it, Penelope? You're supposed to be going to sleep."

"I'm scared." The girl's lower lip trembled, and Jade moved closer. How could she have forgotten that Penelope was afraid of the dark?

She held out a hand to the little girl and led her to the rickety-looking porch swing. She sat tentatively, and when it held, she pulled Penelope onto her lap. They sat like that for a couple minutes, listening to the squeak of the swing, as Jade tried to figure out what she could possibly say to help Penelope sleep.

"See all those stars?" Jade pointed to the night sky, which was filled with more stars than she had probably ever seen in her life. They made her feel small and yet important all at once.

Penelope nodded. "They're so far away."

"Yes, but—" Jade swallowed, hoping she wasn't about to accidentally say anything blasphemous. She wasn't exactly fluent in God talk. "Do you know who made them?"

"God made everything." Penelope said it with such conviction that Jade almost envied her. Had she ever been that sure about anything in her life?

"Right. And remember what Pastor Dan said in his devotion tonight?"

Penelope didn't say anything, so Jade answered for her. "He said that God is your Father, and he'll never leave you. So, if God made the stars and—"

But she broke off as Penelope sniffled and a drop of water fell on her shoulder.

"Pen?" She held the little girl back to examine her. Silent tears slipped down Penelope's face. "Oh, Penelope, what's wrong?"

Penelope nuzzled into Jade's neck, leaving her skin wet, and Jade tightened her arms. Just when she'd thought she was getting the hang of this camp leader thing, she went and made a little girl cry.

"My daddy left," Penelope finally said.

"I know." Jade rubbed a hand up and down Penelope's back. It'd been insensitive of her to mention fathers when she knew Penelope didn't have a father at home anymore.

"Does that mean God is going to leave me too?"

"What?" Jade stopped rubbing Penelope's back so she could adjust their positions and look the little girl in the eyes. "Of course not. Pastor Dan said God will never leave you." Jade only hoped she was getting that right—and that Penelope didn't ask for too many more details.

"That's what my daddy used to say too. But then he left." Penelope swiped a finger under her runny nose.

"Well—" Jade tipped her head back, thinking. "The thing is, God is even better than our daddies. And when he promises something, he always has to keep his promise."

"He has to?" Penelope's eyes widened.

Jade nodded. She was pretty sure that was how it went.

"Did your daddy keep his promises?"

The question hit Jade right in the gut. She hadn't thought about her dad in years.

"No, he didn't. He left when I was a little girl. Littler than you, actually. But I had a great mommy just like you do."

Penelope looked thoughtful. "But God never left you?"

Jade had to think about that one. Had God ever left her? He'd sure felt far from her for many years.

But maybe it wasn't that he'd left her so much as she'd left him. She'd wanted to live her life the way she wanted to live it, so she'd pushed him away. But lately, since she'd been home, she'd started to wonder if he was still there, waiting for her to come back.

Penelope was still watching her, so Jade finally gave her as honest an answer as she could. "No, I guess maybe he never did." She slid Penelope to her feet. "Come on, let's get you to bed. Do you think you can be brave and sleep now?"

Penelope nodded and let Jade lead her into the cabin. They tiptoed past the other sleeping girls, and as Jade tucked the blankets around her, Penelope reached up to hug her again. "Goodnight, Miss Jade. I love you."

Moisture gathered behind Jade's eyelids. When was the last time anyone besides Vi had said those words to her?

"I love you too," she whispered into Penelope's hair.

The little girl gave her a sleepy smile and rolled over, leaving Jade to watch her fall asleep.

Chapter 18

*J*ade was pretty sure this wasn't how scrambled eggs were supposed to look. Liquid seeped from the grainy, almost white lumps in her pan.

Oh well. There wasn't much she could do about it with hungry campers lined up for breakfast. They'd just have to fill up on Grace's perfectly golden pancakes.

Jade had no idea how the other woman did it. Grace had been in about a million places at once as the two of them managed breakfast duty while Dan and Tyler led the morning devotion.

It had been all Jade could do to man her egg station. And look how that had turned out.

"Good morning." Dan reached them, offering a warm smile. "Everything go all right last night?"

"Perfect." Grace slid three delicious looking pancakes onto his plate with a bright-eyed smile.

"We had one little issue in my cabin." Jade fought to suppress a yawn but failed. "Penelope was scared of the dark, but we talked for a bit, and she went to sleep."

She cringed inwardly as she scooped a large pile of eggs onto Dan's plate.

To his credit, he didn't blink. "Thanks." Despite the mess on his plate, his smile was genuine.

"You might want to take some more pancakes and ditch the eggs." Jade wrinkled her nose at the egg juice that was spreading to fill his plate.

"The eggs look great. Thank you for making them."

Jade waved him off. "Pastors aren't supposed to lie, you know."

"No lie." He grabbed a fork and stabbed a big bite. Jade winced as he shoved it in his mouth. She hadn't been able to bring herself to taste them.

"They're better than they look." He grinned at her and stabbed another forkful. "See?"

Jade rolled her eyes, but her cheeks grew warm.

She brushed off the compliment. "So what's on the agenda for today?"

"Not much. Some swimming, hiking, high ropes, crafts—"

Jade's head jerked up. "What did you say?"

Dan wrinkled his brow. "Crafts?"

"No." She brandished her spatula at him. "Before that."

"Oh. High ropes. It's this course where you—"

But Jade held up a hand to stop him. "I know what it is. But I did *not* know I was signing up for that when I agreed to come. You probably don't remember the time freshman year when I totally froze on that high ropes course we went to for phys ed, but I swore then that there was no way I would ever do something like that again." It had been the single most embarrassing moment of her high school career. Everyone had seen her weakness and her need for help.

"I remember." Dan's voice was quiet. "It wasn't that bad."

Jade groaned. "It was worse."

"Yeah, it was."

She hid her face in her hands. Even Dan couldn't deny that she'd made a fool of herself. Mr. Henning, the phys ed teacher, had been forced to climb up and lead her down one step at a time. It'd taken her two days to stop shaking afterward.

"But look at it this way." Dan's voice brimmed with optimism. "It's a chance to redeem yourself. Prove to yourself you can do it."

"But I can't." Jade wanted to stomp her foot.

Nothing he said was going to get her up there.

"I believe in you." Dan gave her a look and moved off to find a seat.

Jade sighed. That line came close to making her want to try. But not close enough.

She managed to make it through hiking and swimming—and even found she was halfway decent at helping the kids with their crafts—but when they got to the high ropes course, the shaking started.

She tried not to let the kids notice as she directed them into a line.

"You don't have to do this if you don't want to." Dan's voice was low in her ear, and she didn't turn around. She simply pressed her lips together and nodded.

She was relieved. Of course she was. But that didn't explain the small dip in her stomach. Was it because she didn't want to disappoint Dan? Or maybe for once she didn't want to disappoint herself. Still, it was probably better if she didn't try. Because if she did try, she would likely only fail again.

"Miss Jade?" Penelope grabbed her arm. "It's too high. I'm scared."

"Oh, it's not that high." Jade crossed her fingers, hoping the little white lie was innocent enough. Besides, too high was relative. "I promise you'll be fine. You're so brave, remember?"

"I'm not brave about this." Penelope stuck out her lower lip. "I'm scared about this."

"Well—" Jade took both of Penelope's shoulders in her hands. "That's good."

"It is?" Penelope seemed unconvinced, and Jade thought fast.

"Yep. Because the only way to be brave is to do something you're scared of."

Before Dan could say anything, she raised her head to meet his appraising look. "Yeah, I heard myself."

He grinned at her, and she turned to Penelope with a resigned sigh. "That's why I'm going to go up first to show you how to be brave. Because I'm scared too."

Dan was pretty sure he'd been holding his breath for at least five minutes. His eyes were locked on Jade's form as she grabbed the rope above her head. With each step she'd taken up the rope ladder, he'd been sure she was going to give up and turn around. But she'd made it to the top. Now all she had to do was step out onto that thin rope.

Dan double-checked the belay line in his hands. He was sure she wouldn't fall, but if she did, he'd be there to catch her.

As Jade placed a foot onto the rope, the kids let out an encouraging cheer. Dan yelled along but didn't take his concentration off Jade as she took first one step and then another.

She was doing it! If he had a hand free, he'd pump it in the air. But he had to settle for the biggest grin that had ever stretched his face. He hadn't been this proud the first time he'd accomplished this course himself.

Climbing, camping, all this outdoorsy stuff was square in the middle of his comfort zone. But for Jade—wow—her comfort zone had to be so far from this that it looked like a dot from here.

Dan fed out more line as Jade approached the middle of the rope, where it started to slope uphill, increasing the difficulty. Jade hesitated a second, then lifted her left foot. But as she did, her other foot slipped. She screamed as she started to fall to the side. Around Dan, several of the kids screamed as well.

Before he could register what he was doing, Dan had pulled on the rope with his brake hand. The belay device reacted just as it was supposed to, locking the rope in place. Jade's feet hung only a few inches below the lower rope, her hands still gripping the upper rope. She scrambled to replant her feet.

Even from here, he could see the trembling in her legs. His own heart was thundering at supersonic speeds, but he forced his voice to come out calm and controlled. "You okay, Miss Jade?"

He saw her helmet bob once, but her shaking didn't ease, and she didn't say anything.

Dan waited, giving her time to shake it off—and giving himself a second to get his heart rate under control.

After a few minutes, the kids around him started to murmur.

"Is she stuck, Pastor Dan? I could go get her." Penelope had sidled up next to him and shielded her eyes against the sun as she peered up at Jade.

"That's very brave of you, Penelope." Dan kept his eyes fixed on Jade. "But I think Miss Jade is braver than she realizes. Just like you. I bet she can do it."

"You can do it, Miss Jade," Penelope yelled.

On the rope, Jade's helmet shook back and forth.

"She can't," Penelope whispered.

"Jade!" Dan moved so that he was standing where she could see him. "Look at me."

She gave her head a minute shake. "I can't look down." Her voice was so quiet he could barely hear her.

Dan tightened his grip on the belay rope. "Look at me. I'm right here."

He waited, holding his breath again. She stared straight ahead for another thirty seconds, but finally she tilted her head slightly downward.

He started talking the moment she made eye contact. He didn't know how long she'd give him. "I've got you." He held up the belay line. "I'm not going to let you go. I'm not going to let anything happen to you. I promise."

He waited, trying to ignore the doubts that she'd trust him. He wasn't sure she'd ever trusted anyone, really.

After several seconds, she lifted her head. When she didn't move, he called Tyler over. He'd have to hand off the belay and go up there to help her down.

But before he could pass the equipment off, Jade took a tiny step. Then another. And another.

The kids broke into wild cheers and chanted, "Go, Miss Jade. Go, Miss Jade."

Though he was too far away to see her face clearly, Dan was almost sure it had relaxed into a smile. And when she finally climbed down ten minutes later, he was certain of it.

The kids all swarmed her with hugs and high fives, but Dan resisted the temptation to do the same, instead concentrating on cleaning up the equipment.

When she passed him her safety harness, she said a quick, low "thank you."

But that radiant look on her face right now—that was all the thanks he needed.

Every muscle in Jade's body protested as she lowered herself onto the tree stump in front of the dying campfire.

She'd gotten all the kids tucked into bed without incident tonight, but she'd felt like she needed a little time to decompress before she went to sleep.

"Hey." Dan stepped into the clearing, and she jumped.

"Sorry." He gestured to the pail of water in his hand. "I was going to put the fire out."

"Oh. Sorry." Jade moved to stand, but Dan motioned for her to sit.

"It can wait." He set the pail down and pulled a stump over next to hers. When he sat, their knees were only a few inches apart, and Jade readjusted to put more space between them.

"Quite a day, huh?" Dan picked up a thin stick off the ground and twirled it between his fingers.

Jade gave a sharp laugh. "You could say that. I'm sorry I'm not very good at all of this." To her surprise, the back of her throat burned, and she had to swipe a quick hand under her eyes.

"Jade, what is it?" Dan swiveled on his stump so that he was facing her head-on, his brow creased in concern.

The look was too much, the connection too strong. She looked away, blinking hard. Why was she being so stupid and emotional about this? It was just a silly church camp. It wasn't like it meant anything.

"It's nothing." But she couldn't lie to him this time. Not when he was looking at her like that. Like he really wanted to know what was troubling her.

"Let's face it. I'm not cut out for this." The admission stung more than it should. Why did she suddenly want to be the kind of person who could handle camping and working with kids and making a difference?

"Is that all?" Dan nudged her shoulder. "I was afraid it was something serious, like you wanted to bail on me."

Jade opened her mouth, then closed it. It *was* serious. She shouldn't be here. She was probably the worst camp leader the kids had ever had. For all she knew, she was harming their faith instead of helping it.

"I know you don't see it yet, but I do." Dan turned to the fire, which had lowered to a few flickering embers.

Jade waited for him to make sense of that cryptic line, but when he didn't say anything else, she sighed. He was going to make her ask.

"See what?" She tried not to sound too curious. She didn't want to give him the satisfaction.

"Your gifts," Dan said simply, as if that were any clearer.

"What gifts?" Had he gotten her something? That would be awkward.

"Well, for starters, you're great with the kids. They all love you. And as much as you try to hide it, you have a big heart for them."

Oh. *Those* kinds of gifts.

Dan turned his head to give her a smile that made her pulse speed up nearly as much as it had when she'd slipped on the ropes course.

She reminded herself that he was just being nice.

"And—" Dan continued. "You're willing to try new things and push out of your comfort zone and—"

"And I screamed at ladybugs, massacred the eggs, and froze on the ropes course," Jade filled in, hitting him with a scowl. He needed to stop looking at her through rose-tinted glasses. If he wanted to talk about the perfect camp leader, he should go find Grace, who'd set a new record on the high ropes course after Jade had finally gotten down.

But he shrugged. "Those things aren't what matters. You're being a Christian role model for these kids."

She almost snorted. Christian role model was the last thing she would describe herself as.

"I'm serious, Jade." Dan's gaze landed directly on her, and she found she couldn't break it. "You have no idea the impact you're having on these kids just by being there for them."

Jade studied her chipped fingernails. Whether she was a good influence on the kids or not, she owed Dan a thank you. "Thanks for talking me down up there. I was half afraid we'd have to call Mr. Henning to come get me down again."

"Thanks for trusting me." Dan's voice went soft, and Jade turned to look at him.

He was watching her with a hint of that look he used to give her. The one that said he wanted to know her—really know her, not assume he knew her based on what he'd already seen or heard from others.

"You're the only one I would have trusted." She probably shouldn't have said it out loud, but for some reason it was suddenly important to her that he know. She wasn't sure why she'd trusted him. Other than the fact that he was the one person in the world, aside from Vi, she knew would never do anything to hurt her.

But now that the words were hanging between them, she wished she could draw them back in.

"Anyway, I guess I have trust issues." She attempted a lighthearted laugh but failed miserably.

The truth was, she didn't want to be like this. She didn't want to be afraid that the moment she let down her guard with someone, they'd take off on her. Didn't want to always be the first one to bail so the other person couldn't.

"Why?" Dan asked.

"Why what?"

"Why do you think you have trust issues?"

She scratched at a mosquito bite on her leg. "It's just who I am, I guess."

"Jade." Dan's voice held that tone he'd always used to call her out when she put on what he called her "tough guy" act.

"I don't know." She dragged her fingers through her hair. How many sleepless nights had she spent trying to figure out why she was so broken? "Blame it on my dad, I guess."

"He left when you were little, right?"

"Yeah." Jade didn't know what was going on. She almost never talked about her dad, and now this was twice in two days that she'd mentioned him.

"He didn't say goodbye. We came home from school one day, and he was gone." Jade bit her lip. That sounded a little too familiar.

But Dan was too good of a guy to point out that she'd done the same thing to him.

"That must have been awful." He looked like he was going to reach for her hands, so she tucked them under her legs.

"It was no big deal. I don't know why I brought it up." It was time to shut this conversation down before she let herself get drawn into wanting something she couldn't have.

"Jade—"

But she jumped to her feet. "I should get to bed. That awful wake-up bugle of yours comes painfully early."

He stood too, still eying her, and she shifted on her feet.

"I know you don't think you're good at this." He gestured at the woods and cabins surrounding them. "But you are. And—" He scuffed his shoe on the ground. "I'm glad you came."

"Yeah. I'm kind of glad too." She tapped his foot with hers, then turned to walk to her cabin.

The night had grown chilly, but she barely noticed, with Dan's words warming her from the inside.

Chapter 19

*W*ow.

It was the only word that came to Dan's mind as he watched Jade cross the clearing in the early morning light. Her face was animated as she chatted with the group of girls surrounding her. In the four days they'd been at camp, he'd seen a more dramatic change in her than he'd perhaps ever seen in anyone in his life.

She'd lost the sullen look that had been her nearly perpetual expression as long as he'd known her. Now it was only in rare moments that he caught her without a smile. And when she was with the kids, she seemed to almost glow. Working with them definitely brought out the best in her.

"Good morning, Pastor Dan." Jade directed her smile toward him but didn't look him in the eyes.

Which didn't keep his insides from lighting up—something that had been happening more and more lately.

Jade shepherded the girls to sit behind the boys, who were already seated on the ground. Since Tyler and Grace were on breakfast duty today, he and Jade would oversee the morning devotion.

Once the girls were all seated, Jade lowered herself to the ground in the back row, but Dan shook his head. She may have assumed she was only here as an observer, but she was wrong.

"Uh, Miss Jade?"

"Yes, Pastor Dan?" Still that beautiful smile. Still not looking him in the eyes.

"Usually the devotion leaders sit up here." He patted the top of the picnic table, right next to where he was sitting.

If it weren't for the fact that the kids were watching him and the fact that he didn't want to embarrass her, he'd have burst into laughter at the way her eyes widened and her chin dropped.

"Oh, I thought I'd—"

"Make me do all the work?" Dan grinned at her as the kids giggled. "Not a chance. Come on."

Jade's mouth closed into a tight, unhappy smile. She wasn't comfortable with this. He knew that.

But he also knew she could do it, even if she didn't realize it yet.

Keeping her back to the kids and her teeth clenched, she leaned toward him. "I have no idea how to lead a devotion." If he read her expression right, she was ready to punch him.

"You'll be great." Dan passed her the Bible, which he'd already opened to the day's reading. "Start right there." He pointed. "Psalm twenty-five, verses four through seven."

Jade hit him with one more disapproving look, then yanked the Bible out of his hands and spun to face the kids. He had to give her credit— the kids would never know by looking at her that she'd wanted to poke his eyes out a second ago.

Probably still did.

But this would be good for her. He knew it would.

Please let it be. He sent up the quick prayer as Jade began to read.

"Show me your ways, Lord, teach me your paths." Jade's voice shook slightly, and her finger traced a line under the words. "Guide me in your truth and teach me, for you are God my Savior, and my hope is in you all day long."

Her voice had grown stronger as she read. She picked her head up to survey the kids, who had all quieted and were listening attentively.

"Remember, Lord, your great mercy and love, for they are from of old. Do not remember—" Jade paused, and he could tell she was letting her eyes scan ahead. She swallowed, but when she spoke, her voice was clear. "Do not remember the sins of my youth and my rebellious ways; according to your love remember me, for you, Lord, are good."

As Jade finished the verse, she closed her eyes. It may have been a trick of the rising light, but when she opened them again, he was almost sure they sparked with unshed tears. He blinked away the sudden emotion that overcame him as well.

He never failed to be moved when he saw God's Word taking hold in someone's heart. And the fact that someone was Jade right now was the answer to about a million prayers he'd offered for her over the years.

He cleared his throat and turned his attention to the kids. "Does anyone have any questions or anything they want to talk about from those verses?"

A few of the kids raised their hands, and Dan allowed himself an internal fist pump. It was early, these kids hadn't had breakfast yet, and here they were, eager to discuss God's Word.

He called on Oliver, a precocious eight-year-old he'd had to get out of more than one sticky situation this week.

"That sounded like a prayer, not the Bible," Oliver said.

Dan nodded. "Good observation, Oliver. That's what the psalms are—prayers and songs to God."

Henry, Oliver's cohort in crime, raised his hand. "Whose prayer is it?"

"King David." Jade answered before he could, and his head swiveled to her in surprise.

She looked as shocked as he felt. "Right?"

"Yeah. It's King David's prayer."

"But why would a king need to pray that?" Henry called out without raising his hand. "He's the *king*."

Jade kept her eyes on Dan, clearly waiting for him to take this one, but he gestured for her to go ahead.

She licked her lips. "Well—" She stopped, her eyes pleading for him to step in and help. But he knew she knew this.

"Well—" She dragged the word out. "Everyone needs to pray—even kings."

Henry nodded, apparently satisfied, and Dan got ready to call on another student, but Jade tapped the Bible she still held.

"I mean, even kings sinned, right? And if I remember correctly from my Sunday school days, David sinned a lot. So I guess he needed God's forgiveness a lot." She looked at Dan meekly. "Or am I totally off base here?"

"You're right on base."

Her face relaxed, and she pointed to Samantha for the next question. Dan sat up, on alert. He'd counseled Sam after the young teen had been picked up for shoplifting. She could be tough to get through to.

"But God can't really forget, can he?" Sam's voice was defiant, as if challenging Jade to answer the question.

"What do you mean forget?" Jade's tone was gentle and non-defensive, and Dan could have hugged her. Any other tone likely would have made Sam shut down.

"I mean, David's praying that God won't remember the sins of his youth. But good luck with that. I mean, he's *God*. He's perfect. So he can't forget, right?"

Jade pointed at Sam. "*That* is an excellent question. In fact, I was wondering the very same thing. Pastor Dan, could you help us out here?"

Dan leaned forward with his elbows on his knees. "You're right." He sought out Sam's eyes. "God is perfect. So I guess that means he never forgets anything. Which would be a great skill to have when it comes to a science test, right? How many bones does a giraffe have? God knows because he created them, and he never forgets a single detail."

Sam's face fell, and Jade slid closer to Dan on the picnic table, pointing to a verse in the Bible. But Dan kept going, giving each of them a gentle smile. "But God would totally bomb a test where he had to name each one of our sins. Because when he looks at us, he sees Jesus. He sees the perfect life Jesus lived for us and the innocent death he died to pay for our sins. Jesus took them all away. They are gone. God can't remember them because they don't exist anymore."

Sam nodded, looking relieved, but Jade frowned at him. "Why would he do that?"

Dan leaned close enough to read the Bible over her shoulder, his finger landing at the end of verse seven. "According to your love."

Jade lifted her eyes to his. There was still doubt there, but behind it, there was something more.

Something that looked a lot like hope.

The big dinner bell outside the mess hall clanged, making both of them jump.

"Okay, campers, off to breakfast and then we've got all kinds of stuff planned for today, since it's our last full day here."

As the kids scampered toward the food, Jade passed him his Bible. "Sorry I didn't have all the answers."

He almost reached to tuck a stray hair into her ponytail but stopped himself at the last second. "It's okay not to have all the answers. It was actually good for the kids to see that faith doesn't depend on knowing everything."

"And you really believe God forgets about all our past sins?"

Her gaze was intense, but he returned it without flinching. "I really believe that."

"Well." Jade started toward the mess hall. "Even if God forgets, people don't."

Dan thought about arguing. About saying that he'd forgotten.

But no matter how much he wanted that to be true, it wasn't.

Chapter 20

S weat rolled down Jade's neck, and she took a swig from the water bottle on her hip. They must have hiked at least four miles already, and the girls in front of her were starting to lag. Their chatter had long since quieted, and now they simply plodded, one foot in front of the other.

But the long walk was exactly what Jade had needed. She tipped her face skyward, taking in the tops of the trees that arched over the trail, spots of flawless blue sky showing through the foliage. It didn't take much effort to believe in God when she was surrounded by all this majesty.

On the first day of camp, she'd watched her feet as she walked, simply hoping to survive the week. But now that camp was almost over, she found herself wishing it could last longer. Church camp was nowhere near where she'd imagined her life taking her, but after spending most of her life feeling directionless, it was nice to wake up each day with a purpose. She wouldn't miss the bugs, but these kids had grown on her, and she didn't know how she would fill her days without them. Plus, she'd finally mastered cooking scrambled eggs and putting together woodsy crafts—and she'd even managed to complete the high ropes course yesterday with a respectable time. But her most shocking accomplishment of all had to be this morning's devotion. She'd never imagined she could enjoy reading the Bible, let alone talking about it. But now that she'd done it, she found she kind of craved a chance to do it again. But once she returned to her real life, all of this would be only a memory. There was no way to make it last.

"Miss Jade, Penelope's off the path." Melody's voice cut into her thoughts.

She dropped her eyes to the girls. Sure enough, Penelope had wandered a few steps off the trail to a patch of purple coneflowers.

"Aren't they pretty?" Penelope asked, reaching to touch the petals.

"Let's keep going, Pen." Jade stopped to wait for the little girl, letting her gaze drift to the lake below. They'd kayaked across it yesterday—something else she'd never thought she'd enjoy.

"Ouch!" Penelope's scream made Jade's head snap to her.

"What happened?"

Penelope stood in front of the flowers, her right hand clutching her upper left arm. Her face was scrunched in pain, and tears ran down her cheeks as she continued to scream.

Jade ran to her side and crouched next to her, reaching to lift Penelope's hand off her arm so she could take a look. But Penelope tightened her grip and refused to let go.

"Pen, you have to let me see it so I can help." Jade pried the little girl's hand off, but Penelope clapped it right back onto her arm.

"Madison," Jade called to her oldest camper. "Run ahead and get Pastor Dan. The rest of you stay put for a minute."

Dan's group was in the lead, so they were probably at least a quarter mile ahead. Madison sprinted off, and Jade lowered herself to sit on the ground next to Penelope. The little girl was crying so hard she was shaking, and Jade wrapped her arms around her, pulling her in close. If only she could do more to make the small girl feel safe.

After a few minutes, footsteps pounded toward them.

Thank goodness. Dan would know what to do.

"What happened?" Dan crouched at her side, worry filling his eyes.

"I don't know. She was smelling some flowers, and I looked away for a second, and then she started screaming."

Why had she looked away? Penelope was her responsibility, and she hadn't protected her. Dan never should have trusted her with the kids.

Dan turned to Penelope. "Do you think I could peek at your arm?"

Penelope shook her head.

"What if Miss Jade looks at it? She'd never do anything to hurt you, right?"

At Penelope's slow nod, Jade let out a breath.

"Good girl." Jade smoothed Penelope's hair off her cheek. "You're so brave."

Penelope lifted her hand to reveal a small red dot with a white center. Jade breathed a sigh of relief. "Okay, sweetie. You have a bee sting. Pastor Dan is going to remove the stinger, and then it will feel a lot better."

But Penelope squirmed away as Dan reached to touch her arm.

She buried her face in Jade's neck. "I want you to do it."

Jade grimaced. She'd had an allergic reaction to a bee sting once as a kid. It hadn't been too serious, but it was enough for the doctor to prescribe her an EpiPen. Which she should probably have with her now, come to think of it. Instead of in her purse back in the cabin.

She pushed the thought aside. What were the odds that she would get stung by a bee too?

But no one had ever told her if it was dangerous to simply remove a stinger from someone else.

Penelope's fresh wails made the decision for her. "Okay, sweetie. I'll get it out. But you have to be super brave and hold very still."

At Penelope's nod, Jade shifted her so that she could reach her arm, then placed her fingernail at the edge of the stinger and scraped.

Penelope screamed, and Jade almost pulled her hand away, but she made herself keep going. Stopping now would only make it worse.

Finally, the stinger was out, and Jade flicked it to the side of the trail, wrapping Penelope in a big hug. "You did it. Does it feel a little better?"

Penelope nodded, and Jade stood up.

Dan met her eyes, looking at her with . . . what? Admiration, maybe. She looked away.

His admiration was the last thing she deserved.

"Let's head back to camp and get some medicine on that to make it all better." He smiled at Penelope, who offered him a wobbly return smile, even as tears continued to drip down her cheeks. "How about if I walk with you and Miss Jade?"

In spite of herself, Jade was relieved. If Dan was with them, at least nothing else bad would happen to Penelope. Brianna had been right not to want her daughter in Jade's care.

They set out again, Dan and Jade falling in with Penelope behind the rest of the group.

Penelope clutched Jade's hand as they walked.

The silence stretched between them until Jade couldn't stand it anymore. "I'm sorry I didn't watch her more closely."

Dan reached a quick hand to rest on her shoulder before pulling it back. "Kids get bee stings, Jade. There's nothing you could have done to prevent it."

Jade nodded but looked away. Why was this man always so kind to her? Why did he always see the best in her? Even when there was so little good to see.

Penelope tripped, and Jade tugged her hand to keep her from falling. "You okay, sweetie?"

"I feel kind of funny."

Jade stopped and squatted at the girl's side. Penelope's face was red and splotchy, and Jade tried to remember if she'd gotten sunburned earlier.

"Funny how?"

"Like I'm spinning. And my tummy hurts." Tears welled in her eyes again, and Jade leaned in to hug her.

"It's going to be okay." She sized the girl up. Penelope was small, but not *that* small. She wasn't sure she could carry her all the way to camp.

But she could at least get her partway there. "How about I give you a piggyback ride?"

But Dan reached a hand to stop Jade from picking Penelope up. "Is it okay if I give you the piggyback ride, Penelope? I'm a little stronger than Miss Jade."

Penelope coughed but nodded, and Jade helped her onto Dan's back. The little girl's cough seemed to get worse as they walked.

"Does she have a cold?" The words came out in puffs as Dan kept going with Penelope on his back.

"I don't think so." Jade bit her lip, anxiety coursing through her. Something wasn't right, but she didn't know what it was.

"How you doing, Pen?" She couldn't help asking every few minutes.

"I'm . . . okay," Penelope answered for the third time. But something about the way she hesitated between words drew Jade up short. She set a hand on Dan's arm to stop him.

"Let's give her a break."

Dan stopped and eased the girl to the ground.

Jade helped her lie back and lifted her water bottle to Penelope's lips as Dan jogged ahead to check on the other hikers, who'd kept up a faster pace.

As Jade capped the water bottle, Penelope pulled at her t-shirt, as if it were too tight. "I want to breathe."

Something cold washed down Jade's back as she watched the little girl.

"Dan!" Jade had never screamed louder in her life. She scrambled to her feet, sucking in air to scream again, but Dan was already sprinting back to her.

Jade pulled out her phone and dialed 911.

If she was right, Penelope didn't have much time.

But there was no sound from the phone. Jade yanked it away from her ear.

No service.

"Aargh."

Now what? They had to be at least a mile from camp yet. By the time they got Penelope back, it might be too late.

"What's going on?" Dan's usually calm expression was twisted into a look of fear. It was the first time Jade had ever seen him anything less than collected, and it shook her. But it also spurred her into action.

"Is Penelope allergic to bee stings?"

"I don't know. I don't think so. Her mom didn't say anything—" Dan's head swiveled, as if he was looking for the answer in the bushes that surrounded them.

"Dan." Jade's voice was sharp. He had to get it together. "I think she's in anaphylactic shock."

He blanched, but his eyes locked on hers, and he nodded. "What do we do?"

"I have an EpiPen in my purse. It's on my bunk. You need to run and get it."

Dan was sprinting down the trail before she could finish.

"And have someone call 911 as soon as they have a signal," she hollered behind him.

She dropped to her knees next to Penelope. There had to be something she could do to help her.

She tried to remember what the doctor had told her when he'd diagnosed her allergy, but her own reaction had been so mild, and her mind was stuck on the image of Penelope struggling for air.

Think, Jade.

Raise her feet. She should raise Penelope's feet to help her circulation.

She peered around wildly, her eyes landing on a fallen log off to the side of the trail.

She lunged for it and lugged it toward Penelope. It was heavier than she'd expected, but she used every ounce of energy she had left to maneuver it into position. She piled her pack on top of it, then gently lifted Penelope's feet onto it.

She moved to Penelope's side and brushed the hair off her face, grabbing the little girl's hand in hers. "It's okay, kiddo. You're going to be fine. You just hold on for a few minutes, and Pastor Dan will be right back with some medicine for you." Somehow, her voice was steady, even though she was certain her whole body was shaking.

Penelope nodded, her lips slightly swollen.

Jade bowed her head and brought Penelope's hand to her cheek. "Hurry, Dan," she murmured. "Please let him hurry." She only hoped he'd kept up with his running since his days as a track star.

"Oh no."

"Is she okay?"

"Why are her feet on that log?"

Jade looked up at the chorus of voices. The rest of the campers surrounded them, and some of the younger girls started crying.

Grace knelt and rested a hand on Jade's back. "Dan told us what happened as he ran past, so we came back. What can we do for her?"

"Pray." The word was out before Jade could think. But she knew, somewhere deep in her heart, that prayer was what Penelope needed more than anything right now.

Grace told the other children to fold their hands. Then, with her hand still on Jade's back, she started to pray. "Dear Heavenly Father, please hold Penelope in your loving arms. Protect her and keep her safe. We pray that you would give Pastor Dan swift feet to bring the medicine Penelope needs and that you would help Mr. Tyler's phone get a signal so he can call for help."

Jade squeezed her eyes shut and let Grace's prayer wash over her. Did she even believe it could make a difference?

She wasn't sure, but right now, it was all she had.

Grace's hand was firm on Jade's back as she continued with her prayer. "Most of all, we ask that you would help us all to trust in you. To trust that just as you are the all-powerful God who created this world, you are the loving Father who created each one of us and watches over us daily. To trust that you love us without condition and that in you we have the promise of eternal life, whenever you choose to call us home to you."

The tears were coursing down Jade's cheeks now, but somehow she was more at ease than she had been in months. There was nothing she could do in this moment.

So she had to do the only thing there was left to do.

She had to trust.

The group fell silent, most of the campers standing with their hands folded, a few hugging each other and whispering, all of them watching Penelope. With every movement of the little girl's chest, Jade gave a prayer of thanks.

Just let her keep breathing. The words circled through her mind in a continuous loop.

"Here he comes."

Jade's head popped up at the shout. The campers all cheered Dan on as he closed the remaining yards, holding the EpiPen out to Jade like a relay baton, a look of sheer determination on his face. Jade didn't know how much time had passed, but she'd be willing to bet that his run had broken the records he'd set in high school.

The moment the EpiPen hit her hand, she pulled off the protective cap and jabbed it into Penelope's leg. The little girl flinched but didn't have the energy to cry out.

Jade held completely still, vaguely aware of Grace's hand on her back, of Dan standing above them, breathing heavily. But mostly watching Penelope's chest.

After a few seconds, the little girl's breathing eased, her chest rising and falling more deeply. The swelling in her lips went down.

"Thank you, Lord." Jade wasn't sure if she'd spoken the words aloud as she bent in half and kissed Penelope's cheek.

She jumped to her feet. "She needs to get to a hospital. She could relapse and need another dose."

"Tyler got a signal when we were halfway to the cabins. He said they were sending flight for life since we're too remote for an ambulance. They're going to land in the clearing by the lake."

Jade nodded. "We should get her there. Can you carry her?"

But Dan was already scooping Penelope into his arms. "Let's go."

Chapter 21

The flight nurse circled his hands and pointed down, and Dan nodded, glancing out the window to see the hospital below at last.

He let out the breath he'd been holding the entire chopper ride.

Thank you, Jesus.

They'd had to give Penelope two more shots of epinephrine on the way here, and each time, Dan had been sure his own heart was going to stop. He was responsible for this little girl, and if anything happened to her . . .

But nothing had happened to her.

No thanks to him. He'd had no idea what was wrong with Penelope or what to do to help her. He'd promised the parents of these children that he'd keep them safe, and the first emergency that had come up had left him helpless.

But not Jade.

Thank you, Lord, that she knew what to do. It was at least the tenth time he'd uttered that prayer since the moment she'd said the words anaphylactic shock. He didn't know how she'd known what to do or why she happened to carry an EpiPen, but he trusted that God had brought all that together at just the right time for a reason.

Jade had accepted his decision to be the one to ride with Penelope with a resignation that had almost broken him. He knew how much she cared about this little girl. And after the bond she'd formed with

Penelope, she should be the one here with her. But he'd also known how it would look to Brianna if Jade was the one to greet her at the hospital with her daughter, when she'd specifically asked him to keep Penelope away from Jade.

The moment the chopper landed, a team unloaded Penelope's stretcher, and Dan followed them into the building. He was here often enough to visit sick congregation members, but he never quite got used to the unnatural smell of the place.

"I'm going to go check if your mom is here yet. I'll bring her to you." He squeezed Penelope's hand, grateful that her return squeeze was strong.

The moment he stepped into the waiting room, a blond blur rushed him. Brianna stopped inches from him, her normally pristine makeup smeared in streaks under her eyes and across her cheeks. "Where's Penelope? Is she okay?"

Dan set a comforting hand on her shoulder. "She's doing much better now. They want to observe her, but they think she's past the worst of it. I'll take you to her."

As he led her through the hallways, he filled her in on what had happened.

"I didn't know she was allergic to bees." Brianna's face paled when Dan told her about the bee sting and Penelope's reaction.

"The flight nurse said that's pretty common. You can't know until someone has a reaction, unfortunately. I had no idea what was wrong, either. It was Jade who figured it out."

Brianna froze, the click of her heels coming to a sudden halt. "She was with Jade?" She threw her hands in the air. "I thought I made my feelings about that clear. If she hadn't been with Jade, she probably—"

"She'd probably be dead."

Brianna gaped at him, grabbing the wall for support. "Dead?" She said the word as if she'd never heard it before.

"Yeah." Dan ran a hand through his hair. He had to get his personal feelings under control before he said something he'd regret. "She was in anaphylactic shock. If Jade hadn't realized that's what it was, if she hadn't had an EpiPen along, if she hadn't done first aid . . ."

"I didn't realize." Brianna hugged her arms around her middle and bent over at the waist. "I could have lost my baby."

Compassion rose in Dan's chest, and he moved closer, placing a light hand on Brianna's back. "But you didn't. God protected her. And he used Jade to do that. That's something to be thankful for."

Brianna didn't look at him. "Can I see Penelope now? I really need to see her."

"Of course." Dan steered her to Penelope's room. "I'll be in the waiting area if you need anything."

Brianna stepped into the room, then seemed to think twice. She stopped, turned around, and gave him a quick hug. "Thank you for keeping my little girl safe."

He returned her hug. "Thank God for that." He let her go and started down the hall. "And Jade."

Fire burned behind Jade's eyelids, but even though the bus was unusually silent—the kids much more subdued than they'd been on the way to camp—she couldn't close them.

Every time she'd started to fall asleep last night, she'd seen Penelope strapped to that stretcher, being loaded onto the helicopter. Eventually, she'd given up on sleeping and spent the night watching the stars until they'd faded in the gray dawn light. She'd tried to find the majesty of God she'd seen in the forest, but it was all tainted now.

Dan could say God loved them all he wanted, but if that was true, why had he allowed this to happen to Penelope?

This morning, Tyler had led the kids in a short devotion, then he, Grace, and Jade had agreed it was best to skip the few activities that had been planned and head home. The kids were all too worried about Penelope to have any fun, and they wouldn't be able to get an update on her until they got within decent cell range. Apparently, it had been a fluke that Tyler had gotten a signal to call for emergency services yesterday, since none of them had been able to get any reception since.

Jade leaned her head against the window, the trees outside a blur of brown and green. How had she thought yesterday that she'd found purpose in working with these kids? It turned out that getting close to them could be just as painful as getting close to anyone else.

"I've got a signal." Grace's shout from the front of the bus drew everyone's attention. All around Jade, the kids shifted in their seats, everyone leaning forward as if their proximity to the phone would help Grace's call go through.

Jade's heart sped up, but she resisted the urge to pray. If God wanted to try to convince her he loved her, he could go ahead. But she was done begging him.

"It's ringing," Grace called. A second later, she held up a finger for silence, even though no one was talking.

"Hi, Pastor Dan, it's Grace." Her voice carried to the back of the bus. "We're almost back to Hope Springs, but I have a bus full of kids here wondering how Penelope is doing."

She kept her finger poised as she listened. But Jade doubted anyone on the bus was so much as breathing. She knew she wasn't.

After a few seconds, Grace's face relaxed. "She's doing great," she called out.

The kids erupted in cheers, and several of the girls exchanged hugs.

Jade leaned her head on the window and closed her eyes, ignoring the tears that slid out from under her lids.

It couldn't have been more than a few seconds later that one of the kids was shaking her shoulder. "Miss Jade, wake up. We're home."

Jade peeled her eyes open and waited for them to focus. The bus had stopped, and kids were waiting in the aisle to get off.

She glanced out the window. Dan must have contacted the kids' parents to let them know they'd be back early, as parents milled in the church parking lot, waiting for their kids and hugging them extra tight when they found them.

Once all the kids had disembarked, Jade made her way up the aisle, checking each seat to make sure no one had forgotten anything. By the time she got off the bus, the parking lot was empty, aside from Grace and Tyler.

Grace wrapped her in a hug the moment she stepped onto the pavement. "I'm so glad you came along. If you hadn't . . ." Grace squeezed tighter. "But you did, and thank the Lord for that."

When Grace released her, Tyler gave her a quick hug too. "Get some sleep."

She nodded numbly.

"Where's Violet?" Grace looked around the empty lot. "Do you need a ride home?"

"No thanks." She hadn't called Vi to let her know they'd be back early. She didn't want to make her sister leave the store in the middle of the day. "I think I need the walk." What was a couple miles compared to the distances they'd hiked at camp?

Grace gave her another hug, then headed for her car, while Tyler made his way to his truck.

Jade lifted a hand to wave to each of them as they pulled away. Then she started walking.

But instead of heading for the road, her feet took her toward the beach. The events of the past few days swirled through her mind, and she needed some time to sort them out.

The waves pulled at Dan's feet, beckoning him farther into the water. He'd love nothing more than to dive in and forget the past twenty-four hours had ever happened.

He should be up in the parking lot, making sure all the kids got picked up, but he trusted the rest of his leaders to take care of that. He couldn't handle the thought of facing the parents right now. Calling to tell them what had happened and request that they pick their kids up early had been humiliating enough. No one had come out and said it, but he knew they were thinking it—if his dad had been in charge, this never would have happened.

He kicked at the water, sending a spray into the air in front of him.

"Good to know it's not just me you splash."

He spun, a smile almost lifting his lips at the sound of her voice. "How'd you know I'd be down here?"

She walked toward him, balancing on the thin border where the water barely kissed the sand. "I didn't. Just felt like I needed a walk."

"Me too."

As she reached him, they fell into step, the same way they had dozens of times before.

"So she's really all right?" Jade grabbed his arm, and he stopped walking so he could look her in the eyes.

"She's great. They released her this morning. She—"

But the hug she launched at him was so powerful, it knocked the air out of him.

"Oh, thank goodness." Her words were a half sob.

Before he could decide whether to return the hug, she'd let go.

"Sorry, I was just so worried—" Jade ran a hand over her wrinkled shirt and started walking again.

"I'm sorry we couldn't both go to the hospital with her. I would have had you go, but—"

Jade waved him off. "You did what you needed to do."

They walked in silence for a few minutes.

"You believe in God, right?" Jade finally asked.

"Of course." He debated with himself a second before asking, "Do you?"

Jade's feet slowed. "I thought I was starting to. But then this happened. I mean, what kind of God lets a little girl get sick like that?"

Dan considered her question. A flippant answer wouldn't do any good here. "This world isn't a perfect place. It's tainted by sin. Which is why bad things happen." Before she could take his comment as meaning that it was her sin that had caused it, he continued. "Even things that are no one's fault."

Jade looked thoughtful, as if she were considering his words. "But he could have made it not happen, right?"

"He could have." Dan leaned down to pick up a shell and passed it to her, delighting in the look of surprise in her eyes. "But he has a bigger plan at work than we can see. He tells us that in all things he works for the good of those who love him. He can bring good even out of this." He didn't add that he could see some of the good right here, in her, in the softening of her heart even as she asked the hard questions about God.

Now that she'd asked her question, he supposed he could be brave enough to ask his. "How did the parents seem when they picked up the kids? Were they angry?"

Jade gave him a curious look. "Why would they be angry?"

Dan's feet dragged through the sand. "Obviously, the trip didn't go quite to plan. I'm guessing that's the last time anyone will send their kids to camp with me."

Jade's hand on his arm was so light, he probably wouldn't have noticed it if he hadn't seen it, but it pulled him to a stop.

"Dan, you brought everyone home safely. You said yourself that Penelope is fine, and—"

"That's no thanks to me. I had no idea what to do. If you hadn't been there—"

"But I *was* there. And that was because of you."

His head snapped up. Had she meant that the way it sounded? The slight blush of pink in her cheeks said maybe she had.

"Anyway." She started down the beach again. "Why are you so concerned about what they think?"

Dan gave a dry laugh. She had to be kidding, right?

"There are a lot of people counting on me. You knew my dad. He was a giant of the church. Everyone loved him. It's a lot to live up to."

Jade didn't say anything for a while, and Dan let his gaze slide to her.

"I guess I can understand that," she said at last. "But maybe people don't want you to be your dad. Maybe they want you to be you."

"Yeah, maybe. But half of them still remember me as the five-year-old who threw up in front of the whole church when we were singing on Easter Sunday."

"No." Jade laughed but quickly slapped a hand over her mouth. "You didn't."

"You don't remember that?"

Jade shook her head, still laughing, and he groaned. "I really wish I hadn't brought it up then."

When Jade's giggles had subsided, she turned to him, her expression earnest. "But you love it, don't you? Being a pastor."

He ran a hand over his chin. "With all the stress of the past few months, I'd started to forget that, but, yeah, I do. Being at camp with the kids"—and with her, but he couldn't exactly say that—"reminded me why I entered the ministry in the first place. It's probably how you feel about acting."

But she looked away. "I gave up on acting a long time ago."

He stared at her, trying to process. "But Violet is always talking about your auditions and—"

"I lied."

He tried to keep the question from coming out but failed. "Why?"

She sighed and stared out at the lake. "Because I knew otherwise Vi would ask me to come home."

"And you didn't want to?"

Any hopes he'd been beginning to build collapsed like a sandcastle under the waves.

Her laugh was laced with sarcasm. "I never belonged in Hope Springs, Dan. We both know that. I've burned too many bridges. No one wants me here."

"Violet wants you here."

I want you here.

But he wasn't entirely sure that was true. Having her here made things complicated. Messy. Uncertain.

Jade watched him for a minute, as if waiting to see if he had the courage to say more.

When he didn't, she smiled softly and looked over her shoulder, toward the dunes.

He saw the moment she recognized where they were.

"This is it." Her words were almost a whisper, and she took a few steps up the beach toward the dunes.

But then she stopped. "That was a long time ago."

Dan stood at her side. "It was."

But somehow his hand had found hers, and now they were facing each other, holding hands. His eyes went to hers, then slid to her lips.

This was nearly the exact spot he'd kissed her once before. The desire to do it again almost overwhelmed him. If he kissed her right now, would they get a second chance?

Jade's eyes closed a fraction, and Dan leaned toward her. His heart took up the pounding rhythm of the waves.

But maybe instead of a second chance at love, all he'd get was a second helping of heartbreak. She'd said herself that she wasn't made for Hope Springs.

He cleared his throat and stepped back, letting her hand fall. "We should probably get going."

"Yeah." Her eyes opened slowly, and she gave the dunes a wistful glance as they walked away. He almost thought she'd stop and say they should stay.

But she didn't.

And neither did he.

Chapter 22

*J*ade stretched a kink in her back, then bent to slide her roller
through the paint tray again.

She had to hand it to Nate and Vi's friends. They'd joined her
here every moment they could spare in the week since camp. She and
Sophie had pulled down the last of the hideous wallpaper last night.
And this morning she'd started painting the living room the subtle blue
she'd picked out.

She surveyed the enormous room. This was going to be a big job. She
hadn't even completed one wall yet. Dan had said he might come by to
help, but with any luck at least one or two others would be here before
then. She and Dan hadn't been alone since that afternoon last week
when she'd mistaken his kindness for a desire to kiss her. Now there
was this weird tension between them. They should probably talk about
it, but she much preferred pretending it had never happened.

"Good morning."

The voice behind her made Jade jerk upright and spin around. Too
late, she remembered the fully loaded roller in her hand. She watched,
mouth slack, as flecks of blue paint scattered through the air, landing
everywhere—including the hardwood floor and Dan's t-shirt.

Dan stood there for a minute, staring down at his shirt as if he wasn't
sure what had just happened.

"I'm so sorry." But she couldn't hold back the giggle that sneaked
out. The look on his face was too comical.

"It's fine." Dan took a step closer and picked up another roller, loading it with paint. "Now I look like I've been working for hours."

Did this guy never get upset about anything? She lifted her roller to the wall, picking up where she'd left off, but something wet and sticky sloshed onto her forearm. Jade gasped and spun on Dan, who was grinning maniacally.

She held up her now-blue elbow. "You did not just do that."

But Dan concentrated on the up and down motion of his roller on the wall. "Now we're even."

Jade could be mature about this and start painting again. Or—

She lunged forward and painted a stripe down his back.

Before she could retreat, Dan had grabbed both her wrists and snatched the roller out of her hand.

"No," Jade shrieked around a laugh. "I'm sorry. Truce. I give up."

But Dan held her hands above her head. "I've seen how you keep truces." He painted a line down each of her sides.

"Hey, that was two for one." Jade made a futile effort to free herself, but she was laughing too hard to put any strength behind it.

"You're right. That probably wasn't fair." Dan loosened his grip on her wrists, and she lunged for the roller. But in one deft movement, Dan had wrapped an arm around her shoulders and pulled her in close enough to slap paint onto her back.

"Hey." Jade gave a halfhearted wriggle but leaned her head into his chest to catch her breath. She hadn't laughed this much since— She had no idea when she'd last laughed like this.

But as her laughter slowed, she became alarmingly aware of Dan's arms still around her, of his heart beating under her ear.

As if realizing it at the same moment, Dan loosened his grip and gave her a gentle nudge away from him.

But he didn't take his eyes off her. "Now that we both look like robin's eggs, I guess—"

"Oh my goodness! What happened?"

Both of them spun toward the door, where Grace was standing with her mouth open, staring from one of them to the other. Out of the corner of her eye, Jade saw Dan open the space between them. She told herself she didn't care.

"It was my fault." Of course Dan was going to take the blame. He always did the right thing, no matter what it cost him.

"Actually—" Two could play this game. "I started it."

"Oh." Grace's mouth was as round as her eyes, but after a second she seemed to decide it was best to ignore whatever had just been happening between Jade and Dan. A pinch of conscience stirred in Jade's tummy, but she reminded herself she hadn't done anything wrong.

"Well." Grace stepped into the room, holding up a bag. "Leah sent lunch."

The smell of fried chicken drifted through the room. For some reason, it set Jade's stomach churning. Or maybe that was still the effect of being too close to Dan.

"Is it lunchtime already?" She checked the time. "I'm supposed to meet Vi for a dress fitting in ten minutes. And thanks to *someone*, I have to find a way to sneak home and change first so Vi doesn't ask what I've been up to."

"She really has no idea?" Dan wiped the paint flecks off the floor as he talked.

Jade felt her face pull into a frown. "I feel bad, though. I think she's starting to worry that I'm avoiding her."

She'd seen the flash of disappointment in Vi's eyes every time she'd declined to help in the store this week.

"Tell her you're meeting a mystery man," Grace said with a wink and a laugh.

Reflexively, Jade's eyes went to Dan, who seemed to be scrubbing at the paint spots on the floor with more vigor than necessary.

She forced a laugh. "I'm not sure she'd believe that."

Chapter 23

The ball swished through the hoop, and Jared lifted his hands in triumph. "That's three in a row, man. What's up with you today?"

Dan grabbed the rebound. "Nothing's up with me."

Jared checked the ball but didn't move in for the block as Dan made his way down the half-court that had been painted off to the side of the church parking lot for youth group events. For the past year or so, he and Jared had been playing a quick game of one-on-one every Friday morning.

"You know, for a guy who's always encouraging others to talk about their problems, you aren't so quick to share your own."

Dan shrugged. He was here to play basketball, not talk about his problems.

Not that he had any.

"You remember what you told me when I needed someone to talk to about Peyton?"

Dan drove to the basket for a layup. The ball went in easily, only because Jared didn't take so much as half a step to block him.

"Are we playing basketball or talking?" Dan tried to keep the annoyance out of his voice.

But Jared was standing with the ball clasped in his hands. "Talking."

Dan stared at his friend a second, then jogged to the sideline to grab his water bottle.

"You said—" Jared walked over, setting the ball in the grass and grabbing his own water. After a long swig, he continued. "You said you were human."

Dan looked up. Of course he was human. "I don't think I've ever said I wasn't."

"No." Jared scooped the ball up and tossed it from hand to hand. "But you act like you're superhuman. You don't share your problems because you don't want people to know you have any."

"I *don't* have any." But he'd known Jared long enough to realize his friend wouldn't let him get away with that.

He dragged a hand through his hair. "Fine. It's Jade. And Grace."

Jared nodded but didn't say anything, just kept tossing the ball from hand to hand. He was using Dan's own technique of waiting silently to draw him out. Dan would think it was nicely played, if it weren't so frustrating.

Jared was right. Dan didn't want anyone to think he had problems. After all, he was the pastor. He was supposed to solve everyone else's problems, not come to them with his own.

But Jared was a good friend. And Dan did need some advice.

He reached to steal the ball from Jared and started dribbling. "Not many people know that Jade and I went on a few—I don't know if you'd call them dates—but we spent some time together at the end of high school, right before she left Hope Springs. We were actually getting pretty serious. At least that's what I thought. But then—" Dan gave an extra-strong dribble that made the ball bounce up to his head. "Then she left. And it seemed pretty clear the path God had laid out for me. And then Grace moved here, and everyone kept telling me how perfect she is for me. But now Jade is back and—" He caught the ball and shrugged helplessly. Why was this all so confusing?

"And you still like her."

Dan nodded. "Quite a lot, actually. But Grace is the smarter choice."

Jared snorted. "Spoken like a true romantic. I believe the exact words you asked me were, 'Do you love her?' So I'll ask you that too."

Dan shook his head. He liked Grace well enough as a friend, and he certainly appreciated all her work at church. But what he felt for her was nowhere near love. As he'd eaten lunch with her at Nate and Violet's house yesterday after Jade had left, he couldn't help mentally comparing the two women. In his mind, Grace came out ahead every time. It was as if God had created her to be a perfect pastor's wife. She was warm, open, hospitable, a natural when it came to serving at church—and she even played the piano and sang in the choir. In short, she was everything Jade wasn't. But no matter how much he told himself all of that, he couldn't get his heart on board.

"Maybe I could grow to love Grace. If I try hard enough, you know? I mean, her dad was a pastor, she grew up in the church, she's right at home jumping into ministry. She's the perfect match for a pastor." So what if he didn't see fireworks when her arm brushed up against his? There was more to a relationship than that. She was the sensible choice. The choice everyone would approve of.

"And Jade? Do you love her?"

Dan wanted to say it was way too early to call what he felt for Jade love. And yet he knew it wasn't too early. He'd never fallen out of love with her in the first place. He never would.

But love wasn't everything. He had his responsibilities to think about. And his first responsibility was the welfare of his church.

"I'm trying to keep everything going here, trying to show everyone that I can handle things on my own, trying to live up to what my dad started."

"Okay—" Jared attempted to steal the ball, but Dan pivoted too quickly for him. "Nice. But what would dating Jade have to do with any of that?"

A hollow opened in Dan's stomach. He didn't like to think it, let alone say it out loud. But he had to get it out there. "I care about Jade.

A lot. But you know what her reputation was in high school. And I've heard whispers even now. I try not to pay attention to them. But I don't think the congregation would ever accept me dating her."

This time Jared was successful in stealing the ball. He placed it deliberately on the ground and braced his foot on it. Then he gave Dan a piercing stare. "I hate to throw your own words back at you, but a few weeks ago, you preached a sermon about the kind of people Jesus hung out with. They weren't the people with the best reputations."

Dan looked away, toward the lake where he'd been so tempted to kiss Jade the other day.

"I know." He couldn't deny that Jared was absolutely right. "But Jesus didn't have a whole church just waiting for him to mess up so they could point out he wasn't as good as his father."

"Sounds to me like it's not Jade's reputation you're worried about. It's yours." Jared picked up the ball and passed it to him, hard.

Dan caught it with a grunt.

"Maybe God brought Jade back so you could have a second chance. Maybe not. But you owe it to yourself—and to her—to find out."

"Yeah, maybe."

Dan lobbed the ball absently toward the hoop. It clanged against the rim, then bounced off in the other direction. Which was probably exactly what would happen with Jade if he told her how he felt.

"You don't think so, do you?" Grace's voice cut into Dan's thoughts and he realized that he'd lost track of their conversation for the fifth time since they'd arrived at the Hidden Cafe.

He scooped up a forkful of French toast to give himself a moment to return his focus to her. "I'm sorry. What was that?"

"You seem sort of distracted this morning. Is everything all right?"

"Sorry. Just have lots of things on my mind." After a sleepless weekend, he'd gotten up this morning certain of his choice. He had to do what was best for the church. So he'd called Grace and invited her to breakfast. Too bad he'd proceeded to spend the entire meal thinking about Jade.

He had to snap out of it. "What were you saying?"

Grace waved a hand in the air. "Nothing much. I was just talking to hear my own voice, as my mama would say. Is there anything I can do to help? With whatever's on your mind, I mean."

He sincerely doubted that. "It's nothing." He grasped at the thread of conversation he remembered. "You were saying you think we need some more people to help with VBS?"

"Oh yeah." She nodded. "I have all kinds of new things I want to try. I thought maybe Jade could help with the crafts and . . ."

She was still talking, but his mind was gone again, drifting to Jade. He hadn't seen her for a couple of days now—Violet had said she wasn't feeling well yesterday, so she hadn't been in church—and he missed her.

"So you're on board with that?"

Dan blinked at Grace. "Yeah. Sounds great. Just let me know if you need anything else."

He finished the last bite of his French toast and signaled for the check.

"Now what?" Grace asked.

Dan's mind drew a blank. Now what *what*? And then he realized she meant now what should they do.

"Oh. I— Um—" He hadn't thought beyond the meal. He'd planned to go to the office afterward. But apparently Grace had taken his invitation to breakfast as an offer to spend the whole day together.

Both of their phones dinged with a text, and Dan breathed a silent thanks.

The message was from Jade, to their group chat about Violet and Nate's house. *The house is open if anyone wants to paint today. I'm still not feeling the best, so I won't be able to make it.*

"Oh, poor thing." Grace clicked off her phone. "Hope she feels better soon."

Dan nodded, but the worry that hummed through him, the desire to be with Jade and make her feel better, told him what he hadn't wanted to admit.

He was with the wrong woman.

"I'm sorry." He didn't have any desire to hurt Grace, but it wasn't fair to let her believe there was something here that wasn't. "I think you're a wonderful woman, and I am so grateful for everything you've done for our ministry. But—"

Her bright blue eyes fell on him, and he had to look at the floor. He'd had a lot of unpleasant conversations with people in his day, but this was one of the worst.

"The thing is, I just don't feel that way about you. I'm sorry." He kept his hands folded in his lap.

Grace gave a soft laugh. He'd been prepared for a lot of reactions from her. But not that one.

He ducked his head. "Sorry. Was I totally off base in thinking you liked me?" He groaned. "I was, wasn't I? That's embarrassing. I don't have a lot of experience with this sort of thing. Can we just pretend none of this ever happened?" Or better yet, they could both hit their heads against the table and get amnesia.

"No, no." Grace shook her head. "Sorry. You weren't wrong. I did like you. Do like you." Her face grew fiery, but she didn't look away. "But I told your sister it was never going to happen. It's pretty clear your heart already belongs to someone else. I'm just surprised it took you this long to realize it."

He could pretend he had no idea what she was talking about, but he wasn't going to insult her intelligence like that.

"Thanks for understanding." A twinge of regret pinched at him. His life would be so much easier if Grace were the one he had feelings for. "I hope this won't make things awkward between us. I want to still be friends if that's okay with you."

She slugged his arm lightly. "Try to stop me. Now go get the girl you're really after."

Dan swallowed. The problem was, he wasn't sure she wanted to be gotten.

Chapter 24

$\mathcal{J}$ade stared around the room, trying to place the sound that had made her open her eyes. She pushed slowly to an upright position, waiting for the wave of nausea that had rolled over her every time she sat up this morning. She hadn't been feeling the best the last few days, and yesterday she'd finally given in and stayed in bed instead of going to church.

She'd thought she was doing better last night, but when she'd woken this morning, the prospect of standing had made her nearly vomit, so she'd regretfully bailed on working at Vi and Nate's house. They had plenty of time to get the painting done, but she had been looking forward to seeing everyone.

To seeing Dan.

She silenced the thought.

She hadn't been looking forward to seeing Dan any more than anyone else. In the short time she'd been back in Hope Springs, Vi's friends had started to feel like an extended family.

If she wasn't careful, she was going to start thinking of this town as home.

A soft knock on the apartment door drew her attention. That must have been what woke her in the first place.

She pushed herself off the air mattress. Thankfully, the room didn't spin. "Coming."

She combed her fingers through her hair, but they got stuck halfway. Whoever was at the door was going to have to deal with seeing her like this.

But the moment she opened the door, she regretted that decision. Her eyes landed on the hyacinths Dan held, then swept down to her baggy plaid pajama pants and stained Minnie Mouse t-shirt.

"What are you doing here?" The words came out almost as an accusation, and she berated herself. It was pretty clear he was bringing her flowers, and she was thanking him by yelling at him. "I mean, I figured you'd be at church, doing official business."

"This is official business." He passed her the flowers. "One of my flock is sick, and I came to see how she's doing."

Jade didn't point out that she wasn't technically part of his flock. Or any flock, for that matter.

She lifted the flowers to her nose, taking in their soft perfume. How had he remembered they were her favorite? She'd only mentioned it once in passing years ago, when they'd found a patch of them sprouting on a dune.

"So, can I come in for a minute?"

"Oh." Jade jumped back. "Sorry. Of course. Have a seat." She gestured to the living room. "I'm just going to put these in some water."

In the kitchen, she dug around the cupboards until she found a suitable vase. While it was filling, she yanked her fingers through her hair a few times, trying not to cry out as they snagged on snarls. She almost always kept a rubber band on her wrist for emergency ponytails, but of course today was the one day she hadn't.

When the vase was full, she added the flowers and carried it to the living room. Dan was seated on the couch. She set the flowers on the table next to it, then shuffled across the room to sit on the chair farthest from him.

"Sorry, I wasn't expecting visitors. I'm still in my pajamas, and my hair—" She touched a self-conscious hand to her head.

"You look . . . fine."

Jade laughed and eyed him. "Careful. Your high praise will go to my head."

Dan grinned. "Actually, you look beautiful, but I wasn't sure how to say that."

"Oh." A smart remark would be helpful right about now. Or, barring that, some way to change the subject. "You do too."

Dan chuckled. "Thanks. That's the look I was going for today."

Jade joined in his laughter. "I mean— Oh, never mind." She threw her hands in the air. She was making a complete fool of herself. And the odd part was, she didn't care. She felt comfortable here with him, pajamas and messy hair and all.

"But seriously, how are you feeling? Any better?" Dan's mouth turned down, and Jade had to force herself to take her eyes off his lips.

"Much better, actually. Must have been something I ate. The weird thing is, I'm starving now." She got up and moved toward the kitchen again. "Want anything?"

"No thanks." Dan's voice was relaxed and easy. "I had breakfast with Grace a little while ago."

Jade's back stiffened, and she stopped rummaging through the cupboards for a second. Why was she surprised? Everyone could see that Dan and Grace were perfect for each other.

She dug through the food for another second, then slammed the cupboard shut. Why was there nothing that looked good?

She returned to the living room emptyhanded and flopped onto the chair with a dejected sigh.

Dan raised an eyebrow. "I thought you were starving. Where's your food?"

Jade lifted a shoulder. "Nothing here looks good."

"What are you in the mood for?"

Jade didn't even have to think about it. "Ice cream."

"The Chocolate Chicken it is. Let's go." He stood and held out a hand to help her up.

She only hesitated a second before setting her hand in his. His fingers closing around hers felt like the most natural thing in the world. She pulled her hand away the moment she was on her feet. No point in getting used to that sensation.

"Give me a second to change and do something with this hair." It was bad enough Dan had seen her looking like this. No way was she going in public.

"I like the jammie look on you. But if you want to change, go for it."

She shot him a mocking grin and disappeared into Vi's room.

Ten minutes later, she emerged wearing a pair of cutoff shorts and her favorite yellow tank top. She'd thrown her hair into a messy bun. It wasn't stellar, but it would have to do.

Dan surveyed her. "I think I liked the jammies better, but this is good too."

She swatted at him. She'd seen the appreciation in his eyes as he looked at her. Not the lustful kind of appreciation other men had always directed her way, like they were wondering what she looked like under her clothes. Dan's look was more tender—a look that made her feel sheltered and safe.

Downstairs, she popped into the antique shop to let Vi know she was going out, then followed Dan to the parking lot.

He started for his car, but she grabbed his arm. "Do you mind if we walk? It's so nice out, and I've been cooped up inside all day."

"Of course." Dan matched her pace, and they fell into an easy silence. The day was warm, but a gentle breeze played with the hairs that had fallen out of her bun. Jade tilted her face to the sky and sighed.

"Something wrong?" Dan looked at her with concern.

"Nope. I just feel—" She didn't know how to describe it. "Like I wouldn't change anything right now."

Dan's footsteps stuttered, but he quickly resumed walking, picking up his pace slightly. Great. Now she'd scared him off. Again.

She had to stop implying that she wanted to be with him. It was pretty clear he already had a future. And it wasn't with her.

"I'm glad," Dan said finally, and it took her a minute to figure out what he was glad about.

She should undo what she'd done. But she didn't know what else to say. She couldn't take it back because it was true.

Fortunately, they arrived at the Chocolate Chicken, and the crowds made further conversation impossible. Apparently, ice cream sounded good to everyone on a hot day like today. Vacationing families, local teens, and a few senior citizens filled every last table, and the line to order stretched outside the door.

As they waited for their turn, Dan talked easily with a few people in front of them in line. Jade recognized them from church. She watched as Dan laughed at their jokes, listened to their concerns, offered to pray for them. This all came so naturally to him. Jade hovered awkwardly by his side, saying hi when he introduced her but not saying much else.

More than one person cast a curious eye at her. She knew what they were thinking because she was thinking it too. She wasn't the kind of woman he should be taking out for ice cream. He needed a woman who could support him in the ministry. They all knew who that woman was. And—spoiler alert—it wasn't her.

When they got close enough to see the counter, Jade busied herself examining the ice cream flavors.

"I'll take a scoop of cotton candy ice cream in a waffle cone with chocolate syrup and . . ." She tapped her lip, thinking. "Maybe some crushed candy cane."

Dan gave her a revolted look. "Is that even a thing?"

She shrugged. "It sounds good."

"If you say so." He turned to the high school kid taking their order. "I'll have a double scoop of triple chocolate in a dish."

"A dish?" Jade scoffed. "Does that qualify as real ice cream?"

"Hey, no comments from the woman who ordered the world's weirdest ice cream combination." He took out his wallet and passed the kid his credit card.

"Oh, wait. Let me get—"

But it was too late. The kid was already passing the card back.

Dan winked at her. "You can get it next time."

She told herself that the temporary bump in her heartbeat was not because of those two little words, *next time*.

Three minutes later, when she grabbed her ice cream cone, Jade had to admit that it looked rather disgusting.

"Want to go down to the marina to eat these?"

Jade glanced around the crowded restaurant. "Yeah. It doesn't look like there's a single table open."

"Oh, I'm not worried about that. I just don't want anyone else to have to watch you eat that." Dan gestured at her ice cream cone.

"Haha." Jade gave him her most dramatic eye roll. "It's going to be good. You'll see."

The moment they stepped out the door, the ice cream dripped down her hand, and she had no choice but to take a lick.

She gagged and yanked it away from her tongue. Too late, she realized Dan was watching. She tried to make herself take another lick. But she couldn't do it. How could she have thought cotton candy, chocolate, and mint would taste good together?

To his credit, Dan managed to avoid laughing for all of five seconds. Then a huge chuckle burst out of him. "So not the most delicious thing in the world?"

Jade pouted. She'd really wanted ice cream. But there was no way she could eat this. "I may have been a little off in my calculations. Apparently, watching Top Chef doesn't actually qualify you to choose flavor combinations."

"To be fair, it was unique." Dan chortled again. "I'm sure no one else has ever tried it before."

"Want to trade?" Jade held it out to him as a joke.

"Sure." His answer was instant, and she had to stop to look at him.

"I was joking."

"I wasn't."

Before she realized what he was doing, he'd grabbed the cone from her and placed his dish of decadent looking triple chocolate into her hands.

"Dan, no. We aren't going to switch. There's no way you're going to eat that."

"Nope." Dan tossed the cone into the trashcan they were passing. "I'm not."

Jade's mouth fell open. "I'm not going to eat your ice cream."

"Of course you are. We traded fair and square."

"Not fair *or* square." She would have placed a hand on her hip, but she was afraid of dropping the dish. In which case neither of them would have the ice cream Dan had paid for.

"Come on." Dan laid a hand lightly on the small of her back to lead her forward. The jolt of his touch kicked her legs into gear, but his hand lingered there a second longer than was necessary. When he pulled it away, Jade concentrated on keeping her expression neutral. She didn't need him—and the whole town—knowing how much that simple, protective gesture meant to her.

And anyway, it hadn't meant anything to him. He'd simply wanted to get her moving again. He probably wanted her to finish up the ice cream so he could get back to his office. He had more important things to do than eat ice cream with her.

"Why don't we sit over there?" Dan pointed to the worn wooden bench at the end of the breakwater that protected the marina.

Jade swiveled to survey the area. It was rather exposed. Did Dan really want everyone to see him with her?

Then again, if it didn't bother him, it didn't bother her.

She followed him and settled on the bench, pressing herself all the way to the far side. Was this a standard-sized bench? It seemed way too small.

"Eat up." Dan angled his body toward her and slung an arm over the back of the bench.

Jade inched the last centimeter closer to the other end of the bench and held the ice cream out to him. "I told you, I'm not going to eat your ice cream."

Dan's eyes crinkled in a smile as he leaned closer to her face. All the breath got caught in her lungs. What was he doing? He wasn't going to—

"That would be a lot more convincing if you weren't drooling."

His comment caught her completely off guard, and a laugh burst out of her. But she reined it in and put on a mock hurt expression. "That wasn't very nice."

"I'm sorry." Dan's lips folded into a fake frown and he fluttered his eyelids at her. "Here, I'll make it up to you." Before she could react, he'd reached over, grabbed the spoon from the ice cream, and popped it into her mouth.

"Hey," she protested around the spoon. But a microsecond later, she closed her eyes in bliss as the creamy chocolate coated her tongue.

"Good, right?" Dan pulled the spoon slowly from her mouth.

She nodded, letting the cool cream slide down her throat. When she opened her eyes, Dan was studying her like watching her eat ice cream was the most fascinating thing he had ever done.

"Fine. You win." Jade grabbed the spoon and dipped out a heaping scoop. She lifted it toward her lips but at the last second diverted it into Dan's mouth. "We'll share it."

His eyes widened, but his mouth curved into a grin around the spoon. "Fair enough," he mumbled through the ice cream.

For the next ten minutes, they were busy passing the spoon back and forth, though Jade noticed Dan always took tiny spoonfuls for himself.

When all that remained was a melted soup covering the bottom of the bowl, Dan passed it to her. "The rest is all yours."

Jade eyed him but took it. "You really would have given me the whole thing, wouldn't you?"

Dan shrugged. "Of course."

Jade leaned against the back of the bench and scooped the soupy mess into her mouth. The last time she'd splurged on good ice cream, the guy she'd brought home with her had found it in her freezer and eaten it while she slept.

"Thank you." She licked the spoon clean and set it and the bowl to the side.

Somehow, as they ate, the distance between them had closed, so that Dan's shoulder was almost pressed against hers now.

She should move.

But she was too comfortable like this.

She closed her eyes. The sun baked pleasantly on her hair, and the refreshing breeze slid against her skin. She gave a contented sigh, letting the sound of the waves lapping against the rocks lull her.

Just for a moment, she'd pretend this was her life.

Chapter 25

An itch in the middle of his back was driving Dan crazy, but if he moved to scratch it, he'd disturb Jade. He hadn't realized she'd fallen asleep next to him until her head had slid onto his shoulder.

He couldn't stop looking at her. In sleep, all the guardedness she normally wore like a hockey mask faded away. With the wind blowing tendrils of hair across her cheeks, she looked sweet and almost . . . fragile. Dan resisted the temptation to brush her hair off her cheek and tuck it behind her ear.

He cast his eye on the lowering sun, trying to calculate the time, but he'd never exactly been a Boy Scout. It had to be nearly dinnertime by now. Much as he didn't want to move, he did have to get home and get ready for a meeting tonight. He still had a couple of reports to write up for it.

A gust of wind carried a tendril of hair across Jade's nose, and she shifted on his shoulder. Forgetting his earlier resolve, Dan hooked his finger under the hair and slid it gently off Jade's cheek.

She stirred again, this time blinking up at him, and he pulled his hand back quickly.

Jade blinked again, her eyes clouded with confusion, then bolted upright, wiping at the line of saliva that had trickled down her cheek.

"I'm so sorry. I didn't mean to— Oh my goodness, I drooled on your shirt." She lifted a hand to swipe at a small wet spot on his shoulder.

Dan caught her wrist gently and lowered it to the bench between them. "Don't worry about it. You should see the puddle Nate's dog leaves on me all the time."

Jade laugh-groaned. "Thanks for comparing me to a dog." She swiped self-consciously at her cheek again. "I'm sorry about falling asleep. I don't know what's wrong with me."

"You've been working too hard. And you're sick. You're allowed to fall asleep." Dan stood and held out a hand to help her up, not letting go until he was sure she was steady on her feet. Then he reached behind him to scratch desperately at the spot that had been itching for the past twenty minutes.

But his arm didn't bend like that.

"Here." Her fingers found the exact spot and scratched back and forth.

"Ahh." Dan could have crumpled in relief. "Thank you."

Much as he wanted to stay there with her the rest of the night, he couldn't. "Should we head back? I was going to ask if you wanted to grab some dinner, but I actually have to get to a meeting. Plus, I don't know about you, but I'm still full from that ice cream."

"Dan." Something in Jade's voice made him stop, but he was afraid to look at her. She sounded too gentle, too un-Jadelike.

"What's up?"

She took a step closer, so they were standing side-by-side.

"This was nice." She studied the bench, as if there was still a shadow of them sitting there. "And I appreciate it. But don't you think Grace is the one you should be taking out to dinner?" She didn't meet his eyes.

He tried to tamp down the hope sprouting in this heart. Was it possible she was jealous?

"Jade." He waited for her to look up at him. When she did, her expression was unreadable. But he was used to that. Typical Jade.

"Grace and I aren't a couple."

Jade broke their eye contact and started walking. He fell into step beside her.

"Maybe not yet." Jade's stride was rapid. "But you will be eventually. Everyone sees it. She's perfect for you."

He grabbed her arm and pulled her to a stop. "*I* don't see it, Jade. I know Leah already has Grace and I walking down the aisle. And I couldn't tell you the number of older women from church who have given me their blessing to court her. They've pointed out all her good qualities—she loves ministry, she sings, she plays the piano, she cooks, she—"

"Yeah, it really sounds like you don't see a future with her." Jade's sarcasm cut through his list, and he broke off.

"But those aren't the things I'm looking for." He licked his lips. He had to stop now. Before he went too far.

"What are you looking for then? Because if Grace doesn't meet your standards, I don't know who will." Was that a note of bitterness he detected?

Dan raised his hands helplessly. "I don't have a list. I just want someone who makes me laugh. Someone I can spend time with for hours and never get tired of their company. Someone I look at and think, 'Wow, God really knew what he was doing when he put this person in my life.'"

Someone like you.

But if he said those words, there'd be no taking them back.

"Oh, is that all?" The sarcasm was back, but under it, Dan thought he caught a note of hope.

"Anyway, I told Grace this morning that I thought it was best if we didn't pursue a relationship."

"Oof." Jade let out a breath. "Poor girl. How'd she take it?"

Dan considered. How much did he want to reveal? "Surprisingly well, actually. She seemed to be expecting it. She seemed to think—" But no, that would definitely be revealing too much.

"To think?" Jade prompted.

Dan scrambled for an explanation that was the truth—but not enough of the truth to scare Jade away. "She seemed to think it was for the best too. Anyway, she didn't seem to have any hard feelings, so . . ." What was the end of that sentence? So he was free to marry Jade? Or at least to confess his love for her? Maybe start with dating her?

Jade raised an eyebrow, waiting. Was that a challenge? Did she think he was too chicken to say the rest of it?

He opened his mouth, then snapped it closed. She was right—he was too chicken.

They started walking again, and with every step, Dan's cowardice mocked him.

Tell her. Tell her.

You didn't tell her.

When they arrived at Violet's apartment building, Dan opened the door and stood aside for Jade to enter.

She gave him a long look, then stepped up.

Before he could rethink it, he darted out a hand to stop her. "Actually, there was something I wanted to ask you."

"So ask." Jade's voice was all business, but her eyes brightened.

For some reason, that scared him more than anything else.

"Would you be willing to help out with VBS in a couple weeks?" He shuffled his feet as her face fell. That was so *not* the question he'd wanted to ask, but now that he'd started, he couldn't undo it. "You were so good with the kids, and they really loved you, so I was hoping . . ."

"Yeah, of course. I'd be happy to." Jade reached for the door.

It was halfway closed when he stuck his arm out to brace it open. "Also, one more thing."

She tilted her head, lips in a straight line.

Dan heaved in a quick breath. He wasn't likely to get another chance if he blew it again. "Would you like to go to dinner with me tomorrow night?"

Watching the slow smile spread across her face was like watching the sun rise over the lake on a perfect morning.

"Yeah." Her smile stunned him more than any sunrise ever had. "I would."

Chapter 26

*J*ade did a slow spin in front of the bathroom mirror. She'd taken a few minutes off of working on Vi and Nate's house this afternoon to buy the dress, but now she was having second thoughts.

Maybe it was too much.

She needed another opinion.

"Vi?" She checked the time as she wandered to the kitchen. Fortunately, she'd started getting ready for dinner plenty early, so she could change if Vi gave the dress a thumbs down.

"Whoa." Vi set down the knife she'd been using to chop garlic. "I guess you're feeling better."

"Yep." She'd felt a little off again this morning, but it had passed rather quickly. "Is it too much?"

She spun to give her sister the full effect of the pink off-the-shoulder dress.

"It's not something I would have pictured you wearing," Vi said. "But you look amazing. What's the occasion?"

Jade bit her lip, suddenly feeling shy about telling her big sister she had a date.

"I'm meeting a friend for dinner."

Vi gave her a knowing look. "Is this the same *friend* who brought you those heavenly smelling flowers?"

Jade's face heated way beyond any fever she'd ever had. But she couldn't stop the silly smile that kept threatening to lift the corners of her mouth as she nodded.

"So?" Vi prompted. "Who is he?"

"Uh—" Jade busied her hands straightening a pile of mail on the counter. "It's Dan."

She chanced a glance at her sister.

Vi's mouth widened into an almost perfect *O*, and she dropped her knife. "You like *Dan*?"

Instantly, Jade's hackles rose. "What's wrong with Dan? He's a great guy, and—"

Vi waved her hand. "Nothing's wrong with Dan." She picked up her knife and resumed chopping. "I know he's a great guy. I just didn't think he was your type."

"I'll have you know that we actually dated—well, not really dated, but spent a lot of time together—at the end of senior year."

"You and Dan dated?" Vi shrieked.

Jade pressed her hands down in midair, as if that could calm her sister. "It wasn't that big of a deal. We were just friends."

But the word mocked her.

She hadn't been willing to see it at the time, but she'd realized it after she'd left. She was in love with him.

And it wasn't some high school infatuation. It was that soul-deep love you only read about in novels.

"Did he know you were going to leave?" Vi concentrated on scooping the chopped garlic into a sauté pan, but Jade could hear the hurt.

She touched her sister's arm. "No one knew, Vi. Not even me, really, until I did it."

Vi nodded with a quick sniffle. "Well, be careful. You're leaving again eventually, and you don't want to hurt him." She set the pan on the stove. "Unless you're not leaving?"

Jade shook her head, trying to ignore the hope that had replaced the sadness in Vi's eyes. Of course she was leaving. This wasn't her real life. It was just a break, a diversion.

But something sank in her stomach at the prospect of going back to her so-called life in LA. It was so empty compared to what she had here—her sister and Nate, their friends, who were starting to feel like her friends, Dan, and even church. What did LA have that compared to any of that?

Still, it wasn't like she could just pretend the past hadn't happened, move back here, and live happily ever after.

Could she?

This was really happening. Dan had to keep reminding himself of that as he watched Jade, sitting across the table from him, smiling a real smile at him, laughing that full laugh that made her whole demeanor soften. The setting sun lit her hair and reflected in her eyes as they sat on the patio outside the Hidden Cafe. He'd wanted to take her somewhere nicer for their first real date, but she'd insisted that this was where she wanted to go.

He was glad now that he'd let her talk him into it. She seemed so at ease here, so comfortable. He could sit and watch her all night. He caught his breath as her eyes landed on his.

"What?" She gave him a self-conscious smile.

"What, what?"

"You're staring at me. Do I have spinach in my teeth?" She covered her mouth with her hand, and he impulsively reached across the table, entwining his fingers in hers and bringing their hands to rest between them.

"No spinach. I was just thinking about how much I enjoy being with you."

"Dan." She tried to pull her hand away, looking at the other tables around them, but he wasn't going to let go. She struggled for another second but finally let her hand relax in his.

Her lips slid into a gentle smile. "I like being with you too." She said it so begrudgingly, he had to laugh.

"You don't have to sound so happy about it."

She stuck her tongue out at him. "I tried not to, you know. Nothing good can possibly come of this." She gestured between them. "I'm only here for a couple more months, and you're a pastor and—"

He raised his hand to stop her, then closed it over her other free hand. "We'll let God worry about all of that. For now, let's just focus on being together."

"But—"

"Please?" He stood, pulling her to her feet too. He had all the same fears she did about this—maybe more, since his heart was already fully invested. But he also trusted that if Jade was the woman God had created for him, his Heavenly Father was powerful enough to make things work out.

"Come on. Let's go for a walk."

"I'd like that." She grabbed her purse. "Let me just use the restroom first."

As Dan watched her walk away, he offered a short prayer. *If this is your will, Lord, help me not to screw it up.*

Jade could not erase the stupid grin from her face even as she used the restroom. She'd tried to keep the date from getting too serious by insisting on dinner at the Hidden Cafe, but somehow even the little restaurant had become magical tonight.

The way Dan had looked at her. The way he'd held her hands. How did that simple gesture feel more intimate than anything she'd ever done with any other man?

With everyone else, the sensations had been purely physical. Her mind and emotions had never been part of the picture. And forget her soul.

But with Dan—

With Dan, simply holding hands felt like forging a deep connection. Like something bigger than themselves was bringing them together. Could it be that it was God?

But that was crazy, wasn't it?

God would never intend for someone like her to end up with a pastor.

Jade stood and fixed her dress. She heard the bathroom door open, a woman's voice echoing in the tiled space.

"Did you see who he's with tonight?" The woman's voice was high-pitched and gossipy, and Jade rolled her eyes. How many times had she said that same sentence to her friends in LA? Did she sound as ridiculous as this woman?

She pivoted to flush the toilet but stopped mid-motion as a second woman chimed in.

"Jade Falter?" Her voice oozed disdain. "I guess he doesn't know about her reputation."

"Or he does." Yet another woman, whose voice sounded vaguely familiar, added. "And he's tired of being a good boy."

A chorus of giggles and "Stop" and "That was bad" filled the room.

Jade pressed a hand over her mouth. She was plenty used to being talked about like that. But it wasn't fair to Dan to let them slander his name because of her.

She steeled her shoulders, then flushed and pulled the stall door open.

The three women were still smiling as they reapplied their makeup in the mirror. She only knew one woman's name—Heidi—but she recognized all three from church.

Heidi noticed her first, and her smile disappeared, her eyes widening. The other two women took a moment to realize what was going on, but within ten seconds, they wore matching expressions.

Jade let the silence unreel as she deliberately washed and dried her hands. Tension consumed the space behind her as she pushed out the bathroom door.

Only after it had closed did she let her shoulders fall and allow herself a few quick blinks to clear her eyes.

She'd been delusional to let herself believe anything real could develop between her and Dan. She'd set the course for her life as a kid. And it didn't include a relationship with a preacher.

The smile Dan greeted her with as she met him at the front door almost brought the tears she'd buried to the surface.

"Ready to go?" He reached for her hand, but she pulled it away, gripping her purse instead.

He frowned, studying her. "Everything okay?"

"Yep." She strode ahead of him toward the door. "Let's go."

Chapter 27

The evening still felt warm, but apparently a cold front had gone through Jade. They'd been walking down the beach together for twenty minutes, but every time Dan came within two feet of her, she moved away.

Pretty soon, she'd be walking knee-deep in the water to avoid him. Already her feet had to be soaking from the waves that pounded the sand.

He'd asked a few times if everything was okay, and every time she'd answered with a short "Yep" and kept walking in silence. He was trying to give her the space she needed to deal with whatever it was that had changed between the time she'd left their table at dinner and the time they'd walked out the door of the Hidden Cafe, but that would be a lot easier to do if she showed some small sign that she was still remotely interested in being here with him.

He slowed, then stopped walking, watching the flecks of light spark off her hair as she kept going.

She made it another fifty yards before she seemed to realize he was no longer next to her.

She whirled around and raised her arms out to her sides. "What's wrong?" He could tell she was yelling, but he could barely hear the words over the constant refrain of the waves.

"You tell me," he called back.

She watched him, her hands still raised, and he wondered if she'd heard him. Then she dropped her arms and spun back around, walking farther away from him.

He huffed out a breath. Why was she making this so difficult?

He bent over and dropped his hands to his knees, considering. Maybe he should give up on this whole thing.

But half a minute later, he sprang up and sprinted down the beach after her. He knew how he felt about her, and that wasn't going to change because she spent one evening pushing him away.

In less than a minute, he'd closed the space between them. Although his instinct was to grab her and demand to know what was wrong, he was careful to give her the two feet of space she seemed to need.

"So in case you didn't realize, I'm not terribly experienced at this dating thing." He stuck his hands in his pockets. She had to know that already, but it was still embarrassing to admit.

Jade appeared to be fighting a smile, as the edges of her lips curved the slightest fraction. He chose to take it as a positive sign.

"So if I did something wrong at dinner—if I used the wrong fork or sneezed too loudly or didn't tell you enough times how beautiful you are—you have to tell me so I can fix it."

Jade completely lost the battle with her smile now, but it wasn't the open, easy smile she'd worn at dinner. This smile was laced with sadness.

"There was only one fork," she said, her voice subdued.

"And I don't think I sneezed at all, so that leaves not telling you how beautiful you look enough times. Which is a huge mistake, and I'm so sorry for it. Because you do. Look beautiful."

He risked taking a step closer to her. Miraculously, she didn't move away.

"Dan." The way she said his name like that, like it was goodbye, made his stomach drop.

"What is it, Jade? Why aren't you willing to give us a chance?"

165

Jade's mouth twisted. "There is no *us*."

But he wasn't going to give up that easily. Not this time. "I'd like there to be."

He took another step closer and reached for her hand. He knew she'd felt the connection between them at dinner. They needed to get back to that.

But she yanked her hand out of his. "Don't you understand?" Her eyes were wild and filled with a pain he couldn't comprehend but wanted desperately to erase.

"No, I don't," he said honestly. "I thought things were going well. I thought, when we held hands—" He looked away. How big of a fool had he been? "I thought there was something between us. I thought you felt it too."

"You know who else felt it?" Jade's words were caustic, and he couldn't help but look at her.

What on earth was she talking about? As far as he knew, it had only been the two of them.

"All of Hope Springs, that's who." Jade spun away from him and walked toward the water.

He watched her back for a moment. Her bare shoulders heaved, as if she were trying to catch her breath.

"What do you mean?" He finally let himself walk to her side. An icy wave washed over his feet, soaking the cuffs of his pants.

"Everyone up there saw us holding hands." Jade sounded completely defeated.

"And that's a problem?" He'd understood her desire to keep their relationship secret in high school. After all, she was the cool girl and he was the nerdy preacher's son. But he'd figured they were old enough to be beyond that now.

"Of course that's a problem." Jade fired the words at him.

"Because you're embarrassed to be seen with me?"

"What?" Jade turned sharply toward him. "Why would I be embarrassed to be seen with you?"

He shrugged. "You never wanted to be together in public in high school, so—"

"Because I didn't want my so-called friends to make problems for you. I was afraid they'd scare you off."

Dan opened his mouth to speak, but all that came out was a long breath. All these years he'd been under the impression that she'd been ashamed of liking him and somehow that had been the reason she'd left. But she'd wanted to protect him?

A new tenderness for her filled him. "What is it then? Why don't you want people to see us holding hands?"

"Because of me, Dan." She met his eyes, letting him see everything she was thinking for the first time maybe ever.

She looked tormented. "I'm not the kind of woman you should be holding hands with."

He almost laughed, the statement was so ridiculous. But the look on her face stopped him.

"Why not? It just so happens that you have the perfect hands for holding." He moved closer and slowly reached for her hand, giving her time to pull away if she wanted to.

This time, she let him wrap his hand around hers, and he smiled as the warmth of his skin transferred to her cold fingers. "See?"

She didn't smile back. "You know my reputation, Dan. You pretend not to, but you do."

He squeezed her hand tighter. "I don't see what that has to do with holding hands."

She shook her head. "Don't play dumb. If people see us holding hands, they'll start talking."

Dan laughed. Was that what she was worried about? "I think people have more interesting things to talk about than who I hold hands with."

"Tell that to the women in the restroom." Jade withdrew her hand from his, crossing her arms in front of her.

"The women?" In the restroom? Is that what had transformed her from open, lighthearted Jade into sullen, closed-off Jade? "Who?"

Jade shrugged. "I don't know their names. They're from church, I think. It doesn't matter."

"And they said something to you?" It was probably just a misunderstanding she'd blown out of proportion.

"They didn't know I was in there. They were talking about you and me. Holding hands." She gave him a grim look.

"So what? It doesn't matter if they were talking about us holding hands. I don't care who knows. In fact, I think it's great people know. I'll tell everyone myself." He cupped his hands around his mouth and yelled to the waves. "I held hands with Jade Falter. And I want to do it again."

He grinned at her. "There. Now everyone knows."

"Stop, Dan." Jade's eyes flashed. "They weren't just talking about us holding hands. They implied that you were with me because of my reputation. Because you wanted to do more than hold hands. A lot more." Even in the quickly fading light, he could see the red rise to her cheeks.

His chest tightened. What right did anyone have to make assumptions like that about Jade?

"I'm so sorry." He stepped in front of her so that she had no choice but to look at him. "They never should have— The thing about the church is that it's made up of sinners. Me included. But—"

Jade stopped him with a glare. "I don't care what they said about me, Dan. I'm used to it. But don't you get that if people see us together, my reputation is going to rub off on you? That's why we can't hold hands. Why we can't be together." Her delicate throat rippled as she swallowed, and he wanted nothing more than to wrap her in his arms and make all the pain of the encounter go away.

"You've changed, Jade. You're not the girl you were in high school. We'll just have to make sure everyone sees that. They already know you volunteered at camp, and soon they'll see you volunteering at VBS. They'll realize you're the perfect girl for a pastor in no time."

Jade lifted her head, her eyes wide enough to reflect the full moon that was rising. "And if they don't?"

"If they don't, I don't care. I don't care what they think."

Jade gave a disbelieving laugh. "Yes, you do. It's why you were so worried about how camp went and why you couldn't talk to the parents afterward."

Dan almost flat out denied it, but he stopped himself. She was right.

"I don't care what they think about this, Jade. About us."

"I don't know." She chewed her lip, and suddenly her lips were the only thing he could focus on. He lifted his hands to her face.

"Do you remember the first time we kissed?" he murmured.

She nodded, her eyes softening. "It was perfect."

Dan's thumb slid back and forth on her cheek. "Not true. I had no idea what I was doing, and I'm sure you could tell."

Jade's laugh was low and throaty. "Maybe it wasn't the most technically perfect, but it was still perfect."

Her eyes fell closed, and Dan leaned forward. It had been eight years since that kiss. But in this moment, it felt as if no time had gone by at all.

"Dan." Jade whispered his name.

The last thing Dan saw before he closed his own eyes was the smile playing on her lips.

And he could feel that smile when his lips at last met hers.

All the magic of that first kiss eight years ago was still there—with none of the awkwardness. Jade's hands slid from his shoulders to wrap around his neck, and she pulled him closer. He let his hands travel to her hair, deepening the kiss.

Jade sighed softly against his lips, then pulled back. He pulled her into a tight hug.

"I hope that was better than last time," he said into her hair.

She tightened her arms around him. "Your technical performance has definitely improved. But it was still perfect."

They stood like that for a few minutes, until Jade tried to disentangle herself. But Dan wasn't ready to let her go.

She shook her head but leaned into him again. "Maybe it'd be best if people didn't see us doing that," she whispered.

He turned to look up and down the beach. "I don't see anyone here."

He dropped his head for another kiss.

Chapter 28

Jade twirled her way across the tiny living room of Vi's apartment as she waited for Keira to answer her phone. She must look like an absolute lunatic right now, but she didn't care. She had to do something with all this extra joy building inside her.

"About time you called." Keira's cheerful voice belied her gruff words. "I was starting to worry Hope Springs had finally done you in."

"Nope." Jade lifted a mini replica of the Old Lighthouse off Vi's shelf. Maybe she and Dan could go there sometime soon. "Everything's good here."

"What do you mean everything's good there?" Keira's disbelief sounded through the phone. "Last time we talked, you were ready to hop a plane back to LA."

"Let's just say things are better now." Jade set the lighthouse down and moved to look out the window at the lake. And the beach. The beach where she and Dan had walked every night for the past week and a half. Where they'd kissed every night for the past week and a half.

"What do you mean things are better? Did you fall in love with working in your sister's antique shop or— Oooh." Keira gasped. "Or did you fall in *love*? You met a wholesome Hope Springs guy, didn't you?" She squealed, making a sound Jade had only ever heard from three-year-olds.

"Nope." Jade dragged out her answer. The suspense would kill her roommate, but she couldn't resist. "I didn't meet him. I already knew him. We sort of, almost, dated, I guess, a long time ago."

"You *almost* dated? What does that mean?"

"It's a long story. But the point is, he's still in Hope Springs and so am I for the moment and—"

"Oh my goodness, it's a second chance romance." Keira's shriek was so loud that Jade pulled the phone away from her ear. "I love those."

Jade chuckled. "Slow down, Keira. I—"

But once Keira got going, nothing could stop her. "I'll come for your wedding. Wouldn't miss it. Wait— Does that mean you're not coming back to LA?"

"That was the exact opposite of slowing down. No one's getting married." But she had to admit that the same questions had been going through her head. And she wasn't sure she had the answers yet.

"You're going to stay there, aren't you?" The excitement had partially faded from Keira's voice. "I'm going to miss you."

"I haven't decided anything yet, Keira. At this point, I'm still planning to come back to LA."

"But you're considering staying? For this guy?"

"Yes. No. I mean—" Jade forced herself to slow down and explain. "I am considering staying. But not for the guy."

Keira snorted.

"Well, not *just* for the guy," Jade amended. "My sister's here too, and she has this great group of friends who have welcomed me, and I don't know. . . . It's kind of starting to feel like home here."

"I'm happy for you, Jade." Keira sounded sincere. "I've never heard you call anywhere home. So this is pretty huge."

"Not huge." Jade didn't want to overplay it. "And nothing's decided yet."

But in her heart, she knew—it was huge.

"Ready for this?" Dan's smile as he met her at Vi's car the next morning sent the same pool of warmth surging through her stomach as always. Even after a week of spending every spare moment together, she still hadn't gotten used to that feeling.

He picked up the oversize beach bag she'd packed and leaned down to drop a kiss on the top of her head. Jade squirmed even as she acknowledged the flip in her heart. She still felt slightly uncomfortable about letting others see them together. But Dan's naturalness about the whole thing eased her worry a little.

She caught Vi's grin as she and Nate also emerged from the car.

"Good morning, Dan," Vi called.

"Hmm?" Dan lifted his head. "Oh, morning."

"So are you?" Dan took Jade's hand and drew her toward the ferry landing. "Ready for this?"

This time it was Jade's stomach that flipped. "Have I mentioned I'm not the biggest fan of boats?" Just the thought of getting on the ferry that was supposed to take them to Strawberry Island had left her feeling queasy all morning.

"I know." He leaned over to kiss her head again as they walked. "But I promise not to leave your side."

The tenderness in his eyes unwound something that had been coiled tight in Jade's gut. "Then let's do it."

Dan wrapped an arm around her and held her against his side as they came to the pier where the rest of their friends had already gathered. Most of them already knew about Dan and Jade's developing relationship—a word she had to admit she liked the sound of—and they greeted them with smiles.

"You two are so adorable together," Sophie called when they were close enough.

"We know." Dan squeezed her close, and she swatted at him, but she couldn't deny that the fact that he wanted everyone to know about them meant everything to her.

The only one who didn't seem to approve was Leah, who was busy rummaging in her bag, though Jade doubted she was searching for anything in particular. She couldn't blame Dan's sister for being less than thrilled with her baby brother's choice of women, especially since she'd been trying so hard to set Dan up with Grace.

Thankfully, Dan had been right when he'd said Grace had taken things well. She'd taken it so well that if it weren't for the fact that Jade knew Grace was the most sincere person alive, she'd think it was all an act.

But when Grace's eyes fell on them now, she immediately grabbed her phone. "Y'all need a picture of this." She snapped the photo, then swiped at her phone for a few seconds. "There."

Both Dan's and Jade's phones dinged with a notification, and they pulled them out at the same time.

"That's a great picture. Thanks," Dan said to Grace.

Jade could only stare at the image on her screen. She was looking at the camera, smiling a smile she didn't recognize—one that made her appear completely comfortable and at home.

But Dan wasn't looking at the camera. His eyes were on her, and the look in them made Jade's breath hitch.

She'd seen that look before. That was the way Nate looked at Vi, the way Spencer looked at Sophie, Ethan looked at Ariana, and Jared at Peyton. It was a look that said the words neither of them had spoken yet.

It was a look that said he loved her.

"Don't you like it?" Dan asked quietly enough that only she could hear.

"I love it." She blinked and turned her phone off, tucking it into her pocket.

"Me too." Dan tugged her forward. "Come on, we don't want to miss the boat."

They followed the others, who were already crossing the narrow walkway onto the ferry.

"I really don't like boats." A fresh wave of nausea hit her as she stepped onto the deck of the ferry, and the whole thing heaved under her feet.

"It's going to be great. I promise."

Tucked against the warmth of Dan's side, she could almost let herself believe it.

He led her past the rest of the group to a spot at the front of the ship. Taking his arm off her, he leaned over the railing, stretching his fingers toward the water, as if he could reach the waves, which were at least ten feet below.

"Are you kidding me?" Jade clutched at the railing as the boat dipped in the waves.

"Sorry." Dan pulled himself upright. "My dad used to dare us to touch the water every time we rode the ferry."

Jade softened. "You really miss him, don't you?"

Dan's smile shifted from playful to wistful. "Yeah, I do. But I'll see him again someday."

"In heaven." Jade ran a hand over Dan's smooth cheek. They'd had several conversations about God and life and death and heaven over the past couple weeks, and Jade had felt a joy she'd never known before as Dan told her that getting to heaven didn't depend on what she'd done or not done. It was all about what Jesus had done for her. Part of her knew that was too good to be true. But the other part of her—the part she was coming to recognize more and more—held onto the hope that it was.

"In heaven," Dan repeated, bending down to brush a light kiss onto her lips. "But for now, I think I'm going to enjoy my day on earth. With you."

"Me too." She popped onto her tiptoes to give him another kiss, but just then the ferry's engine gave a loud roar, and the boat surged forward.

Knocked off balance, Jade toppled into Dan, whose arms went around her.

"Wow. I knocked you off your feet, huh?" Dan quipped.

But Jade could only nod, pressing her lips tight together. The boat's movement had set her stomach churning.

"You okay?" Concern filled his voice.

She closed her eyes and leaned into him, trying to fight off the nausea.

But it was a losing battle.

"I need a bathroom," she gasped.

Chapter 29

*D*an stood with his forearm pressed to the outside of the bathroom door, waiting for the sound of Jade's retching to pass. This was her third rush trip to the restroom since they'd gotten on the ferry, and he couldn't have felt more awful if he were the one throwing up.

When she'd told him she didn't like boats, he should have listened, instead of convincing her to come anyway. But he'd been so excited about the prospect of spending an entire day with her that he hadn't been able to resist.

Inside the bathroom, he heard a toilet flush and then the sound of running water. He stepped back from the door to give Jade room to exit.

The moment she did, he gathered her into his arms. "Feel any better?"

Her head bobbed against his chest. "A little." But her face was pale and drawn, and a cold sweat dampened the hair he brushed off her neck.

"Just hold on a little longer. We're almost there." He led her slowly toward the exterior deck again, bracing her against his side to minimize the impact of the ferry's rolling motion.

At least the fresh air seemed to help. A little color returned to Jade's cheeks as he steered her to a row of low benches. He passed her the water bottle Violet had brought her.

"I wish there was something I could do to make you feel better." He hated being useless like this.

"Sitting with you makes me feel better."

Dan looked over at her. Her head was tilted back, her eyes closed, but the slightest smile edged her lips.

Just then, the engine sounds changed as the ferry slowed. Dan watched the approaching island with relief. He had no idea how Jade was going to survive the trip back to the mainland this evening. But they had a whole day to enjoy together before they had to worry about that.

"We can get off this bucket in a few seconds," he told her.

"That's good." She leaned into him, and he rested his chin on top of her head, taking a second to soak in the tropical scent of her hair. On second thought, maybe they should sit here like this all day.

At last, the engines cut off, and the ferry's forward movement stilled.

"Ready to put your feet on dry land?" He held out a hand to help her up, anticipating the moment her fingers intertwined with his.

"Yes, please." She offered him a weak smile and let him lead her onto the pier.

When they'd gathered everyone, the whole group wandered as one down the wide cobblestone street.

"Where to?" Violet asked. "Stores, beach, or food?"

"Beach and food." Sophie veered to the right, where a short boardwalk led down to perfect white sands. "I have such a craving for some of those soft pretzels. Oh, and maybe a chili dog."

Everyone laughed. Sophie had been eating nonstop since announcing her pregnancy, and the latest joke was that maybe she was carrying a best friend *and* a husband for Ariana's baby, since twins ran in Spencer's family.

The others followed, but Jade stopped with one foot on the boardwalk.

Dan stopped next to her. "Not in the mood for the beach?"

She shook her head. "Not really. Would you mind terribly if we did something else?"

"Jade, the only thing I need to make me happy today is to be with you," he said honestly.

When she grabbed his hand, it was all he could do to keep from cheering out loud. It was the first time she'd been the one to take his hand instead of the other way around.

"How about a walk?" she asked.

He lifted her fingers to his lips and pressed a kiss onto her knuckles. "Lead the way."

Jade had no idea where they were. They'd taken a left turn here and a right turn there, until she was hopelessly lost.

"Do you know the way back to the ferry landing?" she asked Dan.

"Nope." He looked completely relaxed. "Does that worry you?"

"Not in the least." As long as she was with Dan, she could be lost in Siberia and she wouldn't mind.

"I figure we're on an island, so if we keep walking long enough, we should come to the water, and we can always follow the shoreline to where we started."

"You have it all figured out, don't you?" she joked.

But he appraised her with a searching look. "I think I'm starting to figure it out."

The intensity of his gaze made her glance away. He'd looked at her like that so often, and yet it caught her off guard every time.

"Look." She pointed to a sign half covered by the dense trees at the side of the road. "Mercy's Bluff. I wonder what that is."

"Only one way to find out." Dan pointed to the faint remnant of a trail that had long since grown over. Six weeks ago, Jade would have wrinkled her nose and said he was crazy if he thought she was going in there.

"Let's check it out," she said.

They cut through the underbrush that had almost obscured the trail, a few times nearly losing it entirely. After a while, Jade picked up a low rumble.

She paused, holding up a hand like a stop sign. "What's that? It's not going to storm, is it?" She lifted her face, but the trees were so thick here that she couldn't make out more than a speckle of sky.

Dan tilted his head to the side, as if straining to hear. "That sounds like . . ." He trailed off and strode forward again, grabbing her hand and pulling her along.

"Was there supposed to be an end to that sentence?" She fought to catch her breath as he pulled her faster.

Instead of answering, he came to a stop so quickly she nearly ran into him. The low rumbling had intensified and seemed to come from below them.

"Dan. What's going on?"

He stepped aside, giving her a full view. She caught her breath.

They were at the edge of a horseshoe-shaped cliff that dropped straight down to the lake. Below them, huge waves smashed against the rock face, sending spray high into the air.

"Wow." The juxtaposition of the power of the waves and the immensity of the water that stretched until she couldn't see it anymore touched on something deep in the middle of her chest.

"Welcome to Mercy's Bluff." Dan spread his arms wide, inviting her to take it in.

But she didn't need an invitation. She strode a few feet closer to the edge of the bluff so she could look straight into the water below.

"I thought you were afraid of heights." Dan's voice was light, but he moved closer and wrapped an arm around her waist, as if to keep her from falling.

But she wasn't scared. Not of this.

She was . . . in awe.

"I bet that rock at the bottom used to look like this." Dan pointed to the jagged rock that jutted out closer to the top of the cliff. "But it's been worn smooth over time." He gestured to the lower part of the cliff, where the water had worn away all the bumps and rough patches.

Jade nodded. She knew how that rock felt. The same thing had been happening to her since she'd come back to Hope Springs.

Jade couldn't stop smiling at herself in the bathroom mirror as she washed her hands. She and Dan had made their way back to the ferry landing—apparently, he'd known the way all along—just in time to eat dinner with the others. Now she only had to survive the ferry ride to the mainland. But somehow knowing Dan wouldn't leave her side even if she was sick made the prospect of getting back on the boat easier to bear.

She ran her fingers through her hair, trying to bring some sense of order to it. But it was way too messy to go for anything but the windblown look.

Oh well.

She had a feeling she could stick a paper bag over her head, and Dan would still find her attractive.

That was one of the things that drew her to him most. Whenever he looked at her, it was as if he was seeing right past her outer appearance to her heart.

Once, that had scared her. It was why she hadn't said goodbye to him in person all those years ago.

She'd been afraid he'd take one look at her and discover the ugly secret swelling inside her.

But now she didn't have any secrets to keep from him. She wanted him to see her, faults and all.

Giving her hair one last tousle, she reached for the door just as it opened and Leah bowled into the room.

"Sorry. I didn't see you." Jade grabbed the door handle. The sooner she escaped Dan's sister, the better. Leah was nice enough, but her feelings about Jade had been plenty clear in the way she'd kept watch over Jade and Dan at dinner.

"Actually." Leah stood in her way. "I was hoping to find you in here. I wanted to talk for a minute."

Jade swallowed. Why did she feel like she was sitting in Principal Jessup's office all over again? "Sure. What did you want to talk about?"

Leah studied her. "First, I want to say I'm sorry."

"Uh—" Jade reached for the door again. "Okay." She had no idea what Leah had to be sorry for, but this conversation had been much easier than she'd anticipated.

She opened the door a crack, but Leah was still talking. "I should have been more welcoming. It's just, I know how devastated Dan was when you left the first time, and I don't want him to go through that again."

Jade let go of the door and stepped farther into the room. "Neither do I."

"But—" Leah stepped forward and grabbed Jade's forearm. "Even I can see how good you two are together. So I wanted to tell you how happy I am for you."

"Thank you?" Jade didn't mean for it to come out as a question, so she tried again. "That means a lot."

"You're welcome." Leah met her eyes. "But that's not all I wanted to say."

She inhaled audibly, clearly uncomfortable. "If you leave again, it's going to break his heart. So unless you're planning to move back to Hope Springs, it might be best to end things now, before this goes any further." She said it without a trace of malice, and Jade could tell she truly only wanted what was best for her brother.

She swallowed past the dryness in her throat. "The last thing I want to do is hurt Dan."

"I'm glad." Leah squeezed her arm, then moved to the sink.

Jade pushed the door open slowly, savoring a deep breath of the damp night air. She didn't want to hurt Dan. Ever.

Which meant she knew what she had to do.

Chapter 30

" $\mathcal{F}$ or you." Dan held out the small paper bag he'd gotten from one of the shops, fighting to keep from grinning at Jade.

Her eyes met his for a second, then dropped to the bag. "You shouldn't have gotten—" She opened the bag, looked inside, and laughed. "It's Dramamine. Thanks." She took out the box and dropped a tablet into her hand.

He held out the bottle of water he'd also grabbed for her.

"You thought of everything." She swallowed the medicine, then fell into step with him as they boarded the ferry. This time she was the one to lead the way to the front railing.

"So," she said as the ferry's engine churned. "I ran into your sister in the restroom."

Dan braced himself. What had Leah done now? "Whatever she said, don't listen to her. She can't help meddling in my life, but she's harmless. Mostly."

Jade studied him, and he wondered what she was searching for. "She said you were devastated when I left last time."

Dan gazed far out over the water, where he could just pick out the pinpricks of light on the mainland. Simply remembering when she'd left made his chest ache. "I was."

"Dan, I'm sorry. I owe you an explanation."

But he lifted a finger to her lips. "You don't owe me anything, Jade. I forgave you a long time ago, remember?"

She opened her mouth to say something, but he leaned down to give her a long kiss. That should quell any lingering doubts she had.

When he pulled away, Jade kept her eyes closed for a second.

"She also said," she continued once she had opened them.

Dan dropped his head. "Are we still talking about my sister?" That was not exactly his idea of a romantic topic of conversation.

"Yes." Jade shoved him lightly. "We are. She also said that if I'm leaving again, maybe we should end this now, before it goes any further, so I don't hurt you again."

Dan's shoulders tensed. He was going to throttle Leah the next time he saw her. Forget next time. He was going to find her right now.

Just because she didn't like his choice of girlfriend didn't give her the right to ruin things for him. It was his life.

"Look, Jade, Leah's an idiot. I'm crazy about you. I know the stakes. I know it's going to be like tearing my heart out when you leave again. But I don't care." He grabbed her hands and brought them to his chest. "I don't care. This is too good to give up on. *We* are too good to give up on."

He let his eyes rest on hers, praying she wouldn't say there was no "we."

"I agree." Jade's voice was barely above a whisper, and he leaned closer to make sure he'd heard right. "That's why I was wondering how you'd feel if I moved back to Hope Springs. Permanently."

It took him a moment to process the words, but the instant he did, he wrapped his arms around her and lifted her off her feet. "You're serious?"

His heart was beating a tap dance all around his chest, and he was smiling so big that the muscles in his cheeks hurt.

"Put me down." But even as she said it, she tightened her arms around his shoulders. "And, yes, I'm serious."

Dan set her back on the boat deck. "Remind me to thank my sister later."

But first, news this good called for a kiss.

Chapter 31

How had she been so happy only yesterday?

Jade pulled the cap low over her forehead as she reached for the package on the drugstore shelf. She watched her hand land on the box and pick it up. But it was as if it was someone else's hand. Someone else's life.

This couldn't be happening to her.

Not again.

She fought the tears that had threatened all morning. She was wrong. She was sure of it. She was only buying the test to confirm it.

She ventured a quick glance around the store before making her way to the counter. Fortunately, everyone else was at church right now.

When she'd woken feeling nauseous, she'd begged off church again, assuring Vi it was just residual effects of yesterday's ferry ride.

But as she'd lain in bed, her mind had flashed over the past couple weeks. She'd been feeling nauseous most mornings. She'd ordered that bizarre ice cream at the Chocolate Chicken. And her emotions were all over the place. Any one of those things by itself, she could have explained away. But the combination of all three had her worried.

Really worried.

So she'd done some quick calculations.

She'd always kept track of her period rather religiously. But she hadn't thought about it once since she'd come to Hope Springs. Six weeks ago. If she remembered correctly, she'd last had her period a couple weeks before that.

"Just this?" The cashier was a cheerful girl who looked to be about a high school senior. The same age Jade had been the last time she'd bought one of these.

She kept her head down and passed the girl some money, her eyes too blurred to tell if it was the right amount. Then she snatched the bag off the counter and ran to the front door, ignoring the girl's cries that she'd forgotten her change.

By the time she got to Vi's, her breath was coming in ragged gasps, even though it was only a few blocks.

Inside the apartment, she made a beeline for the bathroom but drew up short outside it.

She couldn't go in there. Couldn't do this. That little plus sign had exploded her world last time, just as she'd thought she'd finally found happiness.

She couldn't let that happen again.

You have to know. Then you can deal with it if need be. The thought sent a fresh wave of nausea rolling over her. She'd fought for the past eight years to forget what she'd done last time. But she still thought of it every single day. How could she possibly go through it again?

She forced herself to inhale through her nose and let it out through her mouth. She had to get this over with before Vi got home from church.

Her hands were remarkably steady as she pulled the test out of the box. It was as if she'd separated from her body. This was all an act, part of a movie. She was just an actor following a script. This wasn't really her life.

It couldn't be.

She sat on the toilet, stuck the test in her urine stream, capped it, washed her hands, set the timer on her phone for three minutes, and then stood staring in the mirror. In her bloodshot eyes, she saw the reflection of the scared teenager she'd been eight years ago. She'd thought she'd left that girl behind, but apparently there was no escaping who you really were.

The alarm on her phone rang, but she ignored it, letting its constant trill wear on her nerves. Last time, the moment she'd seen the results, she'd known what she needed to do. She'd packed a small bag, scrawled two notes—one for Vi and one for Dan—then jumped on the first bus headed for the airport.

This time, if the test had the same result, she didn't know what she'd do. She couldn't disappear again, at least not right away. That wouldn't be fair to Vi. She had to at least stay for her sister's shower and wedding.

But after that?

After that, she'd have to go. She only hoped she could keep anyone from finding out before then.

Maybe it's negative. The little whisper of hope was even more maddening than the still-chirping timer.

She tapped the button to turn it off, then made herself look down.

The stick was still there.

The results window glared up at her, the plus sign that had materialized seeming to grow bigger and bigger until it took over the whole bathroom.

She folded in half, bracing her hands against the sink.

"Noooo." The word hurt coming out—hurt her throat, but more than that, hurt her heart.

How could she have let this happen? How could she be in the exact same spot today as she was eight years ago?

Her stomach rolled, and she lunged for the toilet.

She knelt there dry heaving for several minutes. But nothing came up. Her stomach was empty. Her mind was empty. Her heart was empty.

When she finally managed to get herself under control, she wiped her eyes, washed her hands, and wrapped the spent test and packaging in the drugstore bag. Her movements were deliberate and methodical, and she wondered with an odd sense of detachment if this was what it was like to be a robot. To not feel, just do.

Evidence in hand, she made her way down the stairs to the dumpster at the far end of the building's parking lot. Once she'd disposed of the test, her feet turned as if programmed by some outside force, taking her down the hill to the beach below.

How could this same beach be the place where her dreams for the future had formed and died—twice?

She dropped into the wet sand.

She'd always known she wasn't good enough for Dan.

The plus sign on the pregnancy test had only confirmed it.

Chapter 32

"How are you feeling?" Dan had been waiting for Jade since the moment he'd opened the church doors for vacation Bible school this morning. He'd been worried when she hadn't been at church yesterday, but when he'd called after the service, she'd flat out refused his offer to come over.

He'd told himself he'd feel better once he saw her, but the way she brushed past him now had him more anxious than ever.

"Let me help you with that." He moved to take the box of crafting supplies she was carrying, but she hugged it tighter to herself.

"I've got it." She picked up her pace.

"So, I was thinking." He cleared his throat. He'd been so sure about asking her the other night, but that seemed to have been a different Jade. "My family has this tradition where we go to my aunt's house every year for a reunion. This will be the first year without Dad, which is going to be really hard on my mom. But I thought it might cheer her up if I brought you. To, you know—" He cleared his throat again. Maybe this had been a bad idea. "Meet her."

Jade kept walking.

"It's this weekend," he added. "So VBS will be done by then."

She finally stopped and looked at him, but her eyes lacked the warmth they'd taken on over the past few weeks. "Sure. Sounds fun." She moved toward the door to the Sunday school classroom they were standing outside of. "I have to get these crafts set up."

"Yeah. Of course." He stepped aside, hovering in the doorway to watch her for a few minutes. She bustled around the room, grabbing supplies and setting them on the front table.

He told himself it was only because she was busy that she didn't glance up at him even once.

But after two more days of VBS, Dan had to admit it to himself—she was avoiding him. He ran through every possible reason but came up empty again and again.

Last he knew, she was planning to move back to Hope Springs to be with him. And now she could barely look at him, let alone talk to him.

The only plausible explanation he'd come up with was that she was afraid. Of what, he wasn't sure. Maybe that he'd change his mind. Or that people would talk. Or maybe she was scared because she'd never felt this way about anyone before.

He knew he hadn't. But if anything, it made him feel less afraid than he had in months.

He waited until the kids had all left on Wednesday afternoon, then ducked into Jade's classroom, where she was cleaning up the day's painting project.

Dan collected paint brushes from the tables and rinsed them in the sink. "These turned out well." He nodded toward the mini terracotta pots the kids had painted today.

"We're going to plant mustard seeds in them tomorrow." Her voice was flat.

"That's a good idea." He watched the water flow over the brushes, washing blues and purples and reds down the drain. "I have a meeting later tonight, but I thought maybe we could go grab some dinner before that."

"I have an appointment," Jade mumbled.

"Oh." He fought to keep the disappointment out of his voice, then had an idea. "Is it something for Violet's shower? I could come with you. Especially if it's cake testing."

Jade rewarded his effort at levity with a tight smile. "It's not for the shower. But thanks." She put the last of the paints away. "I'll see you tomorrow." She crossed to the door.

"Jade, wait." He shut off the water and set the brushes down. Drying his hands on his shorts, he stepped toward her, trying not to notice the stiffness in her shoulders.

He stopped a few feet from her, scared that if he moved any closer, she'd bolt. "I've missed you."

Her lips lifted into an imitation of a smile. "We've been together every day this week."

He watched her, but she wouldn't meet his eyes. "Yeah. You're right." He dropped a soft kiss onto her lips, but she barely returned it.

When she pulled away, the sadness in her eyes nearly did him in. Something between them had broken. And he had no idea how to fix it.

She was right here in front of him, but he was losing her as surely as he had the first time.

Jade sat in the car she'd borrowed from Vi, staring through the rain that lashed the windshield in pounding sheets. She could barely make out the squat gray building at the other end of the parking lot.

But she didn't need to see it to know what it looked like inside. She'd been in a clinic like this once before. She'd seen the stark waiting room, the plain white walls, the lonely table surrounded by instruments she wished she could erase from her memory.

The rain kept up its relentless thrashing on the car roof.

I can't do this again.

The thought struck her square in the middle of her stomach—right where she imagined her uterus must be. Right where her baby was.

Her baby.

Even in her head, the words sounded surreal.

193

Just go in there and get it taken care of, and you'll never have to think those words again.

Her hand went to the door handle.

But she couldn't open it.

She couldn't go in there.

She couldn't do it all again.

The weight of the guilt from last time pushed on her every single day. If she added to it, it might sink her for good.

I can't do it. The prayer sounded in her head before she realized that was what it was. *I can't have another abortion. But I can't have this baby, either. You know that. You know I'm not fit to be a mother. Please spare this baby and take it from me right now.*

A dry sob escaped her. It was the worst prayer she'd ever prayed—probably the worst prayer anyone had ever prayed—and she was likely going straight to hell for it.

But please answer it, Lord. I can't do what I did last time. I can't. I need you to do it for me.

She started the car and drove slowly out of the parking lot, squinting through the rain.

If God didn't answer her prayer, she didn't know what she was going to do. There was always adoption.

Or she could keep the baby.

Her lip curled into a sneer. The idea of her as a mother was ludicrous. Look at the mess she'd made of her own life. She didn't even want to imagine how badly she could screw up a baby's life.

Her grip on the steering wheel tightened. It wasn't like it mattered what happened now, anyway.

Things with Dan were over no matter what. She only hoped he would get frustrated enough with the way she'd been treating him that he'd give up on her.

Because she wasn't sure she was strong enough to be the one to walk away this time.

Chapter 33

$\mathcal{J}$ade didn't know how she'd made it through the entire week of VBS. When she was working with the kids, she could at least compartmentalize and allow herself to forget the secret growing inside her womb for a little while. But whenever Dan looked at her with that expression of mixed hope and sadness, it all came back to her.

As she waited now for the last of the kids' parents to pick them up, she pressed a hand to the fabric of her loose-fitting shirt. It was much too early to worry about showing, but she wasn't taking any chances.

When the kids had all finally left, she stood there, staring out the church doors. If anyone had told her a month ago that this place would feel like her second home, she would have accused them of indulging in too much communion wine.

But everything about the church had grown on her—the big, comfortable lobby that invited people to stand around talking after services, the bright sanctuary with the large cross on the front wall, the music, the people, and especially the richness of God's Word. She'd never heard another preacher who made it come alive so vividly—in a way that she could understand how it related to her life.

Dan had a real gift—and she wasn't going to get in the way of his ability to use it.

She took a shaky breath, then made herself walk into the sanctuary, where Dan was cleaning up the props he'd used for his final message to the children.

"Hey there." His face brightened the moment she walked through the door, and she knew it was because this was the first time she'd sought him out all week.

Her heart strained with a wish that things were different. That she'd come in here to tell him she was sorry and things were all better.

But none of her wishes had come true lately, so why should this one be any different?

"Hey." She let herself walk halfway down the aisle but no farther. This would be impossible if they were within touching distance. The slightest brush of his hand against hers, and she'd lose her resolve.

"I just wanted to tell you that I won't be able to make it to your family thing tomorrow." She watched her shoe poke at the crushed cracker crumbs scattered among the flecks of brown and gold in the carpeting.

"Oh."

She could tell Dan was trying not to let her see how disappointed he was—which only made this that much harder.

"Maybe we could do something on Sunday then." Dan's voice was measured, as if he already knew what her answer would be.

She stuffed her own longing into a deep part of her soul. She had to do this for his sake.

"I don't think so," she made herself say. "I don't think we should see each other anymore."

"You don't?" Dan's voice had gone dull, and this time he didn't even attempt to cover the hurt.

She couldn't look at him.

"I don't," she choked out.

Then she turned and ran out the church doors, praying he wouldn't follow.

Chapter 34

"*H*ey, Jade. It's Dan. Again." He closed his eyes, picturing her as he left the message a week after she'd broken things off. Her face had been so twisted with anguish when she'd told him they shouldn't see each other anymore that he hadn't known what to do. His instinct was to follow her, tell her whatever it was that had her spooked, they could work through it. But he'd known he wouldn't be able to reach her. That pushing her would only drive her further away.

His resolve to give her space had lasted all of three days, before he'd decided maybe he was wrong. Maybe what she needed was to know he wasn't going anywhere, no matter what. So he'd spent the past four days calling every few hours. So far, she hadn't answered once. And the one time he'd shown up at Violet's apartment, Jade had opened the door only long enough to tell him she was too busy preparing for Violet's bridal shower to talk.

"I know you're scared," he said to her voice mail now. "But I'm not going to give up on you. So if you want me to stop leaving these annoying messages, you're going to have to answer one of these times." He swallowed the *I love you* he wanted to add and hung up the phone. She was already skittish enough. If he said those three words right now, he might send her flying right back to LA.

He hit the phone absently against his hand as he thought through his next move. It had to be something that wouldn't scare Jade away—

but that would give him a chance to show her what she meant to him. To show her that she was his world.

"I know you feel something for me, Jade," he muttered to the silent phone.

There had to be something he could do to get through to her. Or if he couldn't do it, maybe someone else could help him.

He swiped his phone on and scrolled to Violet's number.

"Dan." Violet's sympathetic tone was enough to tell him she knew what had happened between him and Jade. "How are you?"

"I'm—" He ran a hand through his hair. "I'm kind of going crazy without her, to be honest."

Violet's sigh crackled over the phone. "I know. I can tell Jade is hurting too, but she won't talk about it."

"Yeah, I'm pretty sure you got all the talkative genes in your family."

Violet offered a strained laugh. "Don't give up on her, okay? I don't know what happened, but she needs you."

Dan swallowed. "I'm not giving up on her." Until she came out and told him to leave her alone, he wouldn't give up. And maybe not even then. "I actually called because I need a favor."

"Anything." Vi's answer was immediate.

"Tomorrow, after your bridal shower, could you convince Jade to take a walk on the beach with you?"

"Sure." Violet sounded confused. "I can probably do that. And then what?"

"Well—" How did he say this without sounding rude? "After you get her to the beach, you leave."

Violet's laugh rang through the phone. "Ah, I see. And I assume you'll be there waiting for her?"

"Of course." Not just waiting for her. Waiting for her with a romantic dinner and flowers and music and . . . anything else he could think of to show her his love.

"I'm in." Violet sounded almost as excited about the plan as he was.

"Thanks, Violet. I appreciate it."

"You know I'd do anything for Jade."

"Me too." As soon as Dan got off the phone with Violet, he dialed the florist.

Tomorrow was going to be perfect. The first day of the rest of his life with Jade.

He could feel it.

Jade pretended not to notice the number that flashed on her screen as she applied her mascara Saturday morning.

She'd muted the ringer so she wouldn't have to feel guilty every time he called, but that didn't keep her from noticing when the screen lit up with his number.

Each time, she told herself she wasn't going to listen to the voice mails. But each time she only managed to obey herself for three minutes max before lunging for her phone and listening to his recorded voice as if it were a lifeline.

By now, he should have given up. Or he should at least be sounding annoyed or defeated. But if anything, his messages got brighter and more optimistic with each call.

She finished putting on her makeup, then grabbed the phone, tapping to listen to her newest voice mail even as she chided herself not to.

"Hey, Jade. Dan again. But you probably recognize my voice by now, huh?"

She closed her eyes as the warm tones washed over her. She would recognize his voice anywhere.

"Just wanted to say I'm thinking of you today. And I hope to see you soon. That's all for now. Have fun at Violet's shower."

Jade lowered the phone slowly, resisting the urge to replay the message. She wanted to see him more than anything, but she couldn't let that happen. It would only make everything harder.

She was already exhausted from dodging him all week. How was it that not being with him sapped all her energy?

Over the last couple days, she'd started to have a crazy idea. What if she told him? He would understand, wouldn't he? He was the one who was always preaching about how Jesus forgave all sins.

She picked up her phone and ran her hand over it. Should she call and ask him to meet her later? Was she brave enough to do that?

A knock on the bathroom door made her jump and almost drop the phone.

"You ready, Jade?" Violet called.

"Yep." Jade stuffed her phone in her purse. She'd get through this shower first, then she'd decide whether or not to talk to Dan.

She opened the door to find Vi waiting for her in the hallway, her long, dark curls swept into a neat twist, her skin almost glowing under the white sundress she'd chosen.

"Wow, Vi, you look beautiful." Without thinking, Jade leaned over to hug her sister. The affection that had seemed so foreign to her when she'd first returned to Hope Springs came more naturally every day.

"You look pretty spectacular yourself." Vi gestured to the empire-cut blue dress Jade had chosen mainly because its loose fit hid the ever-so-slight bulge that had started to form in her waistline this week.

She wouldn't be able to hide her secret from Violet much longer. But every time she thought about telling her sister, she broke into a cold sweat.

There wouldn't be any celebration or cooing over her tummy when she announced it. No jokes about how her baby might one day marry Ethan and Ariana's baby.

There would only be shame and regret and disappointment.

Jade forced her thoughts off the baby. That was another day's problem. For today, her focus needed to be on making Vi's shower perfect.

Fortunately, Violet kept up her usual chatter on the drive to the church, where she'd insisted she wanted to hold her shower. Seeing Vi so happy helped Jade forget about her own mountain of problems at least a little bit. Even if she'd lost her brief chance at a happily ever after, she couldn't begrudge her sister this second chance.

Vi pulled into the church parking lot, but instead of getting out of the car, she turned to Jade and grabbed her hand. "Thank you, Jade." Tears sparkled in her eyes. "You have no idea how much it means to me that you came home and that you've done so much to make sure my wedding is special. Honestly, just having you here would be enough—"

"In that case, maybe I'll have Peyton take the cake back." But tears pricked at her eyes too, and she leaned over to pull Violet into another hug. "I love you, big sister."

One of Violet's tears dropped onto her shoulder. "I love you too, little sister."

Jade closed her eyes, but it was too late. A tear had sneaked out and trailed down her cheek.

Thank goodness she hadn't told Vi about her wild idea to stay in Hope Springs. That had only been a temporary delusion. One that was over already. She'd called Keira yesterday to let her know to expect her back in a month after all.

She just had to figure out how to survive in Hope Springs until then.

Chapter 35

"You did a lovely job planning the shower." Sophie squeezed Jade's arm as she walked past.

"Thanks again for taking care of the decorations. Everything looks amazing."

Sophie had transformed the church hall so thoroughly that Jade barely recognized it. Elegant tablecloths were topped by beautiful bouquets of wildflowers, and fairy lights were strung across the ceiling, with ivy trailing down the walls. It looked like they'd been transported to an enchanted forest.

"Did you get some cake?" Sophie held out a plate to Jade, but Jade gestured it away.

"I'm fine for now thanks. I'd better check if Leah needs any more help in the kitchen." But halfway there, she had to stop as a wave of pain tightened her belly. It had been happening for the past couple hours, but so far she'd been able to ignore it.

Now she couldn't deny that the pain was getting worse.

It was probably because she'd been on her feet all day. Once she had a chance to sit down, she'd feel better.

She shoved away the niggling fear that something was wrong with the baby. If God had been planning to answer her prayer to take the baby, he'd have done it by now.

As the pain passed, she stepped into the kitchen. Leah was bustling around, refilling bowls and handing them off to Brianna, who was bringing them to the serving line.

Jade froze.

She'd been disappointed—but not surprised—that Brianna hadn't enrolled Penelope in vacation Bible school. Though she missed the little girl terribly, even when she saw them in church she went out of her way to avoid them. The last thing she needed was a run-in with Brianna.

"Oh, sorry, I was just— Looks like you have everything under control." Jade stepped backward out the kitchen door.

"Jade. Wait." Brianna followed her, and Jade stopped like an obedient schoolgirl.

She deserved whatever horrible things Brianna wanted to say to her. A mother had a right to decide who took care of her children, and Jade had disregarded her request to stay away from Penelope at camp.

She ignored the fresh onslaught of pain in her belly as she waited for Brianna to tear into her.

"I wanted to say—" Brianna fidgeted, eyes on the floor.

"Brianna, I'm sorry. I should have respected your request that I stay away from Penelope. She's your daughter, and—"

Before she could finish her apology, Brianna's arms were around her, nearly smothering her with the strength of her hug. "Thank you." Her voice was muted. "Penelope is the only thing in this world that matters to me, and if I had lost her . . ." She shuddered.

Jade had no idea what to do. She'd been prepared for yelling, even a slap to the face, but a hug was so unexpected that she could only respond by hugging Brianna back.

After a full minute, Brianna pulled away, straightened her shirt, and strode back to the kitchen, leaving Jade standing there, completely dumbfounded.

She made her way over to Vi to ask if she was ready to open her gifts or if she preferred to play the goofy games Jade had looked up online first.

But as she was waiting for Vi to finish up a conversation with an older lady, her insides cramped so tightly that she had to wrap her arms around her middle.

"Excuse me," she managed to gasp to no one in particular, before she rushed for the bathroom.

When she got there, she locked the door and leaned her forehead against it, letting the metal surface cool the sweat beaded there.

The cramp eased slightly, and Jade made her way to the toilet. Her hands shook as she lifted her dress to pull down her underwear.

She blinked at the three perfect red circles that had stained the fabric.

"Oh." All the breath left her lungs as she sat. Her thoughts spun, trying to get a fix on what this meant.

She was pregnant. So she shouldn't be bleeding. But she was.

She didn't want the baby. So she should be relieved. But she wasn't.

At the sight of more blood on the toilet paper, she closed her eyes.

Legs shaking, she pulled her underwear up and washed her hands. Then she stood staring at herself in the mirror. Her face was pale, her eyes too big.

How could she go out there and pretend nothing had happened?

But she had to, didn't she? All those people were here for Vi's special day. And she wasn't going to ruin it. As far as any of them knew, she wasn't pregnant and never had been. She might as well keep it that way. If the blood meant anything, pretty soon she wouldn't be pregnant anymore, anyway.

A knock on the door made her jump. "Coming." She splashed a little cold water on her face to put some color back in her cheeks.

"Everything all right in there, Jade?" Vi's voice was muffled through the door.

Jade dried her face and opened the door, fully intending to tell her sister that everything was fine. But one look at the concern on Vi's face, and Jade crumpled. She could feel the tears working their way up, but she was helpless to stop them.

"What is it, Jade?" Vi's expression morphed to confusion, and she stepped into the bathroom, closing and locking the door behind her. "Is this about Dan?"

But that only made Jade cry harder.

She could barely get the words out past the panic that had lodged in her throat. "I'm bleeding."

"Where?" Vi looked her up and down, as if expecting to find a giant, gushing wound.

Jade raised her hands helplessly, then gestured to her midsection. "I'm bleeding, Vi."

Vi's forehead wrinkled. "Like you have your period? I think I have some meds in my purse if you have cramps. I forgot that you used to get them so bad."

"No, Vi." Jade reached a hand to stop her sister, who had turned to the door, apparently ready to fetch her purse and make everything all better. "I'm bleeding. And I'm—" She swallowed so hard it hurt. Could she really say the word? "I'm pregnant."

Time stopped as Violet just looked at her. It was several seconds before she even blinked.

Jade wanted to beg her to say something, but she had to give her time to process.

She bent double as a fierce cramp ripped through her belly, setting it on fire.

"Let's get you to the hospital." Violet placed one hand on Jade's back and the other on her elbow, steering her to the door.

"No, Vi." Jade planted her feet, but she didn't have the strength to fight Violet and breathe through the cramp at the same time. "You are not going to leave your shower. And neither am I. I'll be fine."

But Vi had already steered her down the hallway to a side door. "Stay here a second while I go tell Sophie. She'll take care of everything."

Jade wanted to protest. But she was in too much pain to do more than lean up against the wall and wait.

Within two minutes, Violet was back at her side, steering her out the door. "It's going to be okay."

"What did you tell them?" Not that it mattered. It wasn't like her secret was going to be a secret much longer.

"I told them to pray."

Jade closed her eyes as she settled into the passenger seat.

Maybe it wouldn't be a bad idea to pray herself. But now that God was in the middle of answering her last prayer, of giving her what she'd thought she wanted, all she could think was, *I take it back, Lord.*

Chapter 36

*E*verything was perfect. Dan had spent the past hour carrying the bistro table and chairs from his patio down to the beach and laying out the meal of seared salmon and scallops. It wasn't super fancy, but he'd prepared it himself, and that had to count for something. He double-checked that he had a lighter for the candles and rearranged the flowers in the center of the table for the fifth time. Maybe he should take them off the table altogether. He wanted to be able to see her while they ate. He gave everything one last glance to make sure he hadn't forgotten anything.

The blanket! He'd planned to lay it out so they could sit on the beach after they ate. But he must have set it down when he was gathering the dishes. He could picture it balanced on the back of the dining room chair closest to the patio door.

He glanced at the time on his phone. The shower should be getting done any moment. He didn't want Jade to walk down here and find him missing. But he wanted everything to be perfect. If he sprinted, he'd only be gone a few seconds.

Mind made up, he dashed down the beach, up the stairs alongside the church, and toward his house. He grabbed the blanket and was back out the door in less than two minutes.

As he sprinted back toward the steps, he peered at the church to check if any shower guests were on their way out yet.

But the parking lot was empty.

Odd.

He glanced at the time again. Maybe the shower had ended early. But if it was done, where was Jade?

His heart dropped. Had she refused to take Violet up on her request to walk on the beach? Had he lost his chance?

He pulled out his phone to call Violet, but before he could dial, it rang.

He had it to his ear before the first tone had finished. "Hey, Violet. She caught on, didn't she? What if I just come over and sweep her away?"

Muffled voices sounded from the other end of the phone, but Violet didn't say anything.

"Violet?"

"I'm sorry, Dan. I should have called sooner, but in all the commotion, it didn't occur to me."

"Commotion?" Dan drew up short, watching the dark church. "What commotion?"

"I had to take Jade to the hospital during the shower."

The words nailed Dan right in the chest, and he was already backtracking to his house. He needed his keys. "What happened? Is she all right?" His chest constricted. Of course she wasn't all right, or she wouldn't be at the hospital.

"She's okay. But Dan—" Something in the way Violet hesitated as she said his name made the hairs on his neck stand on end.

"What's wrong then? Tell me." He needed to know right now.

Violet's sigh was heavy. "She's pregnant. She had some pain and bleeding. The baby has a heartbeat, but it's too soon to say if she's miscarrying."

Dan grabbed blindly for a chair. Jade was pregnant? As in carrying a child? Another man's child?

He tried to swallow, but his throat had gone completely dry. "What? I don't—" He closed his mouth. He didn't know what he wanted to say.

"I'm sorry, Dan. They're sending her home pretty soon, if you want to see her. Otherwise . . ."

Dan stared at the car keys in his hand. Otherwise, what?

"Okay," he said dully. But nothing was okay about this. Nothing at all. Tonight was supposed to be the night he won Jade over forever. And now he was learning that he'd never had a chance. That she was pregnant with another man's child.

"Dan?" Violet's voice was tentative. "Could you pray? For her and the baby?"

Dan scrubbed a hand over his mouth and chin. "Yeah." The word came out all scratchy, but it was the best he could do. "I'll pray."

He hung up and glared at the phone in his hand. Dropping it on the kitchen table, he made his way to the beach and packed up the meal and the candles. He grabbed the flowers out of their vase and chucked them onto the dune.

Why, Lord? he cried out in his heart. *Why did you let me think she was the one when you've known this would happen all along?*

The constant rhythm of the waves was his only answer. He moved closer to the water and plopped into the sand, dropping his head between his knees. He had never felt so defeated in his life.

He didn't know how long he sat like that, resisting the urge to pray, but finally his instincts took over, and he found himself pouring out his heart to his Heavenly Father. *I don't know why this is happening, Lord, but you do. You have promised that you work all things for the good of those who love you. Help me to trust that even in this you can work good—even if I can't see how right now. Please be with Jade and keep her safe. Help her to know that your love surrounds her no matter what happens.* He bowed his head deeper. He didn't know how he could say this next part, but he had promised Violet he would pray for Jade—and her baby. *Please protect the little one inside of Jade. Keep him or her safe until they reach full term, and help Jade to deliver a healthy baby when it is time. Help her to raise that baby to know you.*

He lifted his head and tilted it toward the sky. *And help me to surrender to your will. This is not what I want, Lord. Not what I planned. But I leave it all in your hands.*

Chapter 37

The baby's heartbeat was good. Jade clung to that. When she'd heard it, her own heart had filled her chest until she'd been sure she'd burst. Seeing the tiny form on the ultrasound had undone something inside Jade. This was her *child*. Flesh of her flesh. There was something awe-inspiring and almost miraculous in that.

And now that she'd seen it, she wanted this baby to live more than she'd ever wanted anything in her life.

But even after hearing the heartbeat, the doctor hadn't been able to guarantee that the baby would survive. Jade had wanted to argue with him, to talk him into giving her some kind of promise, but she'd known he didn't have that kind of power. So she'd meekly followed Vi to the car. There was nothing more they could do for her at the hospital.

All she could do was wait.

You can pray too, a little voice at the back of her head whispered as Violet drove her home.

But every time she tried to pray, she drew a blank. How was she supposed to ask God to save this baby when she'd despised the last one he'd given her? When she'd been so concerned with how a baby would affect her life that she'd decided to end its life?

Tears gathered behind her lids, and she closed her eyes. Her sorrow over that one decision would never leave her.

And now if she lost this baby too—how would she ever recover from that?

"We're here." Violet's voice was gentle—too gentle. She'd done nothing but take care of Jade's every need since the moment Jade had told her she was pregnant. She hadn't scolded Jade once or reminded her of what an awful person she was.

Jade almost wished she would.

The second Violet shut off the engine, she jumped out of the car and rushed around to Jade's door. She helped Jade out of the car and up the stairs to the apartment, as if she were an invalid.

Jade should tell her not to, but she didn't have the energy.

Nate stood at the top of the stairs waiting for them, his face lined with worry. He moved to open the door for them and squeezed her shoulder as she passed.

Jade closed her eyes. Why were they being so nice to her? She didn't deserve it. Here they were, doing everything possible to honor God with their relationship, and now Vi was stuck with a knocked-up sister.

Violet shepherded her to the bedroom. "Let's get you settled in so you can rest."

Jade should argue that she didn't need to rest. The doctor had said there was nothing she could do to affect things one way or the other. But that didn't mean she wasn't going to try. If she had to lay in bed for the next seven months straight to keep this little one safe, that's what she would do.

Instead of settling her onto the air mattress, Vi pushed her gently onto her own bed, then bent to take off her shoes.

"I can take off my own shoes, Vi." Jade bent toward her feet, but another pang seized her stomach and she stopped with a grunt.

"Lie back, Jade."

This time she obeyed Vi's command. She couldn't deny that it felt good to be taken care of.

Once Vi had her shoes off, she tucked the blankets around Jade's legs, then scurried around the room, closing the curtains. "Do you want anything? Some water or tea or something?"

Jade shook her head, watching her sister. A question burned on the tip of her tongue, but she was afraid to ask it.

But not knowing the answer was worse. "Vi?" Her voice was barely a whisper, but Vi was instantly at her side.

"Do you think—" Jade licked her chalky lips. "Do you think God is punishing me?"

"Of course not." Vi dropped onto the bed next to her. "Why would you ask that?"

Jade gulped back the tears. If she didn't tell Vi now, she never would. And she had to tell her. Had to confess to someone.

"Do you know why I left?" Even as she said it, her brain screamed at her to stop. Once she told Vi, there was no going back. Her sister's opinion of her would forever be tainted.

"You wanted to pursue acting. And there was nothing wrong with that. I should have been more supportive and—"

Jade dropped her hand onto Vi's lap. "I didn't want to act. I mean, I guess I did a little. But the reason I left the way I did, without telling anyone I was going, is because I was pregnant."

Violet couldn't suppress her gasp this time, but to Jade's surprise she didn't get up and walk away.

"Whose baby—" Vi waved a hand in the air. "You know what, it doesn't matter. What happened? Did you miscarry? Did you give the baby up for adoption?"

Jade grabbed her sister's hand and looked at her, really looked at her, until a mixture of horror and pity swirled in Violet's eyes. "Oh, Jade."

The sobs she'd been suppressing for the past eight years tore loose. "I got rid of it, Vi. I got rid of it, and I can't bring it back."

She buried her head in the pillow, but Vi's arms were around her, pulling her closer. She tried to slide away. She didn't deserve Vi's comfort.

But Vi refused to let go. Instead she clutched Jade, letting their tears mingle.

When they'd both quieted, Violet smoothed a hand over Jade's hair.

"I'm sorry," Jade whispered. "I was so scared, and I didn't know what else to do. I thought if I could just take care of it, I could forget about it and go on with my life as if nothing ever happened." Her lip quivered involuntarily, and she waited until she had it under control again. "But I couldn't. I think about that baby every day. And I regret what I did every single day. And that's why God is punishing me."

Vi wiped at the tears on her own cheeks, then on Jade's. She gave a gentle smile. "He's not punishing you, Jade. What you did was wrong, yes."

Jade closed her eyes. Violet was only telling her what she already knew, but it still hurt.

"But—" Violet wrapped her hands around Jade's. "He's forgiven you, Jade. For everything."

"Not—"

Violet shook her head. "Even for this, Jade. You know how much you love that little one inside you, how you would do anything to protect that baby?"

Jade nodded. It made no sense. This baby was the result of one of the biggest mistakes of her life, and she'd thought she didn't want it. But already she knew she loved it more than she loved her own life.

"That's how God feels about *you*, Jade. He loves you more than you could ever imagine. And he wants to protect you—not just physically but spiritually. Maybe all of this is his way of doing that."

Jade bit her lip, letting the words sink in. "I don't understand why he would do it like this," she finally said.

Vi laughed. "Yeah, we usually don't understand it. But we have to trust that he knows what we need, even when we don't."

"If you say so." But a hint of peace settled in Jade's heart. Somehow, she believed Violet was right about this. More than that, she trusted that God held her and her baby in his hands.

It was a new feeling. One she wanted to get used to.

Dan was stalling, and he knew it. Church had been over for twenty minutes already. He'd spent as little time mingling with his parishioners as possible today, seeking refuge in the small room behind the altar instead.

Most people had already filtered out, but he could still hear Violet's voice. He debated hiding here until she left.

He was sure she was waiting to talk to him about Jade. And that was one topic he had no interest in discussing.

Yesterday's shock of finding out she was carrying another man's baby had worn off sometime in the middle of the night as he stared at the wall in the dark. It had been replaced by anger, hurt, shame—you name it, he'd probably felt it. Most of all, though, he'd felt foolish. He'd ignored every single person who'd told him not to get involved with Jade, who'd reminded him of who she'd once been. He'd thought he knew better, thought she'd changed.

Joke was on him.

And some joke it was.

One that left his heart shredded into a pulpy mess.

It was his own fault. He couldn't blame Jade. Not really. She'd tried to keep him away, tried to warn him that she wasn't the right kind of girl for him.

He should have realized she knew herself better than he knew her. After all, she'd never let him get close enough to think differently.

He slammed down the water bottle he'd just drained and drew in a breath.

He couldn't stay in here forever. He squared his shoulders and stepped into the sanctuary, where Violet was talking in a low voice with Nate.

"You guys getting excited for the big day?" His lame attempt at small talk fell short.

"Hey, Dan." Violet gave him a sad half smile. "I know this is awkward. And I wouldn't ask if I didn't think it was important, but could you come by to visit Jade? I think she's really struggling right now, and she could use someone to talk to."

Dan tried to keep his expression neutral but had to assume he'd failed based on the pity in her eyes. "I'm guessing she doesn't want to talk to me."

"No, probably not." Violet lifted her eyebrows. "But you've never let that stop you before."

He looked away. He couldn't deny that. But this time was different.

"How is she doing?" Much as he wished he could shut off his feelings for her and be indifferent, he couldn't. He needed to know she was okay at least, that she wasn't in danger.

"She's doing a little better. The pain seems to have stopped, but she still has a little bleeding."

Dan had to force himself to ask the next question. "What does that mean for the baby?"

Tears clouded Violet's eyes, and Nate wrapped an arm over her shoulder. "I don't know. The doctors said we'd have to wait and see." She swiped at her cheek. "I know Jade is really worried. The only way I can get her to eat is by telling her it's good for the baby."

Dan nodded. "I have a couple visits to make at the hospital today. But I'll try to come by later this week."

Violet's face fell, but it was the best Dan could offer right now. He wasn't ready to see Jade yet.

"Thanks, Dan." Violet gave him a quick hug. "And for the record, I'm sorry. I had no idea . . ."

"Yeah." Dan returned her hug and ushered them to the door. "That makes two of us."

Chapter 38

" The baby is looking good." The doctor switched off the ultrasound machine. "Heartbeat is strong, all measurements are normal, and since you're no longer bleeding and cramping, I think it's safe to say that this little one is out of the woods."

Jade could have hugged him she was so happy, but she settled for a heartfelt "thank you" as Vi squeezed her hand.

This had been the longest six days of her life. She'd barely ventured from Vi's bed the entire week, and every time she'd gone to the bathroom, she'd held her breath, dreading the possibility that she'd see blood.

"That's good news." Vi pulled her into a hug as soon as she was on her feet. "Let's get you home."

Jade nodded and followed her. Violet hadn't asked once who the father of the baby was or how Jade could have been stupid enough to make the same mistake twice. She'd simply loved Jade and taken care of her. Violet's friends, too, had been nothing but wonderful. Sophie and Spencer had stopped by earlier in the week, and Grace had sat with her nearly all day Wednesday. Peyton had brought her a cake. Even Leah had called to check on her.

The only person she hadn't heard from was Dan.

Not that she'd expected to.

She'd known it was over from the moment Vi had told her Dan knew.

She reminded herself yet again that it was for the best.

But that didn't make it hurt any less.

"Have you heard from Dan lately?" She hated how meek she sounded as she asked Violet the question on the way home from her appointment.

Vi shot her a quick glance, and Jade looked away. "Never mind. It doesn't matter."

"Maybe you should call him."

Jade snorted. "And say what? Sorry I'm pregnant?" She watched the shops roll past as Vi turned onto Hope Street.

"You could tell him how you feel about him. He's hurt right now, but maybe if you talked—"

"It's better this way." She kept her voice abrupt. This conversation was pointless, and she was done with it.

Fortunately, Vi took the hint and remained silent the rest of the way to the apartment.

She finally spoke as she parked the car. "I'm not sure how this fits into your plans, but that's Dan's car." She pointed to the beat-up Camry at the other end of the lot, near the dumpster where Jade had thrown away her pregnancy test.

Jade's heart gave an unwanted leap, but she scolded herself. She had no business being happy to see Dan.

She got out of the car and looked around, half expecting him to ambush her from behind one of the vehicles. But there was no one in the parking lot. He must have gone inside already.

"I can't—" Her heart rate surged. "Can you tell him I'm not here? Tell him—"

"Tell him what?"

She spun toward his voice, her blood pounding so loudly in her ears she could barely hear herself as she said his name.

He walked toward her from the hill behind the parking lot, hands in his pockets.

Jade swiveled in desperation. She couldn't see him right now. Couldn't talk to him. Couldn't bear to feel his disappointment in who she'd turned out to be.

He took a few more steps toward her but stopped a good fifteen feet away, just looking at her.

She dropped her eyes. She'd never be able to meet his gaze again.

"Will you walk with me?" he finally asked.

Every instinct told her to say no. To turn and go in the house and lock the door and not come out until her baby was grown. But she found herself nodding instead.

"I'll be inside." Vi's voice from behind her was quiet, and Jade could hear the worry in it. But she wasn't sure which of them it was directed toward.

Dan waited, his face stony, as Jade closed the distance between them. When she reached his side, he pivoted and started walking down the hill toward the beach. He kept his hands in his pockets, his crooked elbow ensuring she couldn't walk too close. Not that she'd try.

Neither of them said a word as they stepped onto the beach and turned north, away from the beachgoers sprawled in the sand to the south.

Finally, she couldn't stand it any longer. "Do you hate me now?"

"No." His answer was swift but emotionless, and he didn't look at her.

She bit her lip, parsing through all the things she could say. But nothing would be adequate.

"I didn't know," she whispered. "Not at first. Not when we started spending time together. When I found out, I didn't know what to do. I didn't want to ruin everything with you. But I also didn't want to deceive you. I was planning to tell you the night of Vi's shower."

He let out an ironic laugh. "The night I was going to tell you I loved you, you were going to tell me you're pregnant with another man's baby."

Her sharp inhale cut at her lungs. Loved. Past tense.

He had loved her. But he didn't anymore.

Not that she'd expect him to. She only wished she could turn off her feelings for him as easily. She swallowed down the ache at the back of her throat and kept walking.

But Dan pulled up short and turned to her. "I thought you'd changed. You told me you'd changed."

Jade reared back. He may as well have struck her. "I have—"

But he was still going. "I vouched for you. Stood up for you."

"I didn't ask you to do that." Her hands balled into fists. "You did it because you were afraid of what people would think of you. Even when you claimed you weren't."

"Yeah, well—" Dan pulled his hands through his hair. "Guess I was right to be. Do you know how many people have asked me if it's my baby? I had an elder stop by yesterday, talking about disciplinary action. About asking me to leave."

Jade's hands covered her mouth. How did she always manage to hurt the people she loved most?

"I'm so sorry. I'll tell them. I'll stand before the whole church and tell them it's not yours." It didn't matter how much that would humiliate her. All that mattered was making things right for Dan.

"That won't be necessary. I told them it wasn't mine, and they took my word." He stopped short, as if suddenly struck by something.

"Whose is it?" The question came out slow and deliberate. "Someone you're in a relationship with?"

Jade hesitated, then nodded. Better he think that than find out the truth—that she didn't even know the name of her child's father.

Dan's stricken look made her want to take it back.

"Then why did— I thought we—" Dan raked his hands through his hair again. Watching the pain on his face tortured her. How could she have done this to him?

She laid a hand on his arm, but he pulled away. She completely deserved that, but it didn't ease the sting.

Dan stared out over the water. "So now what? Are you going back to California? To be with this guy? With the father?"

Now what? Hadn't she been pondering those two words every minute since she'd found out she was pregnant?

"Yeah." The single syllable sliced her heart open. "I'll go back to California."

Dan gave a sharp nod and started walking again. She gave him a few seconds on his own, then followed more slowly. There was nothing for her in California. Everything she wanted in the world was right here. But she'd blown what she had here.

After a few more minutes, Dan stopped and just stood there.

Finally, he said, "I think we should go back."

His voice was so quiet, so defeated, it was all Jade could do to keep from throwing her arms around him and begging him for forgiveness.

She wouldn't do that to him.

She didn't deserve his forgiveness.

And she wasn't going to ask for it.

Chapter 39

$\mathcal{D}$an escorted Sierra and Colton to the door of his office. The young couple gave him a last wave, then walked down the hallway hand in hand. They'd dropped by simply to thank him for being there for them.

Sighing, Dan wandered back into his office and picked up the Bible on his desk, flipping aimlessly through it. He didn't even know what he was looking for.

Answers.

Yes, answers would be nice. How was it that he had the answers for everyone else, but he didn't have any answers for himself?

He needed someone to tell him how to patch this gaping wound in his heart. Because if it wasn't fixed soon, he might lose all ability to feel permanently.

Actually, what he needed to do was get Jade out of his head. It shouldn't be too difficult, since in the three weeks since they'd last talked on the beach—when she'd told him she was going back to California to have another man's baby—he'd seen her only at church. Even then, she'd taken to slipping in right as the service began and ducking out during the final prayer.

But somehow seeing her less only made him think about her more.

Dan slammed his Bible shut. He was starting to drive himself crazy.

Air. That was what he needed. Maybe a good run too.

VALERIE M. BODDEN

He strode through the hall to the lobby but drew up short the moment he reached it.

Jade was on the other side of the room, bent over the reception table. She didn't notice him at first, and he let himself take a moment to soak her in.

Her hair was pulled back into a messy bun, and she had no makeup on, but she'd never looked more beautiful.

He had to leave.

Right now.

He took a step back and started to turn away, but before he could, her head snapped up, as if she'd sensed he was there.

Their eyes met and held. She didn't smile, and neither did he. From this distance, he couldn't read what she was thinking.

When she straightened, her shirt stretched over her midsection, and he looked away. In case he'd forgotten why he couldn't be with her, that bump should be reminder enough.

"Hi," he finally croaked.

She held up a piece of paper. "Vi asked me to stop by to proof the wedding programs." She sounded defensive, as if he might kick her out otherwise.

"Oh." He couldn't get his feet to move. "How are you feeling?"

He grimaced at his own question but found that he wanted to know.

"Okay. The morning sickness is starting to pass."

"That's good." His feet shuffled forward. "I'm sure you're excited to get back to California after the wedding next week. To see the baby's father again." He hated himself even as he said it. And yet, he had to admit that it was satisfying to get one last dagger in.

Until he saw the hurt look on Jade's face and the tears that overflowed her lids.

"I'm sorry." He moved closer. What was done was done. There was no need for him to be a jerk about it. "That was uncalled for."

She shook her head and wiped at her eyes. "There is no father."

"What do you mean there is no father?" Dan could feel his brow wrinkle. There obviously had to be a father.

Jade had gotten her tears in check, but she looked more lost than he'd ever seen her.

"I mean, I don't know who the father is. He was some random guy who picked me up at the bar one night. I don't even know his name."

Dan's head reeled. Why had she said she was in a relationship with the baby's father? For the past three weeks, he'd believed she'd been stringing him along this whole time—a diversion to bide her time until she went home to her real relationship.

"But you're still going back to California?"

Her laugh was mocking. "What else am I going to do, Dan? Hang out here with a baby everyone thinks is yours? It will be better if I go—for both of us."

Dan pinched his chin. She wasn't wrong. But that didn't eliminate the sharp pain in his chest at the thought of her leaving.

"So you're going to raise the baby on your own? Or are you going to give it up for adoption?"

"I'm going to keep it." Her voice was filled with a conviction he'd never heard from her before. For some unexplainable reason, he was proud of her.

"For the record, I think that's really brave."

She shook her head. "Not brave. I'm totally terrified."

He tried a smile. "I heard someone say once that that's what makes it brave."

He thought she was brave?

Jade scoffed.

Nearly everything she'd done in her life was motivated by fear. And she didn't deserve to have him think otherwise.

"I thought about getting rid of it." She didn't know why she said it. Maybe to shock him—to make him stop being so nice to her when she deserved only his wrath.

"Getting an abortion," she added, in case he didn't understand what she was implying. He needed to know the full extent of her vileness.

Dan's face twitched, but he didn't say anything at first.

She could see him running through the possible responses in his head.

Finally, he settled on, "What made you decide not to?"

The question caught her off guard.

She clutched the already crumpled wedding program tighter but made herself look him in the eyes. "Because I couldn't go through with that again."

The way his mouth twisted told her she'd done it—she'd finally killed every last feeling he had for her.

Good, she told herself even as she felt a fissure larger than this room opening right through the middle of her heart.

"Again?" His voice was hoarse.

She followed a crack in the floor with her toe. "It's why I left. The first time. I was pregnant."

The air between them went completely still. Jade heard the air conditioner kick in, but there was no other sound. She couldn't even hear Dan breathing.

She made herself look up at him.

He was staring toward the wall, his face blank. But a muscle jumped in his clenched jaw.

"I'm sorry." The words were so small, but they were the only words she had.

When Dan still didn't move, she walked to the door.

Before opening it, she glanced back, half hoping Dan would tell her to stop. But she already knew he wouldn't.

Chapter 40

Follow her.

Dan ignored the voice in his head. Following her was the last thing he wanted to do.

When he'd first found out she was pregnant, he hadn't thought things could get any worse.

But now? Finding out she'd left Hope Springs to have an abortion?

That meant she'd slept with some other guy—it didn't matter who—while they'd been together last time.

That fact kept circling through his head. He'd loved her, and she'd never seen him as anything more than a—what? He didn't even pretend to know.

He wasn't sure how long he stood in the church lobby before he dragged a resigned hand through his hair and shuffled out the door and across the parking lot to his house.

But he didn't know what to do there. He tried watching TV, but everything he turned on annoyed him. He picked up a book, but after he'd reread the same page half a dozen times, he set it down. He was getting up to change into running clothes when the doorbell rang.

His stupid heart jumped, but he thrust his hope aside.

There was nothing to hope for now, even if it did happen to be Jade at the door.

"Hey, bro." Leah opened the door before he'd reached it. "Just stopped by to— What's wrong with you?"

"Nothing's wrong with me." Leave it to Leah to sour his mood even more.

"Yeah. That's why you look like you did when Patches ran away."

Dan rolled his eyes. He'd give anything to have his biggest problem right now be a runaway cat.

"What do you want, Leah?" He dropped into the worn chair he'd picked up from Goodwill when he'd first moved in, suddenly sapped of all energy.

"I brought some leftovers from a birthday party I catered, in case you're hungry."

"I'm not." The thought of food made bile rise in his throat.

"It can be your dinner then."

He heard her walk into the kitchen and open the refrigerator, but he didn't follow. Instead, he leaned his head back and closed his eyes. He didn't open them when the couch across from him creaked with the sound of her settling into it.

"So how long are you planning to mope around before you come to your senses?" Leah's voice was lighthearted, but he heard the rebuke in it.

"I'm not moping."

"Look, I know you're hurting." Leah's voice was uncharacteristically gentle, the voice she used with her friends, not her brother. "But did you ever think that maybe she's hurting too?"

Dan ignored the gut punch of her words. He knew Jade was hurting. And not only because of the unplanned pregnancy. She was hurting because of him. But he didn't know what he was supposed to do about it.

He cracked an eye open. "I thought you didn't like Jade."

Leah sighed. "It's not that I don't like her. I just didn't want to see you get hurt."

"Well, I did get hurt. So I guess you were right."

"And, what? You want to hurt her back?"

"No." He opened his eyes and stood to pace the room. He didn't want to hurt her. But he also didn't know if he could get over the way she'd hurt him.

"Then stop acting like a spoiled little boy and forgive her. Work things out."

He stared at his sister. Did she really think it worked like that? "It's not that easy."

"Why not? Do you love her?"

He threw his hands in the air. "She's having another man's baby." He practically shouted the words at his sister. How was she not getting this?

"And?" Leah blinked at him way too calmly.

"And she doesn't know whose it is. Probably some jerk who only wanted to use her." His hands tightened into fists. "Why does she always choose guys like that?"

"She also chose you, Dan." Leah folded her feet under her on the couch. "Twice."

But Dan gave his head a vigorous shake. "No, she didn't. I was just a distraction until another jerk came along."

"Or maybe—" Leah speared him with an intense look. "You were her lifeline and she lost her grip. Don't push her farther away, Dan. Swim out and save her."

Dan shook his head at his sister. Hadn't Jade proven more than once that she didn't want to be saved?

"She told me she was pregnant when she left, Leah. When we were together. She was pregnant with some other guy's baby then too." He could barely say the rest—barely believe it. "She had an abortion."

His sister's expression didn't change. "So, two strikes and she's out? How many times has God pursued you when you've messed up? Or me?"

229

Dan looked away, his jaw working. He'd seen the remorse in Jade's eyes. The shame. The fear. But instead of reassuring her of God's forgiveness, he'd beaten her down further, heaped more shame and guilt on her instead of loving her.

He groaned long and low. He hated when his sister was right.

"Anyway—" Leah uncurled from the couch and stood. "What are you going to do? Pretend you never knew her?"

He shrugged. "She'll live her life, and I'll live mine. Just like we did before. Everything will be fine."

Except it wouldn't be. He knew already that his life would never be fine without Jade in it.

Leah opened the front door. "You know I'm perfectly content being single. But if someone were to come along who was as perfect for me as Jade obviously is for you, I'd like to think I'd be smart enough not to throw it away."

She stepped outside and closed the door behind her, leaving Dan staring at the wood grain.

She couldn't be serious when she said Jade was perfect for him. Jade was nothing like what he'd envisioned in a wife and ministry partner.

She was still young in her faith, she was impulsive, she didn't know the first thing about church procedures.

But she was also eager to learn and quick to jump in and help, and she was great with the kids. She'd be great with her kid too—Dan knew that.

He let out a ragged breath and strode to his Star Wars room. There, he opened the bottom drawer of a filing cabinet and grabbed a tattered shoe box. Dropping to the floor, he lifted the lid off.

There was the hyacinth they'd picked on the dunes. And an almost perfectly intact shell. There were wrinkled papers too—notes Jade had passed him during chemistry class.

He lifted them out and sorted through them. Someday maybe he'd be brave enough to reread everything. But for now, he needed to be reminded of how she'd left last time—of why he was doing the right thing in not being with her now.

Finally, he came to the short note.

The last one he'd ever gotten from her.

He closed his eyes for a second, then made himself read it.

I'm sorry, Dan. If I loved you less, I'd stay. But I can't do that to you. Forget about me and live the life you were made for. I'd only get in your way. Love, Jade

Dan looked up from the note, his eyes falling on the Luke Skywalker figure Jade had been standing here holding just a couple months ago.

This note was the only time she'd ever said she loved him, but he'd completely disregarded it. If she'd loved him, she would have stayed.

But rereading the note now, Dan saw it. She'd left to protect him. She'd known being associated with a pregnant girlfriend would keep him from doing the things he wanted to do, even if the baby wasn't his. She hadn't wanted him to know how she'd failed—hadn't wanted him to have any part of her decision regarding the baby.

An overwhelming sadness rolled over Dan that he hadn't been there for her. Then or now.

She'd distanced herself from him the moment she'd learned she was pregnant this time.

And he'd let her.

He hadn't done anything to support her or love her through this.

She'd been trying to protect him. But it turned out that she was the one who needed protection—from him and his judgment.

But that was going to change.

Right now.

He jumped to his feet and jogged out of the house and back toward his office.

He had a sermon to rewrite before Sunday.

Chapter 41

"Come on, it's starting." Vi hurried Jade toward the steps that led down to the beach.

Today was the annual outdoor church service. It was the one service Jade had always loved, even as a kid.

But she preferred to get to church late these days. That way, there was no danger she'd run into Dan. It was the same reason she made her escape before the final prayer each week.

At first, she'd considered giving up going to church completely. But her tender faith was the only thing getting her through right now, and she wasn't willing to give up the opportunity to have it nourished. Whatever had happened between them, she still appreciated the way Dan shared God's Word. Lately, it seemed that each of his messages contained some truth she desperately needed to hear—which she chose to believe was a coincidence.

She kept her head down as she followed Vi onto the beach to the spot where rows of white folding chairs had been set up. Nate and his worship band were finishing the final verse of the first song as Jade and Violet slid into two empty seats at the back.

As Dan stood to deliver the day's readings, Jade couldn't look away. His eyes looked tired, as if he hadn't been getting enough sleep, but he had the same energy about him that he had every time he was in front of the congregation.

For a second, she let herself wonder what it would be like to serve with him in his ministry. Never in her wildest dreams would she have thought that would be something she'd enjoy. But helping with camp and VBS had given her a different perspective. And much as she'd been afraid to recognize it, Dan might have been right about her gift in working with children. She'd loved every moment of it.

She pressed a hand to the bump in her belly. Hopefully her gift in working with other people's children would extend to raising her own child. The prospect terrified her. She had no idea how she was going to do this alone.

Some nights, when she was so tired she could barely move, she let herself imagine a world in which she and Dan were married, and the child inside her was his and they raised it together.

She shook off the thought and tried to concentrate on the service as Dan stood to deliver his sermon.

"Today's message is from the book of John. Here we read about a woman caught in adultery." As Dan read the verses that described how the law declared the woman should be stoned for her sin, a high-pitched humming started in Jade's ears. She knew he was angry with her, knew he would never forgive her, but did he have to preach a sermon directed specifically at her? In front of all these people?

With her baby bump starting to show, it wouldn't take anyone much guesswork to figure out who he was talking about—if there was even anyone left in this town who didn't already know how she had messed up. Again.

She eyed the chairs between her and the end of the row. She could probably get over there without stepping on too many people's feet.

She shifted and started to stand, but Vi's hand landed on her leg and pressed gently. "Just listen," she mouthed.

Jade stared at her. She wanted Jade to listen to Dan reminding her of what a vile sinner she was? She already knew that. But she lowered herself back to her seat just as Dan was closing his Bible.

His eyes scanned the entire congregation. When they met hers, she felt the sear of the connection, but she didn't look away.

If he had something he wanted to say to her in front of all these people, he could go ahead and say it. It wasn't like the weight of guilt pressing her down could get any heavier than it already was.

"Do you ever read that story and wish the people had thrown their stones?" Dan bent and inspected the beach, then stood, holding up a fist-sized stone. "After all, she deserved it, didn't she?"

He tossed the stone from hand to hand and took a step toward the chairs. "You know that woman caught in adultery? She's here."

Jade flinched. He wouldn't really call her out in front of the whole church, would he? He was too kind, too decent for that. Then again, she'd hurt him pretty badly. That could change a person.

"So what should we do? Should we grab our stones?" He held the stone up again but then lifted a finger. "Before you decide, let me tell you about this woman. She's lied, she's cheated, she's lusted after things that weren't hers, she's hated, she's put anything and everything else before God." He paused, giving them time to absorb the list of her sins. "And do you want to know her name?"

Every instinct told Jade to run before he said her name. But she couldn't move.

"Her name is *you*." But Dan wasn't looking at Jade. His eyes were roaming over the entire congregation again. "Her name is *me*." He pressed a hand to his chest. "We are all that woman caught in adultery. We've all been caught cheating on the One who loves us more than we can comprehend. Every time we sin, every time we choose our way over God's way, every time we put something before him, we're committing adultery against our God. We deserve to be stoned. Worse, we deserve hell." He only hesitated for a second before continuing. "But—"

Jade's pulse quickened, and she leaned forward in her seat. She needed to hear that *but*.

"But listen to what Jesus says to the woman: 'Neither do I condemn you.' Do you hear that? He's saying that to you. To me. He does not condemn us. He frees us. He saves us." He held the rock up, then opened his hand and let it fall to the sand. "Those stones that were poised to be thrown at us? They're on the ground now. And that's where they'll stay. No one can throw them at us. Ever again. Our guilt is gone. We are washed clean in Christ's blood."

Jade let out a breath she hadn't realized she'd been holding. Those words sounded too good to be true. And yet, she knew in her heart that they were true. And that they were for her.

But Dan was still talking, and she didn't want to miss a word of this beautiful message. "When Jesus died for us, he freed us from our sin. He told the woman, 'Go and sin no more.' He didn't mean she had to go show him how good she could be. She didn't have to change to earn his love. It was never about change. It was never about her at all. It was about what Christ had done for her." His eyes landed on Jade, and he held her gaze. "He loved her no matter what. Loved her enough to die for her sins." He paused, his eyes still locked on hers, as she soaked in what he was saying. What it meant for her.

Finally, he pulled his eyes away and let them scan the congregation. "He meant that she wasn't a slave to her sin anymore. She was free to live for him, out of love for him. And so are we. Every one of us. It doesn't matter what you've done. You are forgiven, and you are given the power to live for God. Every last sin is erased. You are a new creation."

Jade's heart had climbed up past her chest, past her throat, and was beating so wildly to get out that she had to leave before she erupted in full-out sobs. It was too much, knowing that she was forgiven. Knowing that she was a new creation in Christ. That her past was erased.

This time when she stood, Vi didn't stop her.

She made it to the car before she collapsed into a sobbing heap.

She was free. She was finally free.

"Thank you, Jesus," she whispered into the empty vehicle.

Dan forced himself to loosen his grip on the hyacinths before he crushed them. He'd seen the look on Jade's face when she'd run out of church this morning, and he'd wanted to follow her so badly he'd almost lost his place in the service.

He could tell the sermon had touched her, but he'd written it for himself. He'd learned in seminary that he should preach to himself first of all, and he'd definitely needed to remind himself of God's forgiveness, of the Savior's refusal to condemn those who believe in him.

All this time, he'd been condemning Jade, but he was just as guilty a sinner as she was.

He'd been so busy worrying about what people would think of him if he was with her that he'd never considered what she was going through. Never paused to tell her she was forgiven, not only by him but by God.

But that was going to change. From now on, he was going to do everything he could to show her how much he loved her. Starting with these flowers and the scavenger hunt he'd spent all afternoon setting up. If everything went well, they'd end up at his house, where Leah would be waiting with a gourmet meal—and where dessert would be served with the infinity necklace he'd bought her.

He parked his car and ran up the steps to Violet's apartment. He couldn't wait another second to show Jade how he felt.

Violet's smile as she opened the door and saw him standing with the flowers bolstered his confidence. Surely, this would be enough to show Jade how he felt. And if it wasn't, he'd come up with an even bigger gesture. And a bigger one after that if need be.

"I'm so glad you haven't given up," Violet whispered, stepping aside so he could come in.

Jade was sitting on the couch, reading a book, but the moment her eyes fell on him, she snapped it shut and pushed to her feet.

"I'll give you two a minute." Violet slipped out the door as Dan entered the room.

"That's all right, we don't need—" Jade started, but Violet had already disappeared into Nate's apartment across the hall.

Dan held the bouquet out to Jade, but she didn't take it.

"What's this for, Dan?"

"For you." He shook the flowers a little, but she crossed her arms in front of her, so that they rested on her baby bump.

This was going to be harder than he thought. But she was worth any effort.

"I was hoping you'd give me another chance. I have a whole scavenger hunt set up—" He passed her the first clue, which she didn't bother to read.

"You made your feelings about me clear when you found out I was pregnant." Jade's brow lowered.

Dan set the flowers on the table and took a step closer to her, but when he reached for her, she flinched.

He stuck his hands in his pockets. "I know. And I'm so sorry for that. I was wrong. That's what the flowers and the scavenger hunt are for. To show you . . ." He trailed off. He could hear how lame he sounded. He'd completely written her off, abandoned her, and he thought a little scavenger hunt was going to make up for that?

"I should have been there for you." His voice was quiet, and he couldn't look at her. "And I wasn't. And I'm so sorry for that. I hope you can forgive me someday."

He turned to the door, leaving the flowers on the table without water.

Chapter 42

"No peeking." Jade felt like Santa, the Easter bunny, and the tooth fairy all rolled into one as she led Vi and Nate up the walk to the front door of their house.

She and Grace had finished the painting yesterday, just in time for Vi and Nate to come home to it tomorrow night after their wedding.

"You can look!" She nearly jumped up and down at the shocked expressions on their faces.

"What—" Vi wandered from the living room to the kitchen, her mouth hanging open. "Where'd all the wallpaper go?"

"Do you like it?" Jade fought back the sudden fear that maybe she'd miscalculated. Maybe Vi had wanted to do this on her own.

"Are you kidding? It's perfect." Vi spun slowly, as if taking everything in.

"You did this?" Her sister was staring at her as if she didn't recognize her.

"No. I mean, yes. I mean, we all did it. Ethan and Ariana and Peyton and Jared and Tyler and Sophie and Spencer and Emma and Grace and Leah and—Dan." She tried not to hesitate before the last name but didn't quite succeed.

She pushed on, so she wouldn't dwell on it. "I hope the colors are okay. They were inspired by that pillow." She pointed to a gray-blue pillow she'd found in Vi's store right after she'd come home.

Or, rather, right after she'd come back to Hope Springs. She had to stop thinking of it as home. LA was home. And she'd be going back in two days.

"This is amazing, Jade. Thank you." Nate's voice was full of emotion as he pulled her into a hug. "I'm not sure what I did to deserve another awesome sister, but I'm glad I did it."

"You take care of my big sister, and we'll call it even." She hugged him back.

"That's the plan." Nate let go of her and smiled at his bride. "Forever."

Jade blinked and looked away. What would it be like to have someone who was willing to love her—faults and all—forever?

Vi crossed the room to hug her too. When she pulled away, she and Nate exchanged a significant look.

"What?" Jade swiveled from one to the other. Were they going to tell her they hated the paint colors after all?

"We were talking, and we'd like you to move in here with us." Vi's smile was wide but tentative. "After the wedding."

Jade stared at her sister. She couldn't be serious.

"You guys are newlyweds as of tomorrow. You don't want me around. Especially not with a baby that's going to disturb you at all hours of the day and night."

"We do want you here. Along with our little niece or nephew." Vi touched Jade's belly.

Jade sighed. They might think they wanted her here, but they'd forgotten about one little detail. "I'm an unwed mother. Wouldn't you be embarrassed to have me here?" She kept her eyes on her belly as she said it.

Vi rested a hand on her shoulder. "That's the amazing thing about God's grace. He can take even our weaknesses and our sins and use them for his purposes. The baby inside you is a blessing. And he or she is a blessing we want to know and spoil."

Jade laughed and swiped at her teary eyes. How had she taken her sister's love for granted for so long?

"Please," Vi pleaded. "It would be the best wedding present in the world."

"Better than house painting?" Jade raised an eyebrow.

"Better than anything." Vi grabbed her hand. "Please at least think about it. I feel like I'm getting a second chance at a family. And I want you to be part of it."

Jade opened her mouth to promise she'd call weekly, but Vi beat her to it. "I want you *here*, Jade. With us. A real family."

Jade turned to Nate. "And you're on board with this? Living with your sister-in-law?"

Nate grinned at her. "I'm afraid so. Can't use me as your excuse."

Jade wavered. She'd been trying to mentally prepare herself for returning to LA for weeks now. But she couldn't deny the hope that filled her at the thought of staying.

Sure, it'd be awkward seeing Dan on a regular basis. But so far, she'd been mostly able to avoid him, and eventually, she'd get over him completely.

Wouldn't she?

She looked from Nate to Vi one more time. Both were watching her expectantly.

"I'll think about it," she promised. Before she could warn them not to get their hopes up, they'd both engulfed her in a group hug.

Chapter 43

"You are the most beautiful bride there has ever been." Jade couldn't get over how amazing Vi looked in her wedding dress, with its delicate beadwork and slight flair.

"You could light up the room with your smile." Nate's sister Kayla maneuvered her wheelchair next to Vi to give her a hug. Jade couldn't have agreed with her more. She and Vi had spent some time at the cemetery this morning, talking about Vi's first husband, Cade, and Jade knew this day was one of mixed emotions for her sister. But now that they were here and she was about to walk down the aisle, Vi was positively radiant.

"What can I say?" Vi's smile grew even larger. "God is good."

Jade nodded. She hadn't thought so a few months ago, but now she saw it in every part of her life. She slid a hand over the seafoam green bridesmaid dress that had been let out to make room for her belly.

"I think we're ready." Sophie passed them their bouquets. Vi had asked each of her bridesmaids to choose their favorite flowers months ago. Which meant Jade was now holding a bouquet of hyacinths that looked a little too much like the bouquet Dan had brought her last week—the one she'd tossed in the trash.

She'd been so tempted to accept them and fall into his arms. But they'd tried too many times already. Clearly, they weren't meant to be together.

There was a knock on the door of the church conference room they'd been using as a makeshift dressing room, and all four women turned toward it expectantly. Jade was closest, so she opened the door.

Then she froze, her limbs going numb.

On the other side of the door, Dan seemed to be frozen in place as well.

He recovered first. Looking past her, he sought out Vi. "We'll be ready for the processional in five minutes. Nate is waiting upstairs."

Violet gave her dress one last check, then squeezed past Jade out the door. Nate had been teaching her to play piano, and the two of them were going to play a duet of Canon in D as the bridesmaids walked down the aisle, before taking their own positions at the front of the church.

"We'd better get lined up then." Sophie passed through the door too, followed by Kayla.

Still, Jade's legs wouldn't move.

"Can we talk for a second?" Dan stepped into the room, and Jade's legs finally came unstuck as she moved to open up more space between them.

"I just wanted to tell you—" Dan's Adam's apple bobbed. "It doesn't matter to me what you did in the past. In high school. That you cheated on me—"

"I didn't cheat on you." She hadn't been planning to tell him what really happened, but it suddenly seemed important that he know.

He tugged on his tie. "Yeah. I guess you can't cheat on someone you're not really with."

"No, Dan." She moved close enough to touch his arm, ignoring the sizzle that went through her fingertips. "I mean, I didn't cheat on you. At least not the way you think I did. I considered you my boyfriend. We were together, and it was the best thing that had ever happened to me. But after my mom died, I got kind of messed up. I didn't want you to see me like that, so I started hanging out with my other so-called friends. One night, I went to a party with them. I was only going to stay a few minutes." She closed her eyes. That one decision had changed the entire trajectory of her life. "But they offered me a beer. I didn't want it, but I figured they'd get off my back if I drank it. So I did. And then they convinced me to do a few shots. Before I knew it, I was drunk."

The look in Dan's eyes—she couldn't place it. Was it worry, anger, fear?

She had to tell him the rest before she lost her courage. "Brett was there. You remember him?"

Dan's nod was short, and his jaw twitched.

"He started talking about how we should get back together. I told him I was with someone else now, but I wouldn't tell him who because I was afraid of what he'd do to you."

"Jade, you didn't—"

She lifted her hand. She had to get through this next part. The part she had never told anyone. "He kissed me and pulled me into a closet. I tried to tell him no, but I was too drunk to put up much resistance." She shuddered. "I stopped fighting, telling myself it was no big deal." She dropped her head. "I never wanted you to know. But now you do."

She watched his feet. They remained planted for two seconds, then closed the space between them. Before she could look up, he'd pulled her tight against him. His palms pressed into her back, and her arms went up to wrap around him.

"I'm so sorry," he murmured into her hair. "If I'd known—" She heard him swallow.

"I should have told you," she whispered. "I shouldn't have left without telling you."

Dan drew in a breath, as if preparing to speak, but the door to the conference room banged open.

"Oh. Sorry." Sophie grinned at the two of them. "But it's kind of tough to have a wedding without the maid of honor and the pastor."

"Coming." Dan gave Jade one last long look. "Talk later?"

She nodded and followed him out the door. Her feelings were completely jumbled right now. But one thing she knew. No matter what happened next, she was glad she'd told him.

Chapter 44

"Could I have this dance?" Dan held out a hand to Jade, nerves winging through his stomach as if he were a gangly teenager again.

Jade shook her head but offered him a smile filled with regret. "What would people think?"

But he was done letting the fear of what people would think keep him from being with her. "That I'm with the most beautiful woman in the room." It wasn't just a line, either. Jade looked stunning in her bridesmaid's dress, which set off the glow of her skin. Her hair was swept up, revealing her perfectly curved shoulders.

He thrust his hand closer to her, but she didn't move.

"Fine. Have it your way. But just remember you brought this on yourself." He trotted up to the stage, where members of Nate's band were providing the evening's music. Fortunately, he knew them all well.

"Hey, Aaron. Can I borrow the mic for a second?" he called as the group finished their song.

"Sure thing, Pastor." Aaron passed him the mic.

"Excuse me." Dan spoke to the crowd without hesitation. One of the perks of being a pastor—standing in front of all those people didn't make him nervous. There was only one person whose reaction he cared about—and he wasn't at all sure what it would be.

As he waited for the room to quiet, he caught Violet's eye, hoping she'd understand why he was crashing her wedding dance, but she gave him a thumbs up.

"First, congratulations to Nate and Violet. I know we are all so happy for them and pray for God's blessings on their marriage." He waited for the applause to slow. "And second, I need your help. There's a young woman here I'd very much like to dance with, but she's a little shy. Could you all help me encourage Miss Jade Falter to give me this dance?" He held his hands up and started clapping, grinning as the wedding guests began to clap along.

At her table, Jade covered her mouth with her hands but not before he saw the smile starting there. He crossed the room, holding his hand out to her as the band played a slow, sweet melody. The crowd continued to applaud, and someone yelled, "Dance with him already."

Dan laughed, but his eyes met Jade's. "I don't think they're going to give up. And neither am I."

Not taking her eyes off him, Jade stood slowly and put her hand in his. He finally breathed out, as the crowd broke into cheers.

"Thank you," he leaned over to whisper in her ear.

"Well, you didn't leave me much choice." But she smiled as he wrapped his arms around her waist and her hands came up to his shoulders. He pulled her in closer, suddenly unable to say all the things he'd been planning to say. Right now, all he could think of was holding her. He prayed this wouldn't be the last time he'd ever have his arms around her, but if it was, he didn't want to forget a moment of it.

Too soon, the song ended, and Jade gently untangled herself from his grasp.

"Thank you." Her voice was full, and he wondered if she was overcome with as much emotion as he was.

He grabbed her hand. "Talk outside?"

She nodded and let him lead her.

But before they reached the doors, Terrence Malone stepped in front of them. Dan tried not to groan at the sight of the church president.

"I won't keep you." Terrence nodded a greeting to Jade, who offered a gracious smile that Dan could have kissed her for. "I just wanted to say that I enjoyed your wedding message today. Your father spoke on that First Corinthians text often, but you brought out some things that I'd never picked up on before." Terrence winked. "Your father would have been proud."

Dan cleared his throat at the unexpected compliment. "Thank you."

Terrence clapped him on the back, then gestured for them to continue out the doors.

The night was cool and damp, and Jade shivered as they stepped into the garden behind the ballroom. Dan slipped off his suit coat and draped it over her shoulders, then wrapped an arm around her. They made their way through the gardens, the fragrant scent of the flowers enveloping them, and he was afraid to break the silence.

When they came to a small stone bench, he gestured to it, and Jade sat. He lowered himself next to her.

"I screwed up." No point in denying it. He'd messed up big time. "I thought I could make it up to you with flowers and grand gestures." He turned his body toward her and took her hands in his. "But what you needed was my constancy. My promise not to give up on you or turn away from you no matter what. If you let me, I'm ready to give you that. To give you me. If you can forgive me."

Jade's smile edged laced with both joy and sorrow. "I forgive you, Dan."

A thousand fireworks burst in Dan's heart. Asking for her forgiveness had been a long shot, but she'd given it so willingly. Hope infused him with new courage. He didn't want to spend another moment without her.

"So, what are you doing tomorrow?"

She looked at him in surprise. "I'm moving, actually."

All the hope that had filled him burst, leaving him as flat as a balloon that had been filled too full and then popped.

He slid as close to her as he could, his knees pressed against hers, and tightened his grip on her hands. She couldn't go. Not when they finally had their second chance. "Please don't go back to LA. I know I messed things up, big time. I let my own petty concerns get in the way, and I shunned you when I should have been holding you close and protecting you, and I'm so sorry."

"Dan, I—"

But he pressed a finger to her lips. "I have to say this, Jade. I should have said it sooner, I know I should have. But I'm saying it now. I love you."

Tears sprang to her eyes, and she opened her mouth, but he had to keep talking. If he let her get a word in, he was afraid it would be to tell him it didn't matter. To tell him she was leaving and would never be back.

"I've loved you since that first day when you told me to ask you out. And I admit that sometimes you confuse me and sometimes I don't know what you're thinking. But I want to figure it out. I want to understand everything about you. And even when I don't understand you, I still love you."

"Dan—"

He cradled her hands against his heart. "The thought of you disappearing and going back to California and living a life that's completely separate from mine—that scares me more than anything. The thought of losing you keeps me up at night. I want you to stay, Jade. I want you to stay and be with me."

He drew in a breath. What else could he say to show her the depth of his feelings for her?

Jade pressed her fingers to his lips. "Dan."

The way she said his name made him stop.

She slid her hand to his cheek. "I'm not leaving. I'm moving in with Vi and Nate. Into their house. They asked me to stay, and I said yes."

Dan stared at her, trying to comprehend what she was saying. "You're not going back to California?"

Her head shake was the most wonderful thing he'd ever seen.

"I belong here," she said. "Hope Springs is home. It's where I want to raise my baby."

"That's—" He wrapped his arms around her shoulders, pulling her close enough that he could feel her breath on his face. "That's good news."

He swallowed down the emotion that had blocked his throat.

But Jade pulled back a fraction, her eyes darkening. "We can't, Dan. It doesn't make sense, you and me."

"Us." He laid a palm against her cheek.

"There is no us," she murmured.

"There's always been an us, Jade. It just took us a long time to realize it. But now that we've found it, I'm not letting it go." He was determined. Nothing was going to change his mind.

"But people will think—"

"I don't care what people think."

Before she could come up with another argument, he slid his arms around her. When she lifted her face, he lowered his lips to hers.

This was right. He could feel it with every fiber of his being. Everything they'd been through had been leading them to this moment.

The kiss ended much too soon for his taste, leaving both of them breathless.

"Now—" Dan wrapped a strand of hair that had fallen from her updo around his finger. "Do you have anything else to say?"

"Yes."

Dan shifted his eyes to hers, half afraid she'd come up with another argument for why they couldn't be together.

But she smiled and brushed a kiss over his lips. "I love you too."

Epilogue

"*D*an, say something."

Dan shook himself. He'd been staring at Jade, but he couldn't help it. She'd completely taken his breath away the moment he'd opened his front door. She was due in two weeks, and her belly protruded adorably from her small frame. But it was her eyes that had captivated him. Every day they got brighter, more joyous.

"Sorry." He leaned down to give her a deep kiss, savoring the warmth of her lips against his. "Come in."

"Have you been outside today? It's beautiful." Jade took off the light sweater she'd been wearing over her flowery maternity shirt. "I don't think there's a single flake of snow left on the ground. And it's only March first. That has to be a new record. Which is a relief because I don't want to deliver this baby in a snowstorm." She pressed her hands to her swollen belly.

Dan covered her hands with his. "And how's our little one today?"

"Busy." Jade rubbed at her tummy. "I feel like an inside out drum. Which made it extremely difficult to concentrate at school today. I'm pretty sure I bombed my philosophy of education test."

Dan dropped a kiss on her nose. "I'm sure you didn't." He'd helped her study for the test yesterday, and she'd known every single question he'd asked. Ever since she'd started working toward her teaching degree, he'd sensed a new purpose in her.

"What's that delicious smell?" Jade raised her nose to the air and sniffed.

Dan had to laugh. If this were a cartoon, she'd be following those little squiggly scent lines to the kitchen.

He took her elbow and led her toward the dining room table.

"Dan!" Jade's gasp made him smile. It was exactly what he'd been hoping for. "I thought we were ordering pizza."

He shrugged as if it had been no big deal. "You deserve something a bit more special than pizza." He dropped a kiss on the top of her head and pulled out a chair for her.

Jade eyed the spaghetti carbonara and garlic bread, then narrowed her eyes at him. "Did Leah bring this over?"

He pressed his hands to his heart. "I'm hurt." But he couldn't carry it off. "Fine, she brought over the pasta. But I made the bread. From scratch."

Jade whistled. "Wow. I'm impressed."

"Maybe you should wait until after you've tasted it to decide that." But inside he was glowing. He wanted everything about this night to be absolutely perfect.

He sat across the table from Jade, and they both folded their hands.

But before Dan could start the prayer, Jade cut in. "Would you mind if I pray tonight?"

He lifted his head in surprise. She'd grown so much in her faith over the past months that he was astounded. It'd been almost like watching a seed sprout and flower into a full-fledged plant. She'd even started attending a women's Bible study, and the two of them had been reading the Bible together whenever they had a chance. But she'd never volunteered to pray out loud with him before.

He had to clear his throat to swallow the emotion. If that wasn't a sign that tonight was the night, he didn't know what was. "Of course."

Jade gave him a hesitant smile, then closed her eyes and bowed her head. He followed suit.

"Heavenly Father," Jade began. "Thank you that we can call you that. Thank you that we can come to you with all our hurts, all our joys, all our needs. Tonight, Lord, I want to praise you for what you have done in my life. I was broken, Lord, you know that. I thought I was beyond repair. But you didn't. You put people in my life to show me your love. It wasn't always easy, and they probably should have given up on me long ago, but they didn't. Thank you for Dan, who has made me happier than I have any right to be. And thank you that you have taken even my worst sins and you have worked them for your good. Thank you for the new life growing inside me. Please help me to be the mother this child needs and to dedicate my life to raising him or her in you. Amen."

Dan lifted his head and met her eyes. The joy in them was brighter than ever.

"That was—" He had to stop to swallow. "That was perfect."

She smiled as he passed her the bread. He would do anything to keep that joy on her face forever.

As they ate, he grew more and more certain.

He'd considered waiting until after the baby was born, to give her time to settle in and get used to being a mother before he asked her to become a wife too.

But he couldn't wait even a day longer. He had to tell her how he felt.

Now.

Tonight.

As soon as the dishes were cleared, he ducked into his bedroom and grabbed the tiny box he'd bought weeks ago. He tucked it into his pocket as he stepped into the living room, where Jade was sprawled in his chair, her feet up on the oversize ottoman.

He paused, soaking up her presence in his house. This is where he wanted her to be always.

But maybe it wasn't the right place for a proposal. "You want to go for a walk on the beach?"

"Sure." She held out her hands, and he tugged her up off the chair. "I'll be glad when it doesn't take a team to get me off the furniture anymore."

"Yeah."

She gave him an odd look. "Are you okay? You look kind of pale and sweaty all of a sudden."

"Yeah," he croaked again. The enormity of what he was about to do had just hit him. He wasn't afraid of the commitment he was about to make—he'd already made that in his heart long ago. But what if she said no? What if she couldn't bring herself to marry him and share in his life in the ministry? Although most people at church seemed to accept that he was with her, he knew there were still plenty who didn't. And while that truly didn't matter to him anymore, what if she thought she'd be protecting him by pushing him away again?

Forcing the worries aside, he led her across the lawn that separated his yard from the church and down the stairs toward the beach.

He had to trust this was in God's hands.

"You're sure you're okay?" Jade was a step in front of him, and she turned to look him up and down, concern pulling at her forehead. "You're so quiet."

"Sorry." He leaned forward to press a kiss onto her hair. "Just thinking."

"About what?" She smoothed a hand against his cheek, and he smiled and gestured for her to continue down the steps.

Much as he was bursting to drop to one knee right here and now, he wanted to wait until they'd reached their special spot. "I'll tell you in a minute."

She gave him a curious glance but continued down the steps.

As they walked, he ran through the options in his head. *Will you marry me?* Traditional but straightforward. *Will you be my wife? Will you make me the happiest man in the world? Will you let me love you forever?*

"Oh." Jade drew up short on the bottom step, and he had to stop quickly to keep from running into her. She inhaled sharply and pressed her hands to her stomach.

"What is it?" Every other thought fled as he stepped down next to her and wrapped an arm around her back. "Is it too far? Do you need to sit down?"

She shook her head. "I'm good." She gestured toward her feet. "But I think my water just broke."

Jade was exhausted, sweaty—and happier than she'd ever been in her life.

Her daughter, Hope Elizabeth Falter, was cradled in her arms, sleeping after an amazingly fast delivery. Dan stood next to her bed, leaning over to stroke the soft auburn fuzz on the baby's head. He hadn't left her side once since he'd sped her to the hospital, probably breaking more traffic laws than he'd ever broken in his life in his rush to get her here on time.

In the moments before her water had broken, Jade had sensed something shift in Dan. His sudden quiet, his almost nervous demeanor, had made her start to wonder if he was going to propose on the beach.

Just the thought had sent tingles all the way to her toes.

But now that he saw her here, with another man's baby—a baby who would never look anything like him, who would always be a reminder that she had fallen short—would he change his mind?

Was he secretly glad that her water had broken when it did? Had it saved him from making a terrible mistake?

"Jade." Dan reached for her hand, and she met his eyes.

What she saw there made her breath catch. He hadn't changed his mind about her—if anything his look held more love than ever.

He took something out of his pocket and lowered himself to one knee at the side of the bed.

With a half sob, Jade adjusted Hope in her arms so that she could lean closer to him. She didn't want to miss a single detail of this.

"I am so happy for you. And for little Hope. And I love you both. And I want to be there for both of you. Forever." He cleared his throat, and his eyes reddened. Jade's eyes welled at the emotion in his voice.

"I want to be your husband, and I want to be Hope's father." He opened the box, but Jade couldn't see the ring through the tears coursing down her cheeks. "Will you marry me?"

If she weren't holding the baby, Jade would have jumped out of the bed and flung herself at him. Instead, she let out the sob she'd been holding back, managing to squeeze out a yes around the cries.

In an instant, Dan was on his feet, leaning over to press his lips to hers. His kiss conveyed all the love words couldn't express.

When he finally pulled back, he took the ring out of the box and gently took her left hand, which was still cradled around Hope. Careful not to wake the baby, he slipped the ring onto her finger. Then he kissed his hand and pressed it lightly to Hope's head.

The baby opened her eyes and looked from one to the other of them, as if trying to figure out what all the commotion was about.

"Hope." Jade whispered her baby's name in awe. As unexpected as she'd been, this little blessing had helped her find her true Hope again. "I'd like you to meet your father. We're a family, you and me and him."

Dan leaned closer and kissed first her cheek and then the baby's. "We're an us."

"Yes." Jade snuggled closer to him and hugged Hope tight. "We're an us."

Thanks for reading NOT UNTIL US! I hope you loved Dan and Jade's story! Catch up with them and all your Hope Springs friends in NOT UNTIL CHRISTMAS MORNING—where it's Leah's chance to find love!

She's a fixer... He's about as broken as they come... Can they learn to turn to God for healing and hope this Christmas?

Leah has always been a fixer. That's why she decided to foster a troubled teen. And it's why she's determined to give him the perfect Christmas. It might also be why she feels compelled to reach out to her grinchy, reclusive neighbor Austin. But she'll have to be careful that reaching out doesn't turn into something more—she's been hurt by crossing the line from friendship to romance once, and she's not willing to let it happen again.

After losing his leg, his friend, and his faith in Afghanistan, Austin figures he's about as broken as they come. Hope Springs is simply a stopping point—a place to rehabilitate his leg, get over the burden of his PTSD, and get back into shape to redeploy. He has no desire to get to know anyone while he's here, least of all the meddlesome—if sweet—woman next door. But when she calls on him to help her make Christmas special for her foster son, something compels him to relent. Soon, his heart belongs to both of them.

But what if Austin is too broken for even Leah to fix? Can the two of them learn to turn to God for hope and healing—and maybe even a chance at love—this Christmas?

Fall in love with NOT UNTIL CHRISTMAS MORNING now!

And be sure to sign up for my newsletter, where we chat about life, faith, and of course books! You'll also get Ethan and Ariana's story (available exclusively to subscribers) FREE.

Sign up at www.valeriembodden.com/gift!

Read on for an excerpt of Leah and Austin's story...

A preview of Not Until Christmas Morning

Please ring.

Austin stared down his computer, perched on the scuffed card table in his cramped eat-in kitchen. These moments before his brother was supposed to call were the hardest. The moments when his mind went to all the things that could have happened to keep Chad from calling.

He folded himself into the rickety chair next to the table, sliding his crutches to the floor and pulling up the leg of his sweatpants. It'd been almost a year, but the jolt still went through him every time his eyes met the rounded end of his left leg. Even though he knew intellectually that his foot wasn't there anymore—even though he accepted it to some degree—it was still surreal every time he saw the empty space where it should be. He rolled the silicone liner over his residual limb, which ended about eight inches below his knee, then grabbed his prosthetic and slid his stump into it, standing to walk in place until the pin on the end of the liner locked with a series of clicks.

He lowered himself to the chair with a groan, tucking his legs under the table as his computer blasted the sharp alarm he'd set to indicate an incoming video call. As always, the sound set his nerves firing, ramping his heart rate to levels it hadn't achieved since the first days of Ranger training. But he wasn't about to lower the volume, in case he was ever asleep when his brother called. If he ever actually slept, that is.

The moment his brother's face filled the screen, wearing the same goofy grin as always, his heart rate slowed, and he could breathe normally again.

"Hey, man, it's good to see your ugly face." There was a delay between Chad's words and the movement of his mouth, but Austin didn't care. Seeing that his brother was still safe—still whole—was what mattered.

"Likewise." He kept his voice gruff, so his big brother wouldn't know how much he lived for these too infrequent calls. It was the only thing he lived for anymore, really. That and getting in shape to redeploy. No matter what the doctors said.

Only two percent of soldiers with injuries like yours return to the battlefield.

Well, Austin was going to be part of the two percent. There was no other option. No way was he going to leave his brother over there alone.

"How are things?" Austin asked the same question every time they talked.

And every time, Chad repeated the same bogus answer: "It's raining peaches." It had been one of their mother's favorite sayings when they were growing up, and after she'd died, Chad had taken it over as if he'd inherited it the same way he'd inherited her curly hair.

Usually, Austin let him get away with it. When he'd been stationed over there, he hadn't wanted to talk about what was happening with anyone back home either. There was just no way to make them understand.

But this was different. He did understand. He'd been there. He'd lost buddies there. Tanner and—

No. He couldn't go there right now.

Austin squinted at his brother, trying to see what he wasn't saying. "Stop churching it up and give me a straight answer. How many missions are you running? You look tired."

Chad's grin slipped, and he ran a hand over his unshaven cheeks. "You know I can't, Austin. I'm fine. We're all fine. God's got our back."

Austin shoved his chair out and pushed to his feet. Supposedly God had their back last year too. Right up until the moment everything blew

259

to pieces. He'd feel a lot better when he got back over there. Then he could be the one who had everyone's back.

"Austin, don't be like that." Chad's voice followed Austin as he took three steps to cross his kitchen.

"I'm not being like anything," he called over his shoulder, loudly so the computer would pick it up. "I'm hungry."

He yanked the refrigerator door open. But aside from a bottle of mustard and a gallon of milk he was pretty sure was at least three weeks old, it was empty.

"Did you go grocery shopping? Got something in there for a change?" Chad's voice carried across the small room, a rough mix of reprimand and concern.

Austin slammed the fridge door shut with a growl, then stood with his head braced against it, the stainless steel cooling his overheated skin.

"Austin—" Chad's voice was gentler now, laced with big-brother authority. "You can't keep living like this, man. Something has to change."

"Yeah." Austin nodded with his head still against the fridge. "I have to get back there."

"No." Chad's voice was firm, and Austin jerked toward the computer screen. His brother's face was grim.

"What do you mean, no?" The snap of his words carried across the room, bouncing off the walls.

Chad had never been anything but supportive of Austin recovering and redeploying. So what was he saying now?

"Maybe you'll get back here, Austin, maybe you won't. But either way, you have to learn to live with it."

"I *am* living with it."

"Yeah? When's the last time you left your apartment or ate anything besides takeout or went on a date or even talked to another human being?"

Austin opened his mouth to respond, but Chad jumped in. "And I don't count."

"I leave my apartment three times a week for physical therapy. I have no interest in dating. I talked to my mailman this morning." He couldn't argue about the takeout, though. Still, three out of four wasn't bad.

"That's not a life, Austin."

He almost argued again. But the little voice in his head that said Chad was right got the better of him. "I know. But what else am I supposed to do?"

"Get out of town for a while. Go somewhere warm. Florida or Hawaii or something. You've got the money from selling Mom's house."

Austin lifted his lip. Go to Hawaii? That was his brother's answer? He had no desire to go to Hawaii.

"Chad, I'm not going—" But he cut off as his eyes fell on the single picture he kept on his refrigerator. A family of four: Mom, Dad, Chad at maybe four years old, and little baby Austin.

He snatched it out from under the magnet and strode to the table, his gait sure despite the uneven floor that often tripped him up. He held the picture in front of the computer's camera.

"Do you remember this?"

Chad squinted, and Austin waited for his delayed answer.

"Yeah. That was right before Dad was called up. I think it's the last picture we have of all four of us together."

Austin pushed aside the familiar stab of jealousy that Chad had four years with their father before Dad was killed in action. Austin had been too young then to remember the man at all.

"What was the name of the town again?"

"Hope Springs? Why?"

Hope Springs. That was right. His parents had grown up there, but after his father's death, Mom had found a job opportunity in Iowa. Every once in a while, she'd tell them a story about the town, though, and to Austin, it had always sounded like the perfect place.

"I'm going to go there." He said it with certainty, as if it were the most logical thing in the world. Even though some part of him knew it was the exact opposite.

"Go where?" Even with the poor video quality, Austin could see Chad's brow wrinkle.

"To Hope Springs." He dropped into the chair next to the card table. "To see where we were born. Where Mom and Dad grew up."

"Okay." Chad dragged the word out, and Austin could tell he was trying to avoid saying a whole lot of other things. "If that's what you want to do. But November in Wisconsin sounds even less pleasant than November in Iowa. I still think somewhere warm and—"

"No." Austin peered at the picture again. This was where he wanted to go. Where he needed to go, even if he didn't know why.

And if he left right now, he could be there before dark.

More Hope Springs Books

While the books in the Hope Springs series are linked, each is a complete romance featuring a different couple and can be read in any order. Wondering whose story is whose? Here's a helpful list:

Not Until Christmas (Ethan & Ariana)

Not Until Forever (Sophie & Spencer)

Not Until This Moment (Jared & Peyton)

Not Until You (Nate & Violet)

Not Until Us (Dan & Jade)

Not Until Christmas Morning (Leah & Austin)

Not Until This Day (Tyler & Isabel)

Not Until Someday (Grace & Levi)

Not Until Now (Cam & Kayla)

Not Until Then (Bethany & James)

And Don't Miss the River Falls Series

Featuring the Calvano family in the small town of River Falls, nestled in the Smoky Mountains of Tennessee.

Pieces of Forever (Joseph & Ava)
Songs of Home (Lydia & Liam)
Memories of the Heart (Simeon & Abigail)

Want to know when my next book releases?

You can follow me on Amazon to be the first to know when my next book releases! Just visit amazon.com/author/valeriembodden and click the follow button.

Acknowledgements

After writing a 70,000+ word book, you would think writing this one-page acknowledgments section would be a piece of cake. But I find that this is always one of the hardest parts of the book to write—not because I don't have anyone to be grateful to but because I have so very many people to thank, and words seem inadequate to express my gratitude. But here goes my best attempt:

First and above all, I thank my Heavenly Father, who gave me this gift of writing and has led me to this point in my life where I can use that gift to serve him daily. I certainly haven't done anything to earn or deserve this privilege—and I stand in awe every day of what he is doing with my books. I thank him for leading me to these stories of hope, love, and redemption. And most of all, I thank him for forgiving every last one of my sins through the blood of his Son, Jesus Christ. I pray that through my books, readers will be reminded that all their sins are forgiven in Jesus as well.

I thank God every day for the blessing of my family. For my husband, who not only sets an example of Christ's love for me every day but who is also my number one fan and strongest supporter—not to mention an incredible book cover designer. For our four children, who have taught me more about love and grace and trust and forgiveness than I'll ever be able to teach them. For my parents, who raised me in a Christian home, where I knew God's love from before I can even remember. For my sister, my in-laws, and my extended family, who have supported and encouraged me as I have worked to get this series into the world.

A huge thank you also goes to my incredible Advance Reader Team: Lisa, Karen Bonner, Cathy D. Massett, Ashley Lundquist, Judith

Barillas, Jennifer Ellenson, Jenny Kilgallen, Rachel Kozinski, Diana, Sandy C., Christine Beck, Shavona Thompson, KP, KVee, Deb Galloway, Mary Heiner, JoAnn Stewart, Melanie Tate, Debbie Mhufhly, Jeanette Huntsucker, Brandi M., Beverly Vice, Debra L. Payne, Becca T., Josie Bartelt, Kori Thomas, Kim, Kari King, Diane Ellsworth, Dawn L., Bonny Rambarran, Diana Austin, Julie Wayner Bult, Patty Bohuslav, BJF, Korkoi Boret, Kathryn Rebernick, and Connie Gronholz. I am humbled just looking at that list of names—each one of you was willing to take time out of your life to read my book, share your thoughts and suggestions, and spread the word. You are all amazing, and I have so enjoyed my conversations with you, not only about my books but about our lives and our walks of faith. You are such an encouragement to me, and I couldn't do this without you!

One of the amazing and unexpected benefits of writing books in the digital age is that I have had an opportunity to connect with readers from around the world. Thank you for being one of them! I know this world is a busy place—and I thank you for choosing to spend some of your time with me and the characters of Hope Springs. I hope you've enjoyed their journey.

About the Author

Valerie M. Bodden has three great loves: Jesus, her family, and books. And chocolate (okay, four great loves). She is living out her happily ever after with her high-school-sweetheart-turned-husband and their four children. Her life wouldn't make a terribly exciting book, as it has a happy beginning and middle, and someday when she goes to her heavenly home, it will have a happy end.

She was born and raised in Wisconsin but recently moved with her family to Texas, where they're all getting used to the heat (she doesn't miss the snow even a little bit, though the rest of the family does) and saying y'all instead of you guys.

Valerie writes emotion-filled Christian fiction that weaves real-life problems, real-life people, and real-life faith. Her characters may (okay, will) experience some heartache along the way, but she will always give them a happy ending.

Feel free to stop by www.valeriembodden.com to say hi. She loves visitors! And while you're there, you can sign up for your free story.

Printed in Great Britain
by Amazon

18038056R00155